NO PLACE LIKE

and other short stories by
southern African women writers

NO PLACE LIKE

and other short stories by
southern African women writers

selected by
Robin Malan

with an introduction by
Rochelle Kapp

David Philip Publishers • Cape Town
Sterling Publishers • New Delhi

Published in South Africa by
DAVID PHILIP PUBLISHERS
208 Werdmuller Centre,
Claremont 7708 South Africa
www.twisted.co.za/dpp

Published in Asia under
Sterling Paperbacks
An imprint of
STERLING PUBLISHERS (P) LTD.
L-10, Green Park Extension, New Delhi-110016
Ph. : 6191784, 6191785   Fax : 91-11- 6190028
E-mail : ghai@nde.vsnl.net.in
http://www.sterlingpublishers.com

Published in Zimbabwe by
BAOBAB BOOKS
4 Conald Road, Graniteside
Harare, Zimbabwe

Published in Namibia by
NEW NAMIBIA BOOKS
Mutual Platz, Post Street Mall
Windhoek, Namibia

Printed in India
Cover design by Karen Stewart

Contents

Introduction

This selection brings together a range of new and established women writers, with pieces drawn from the last fifty years. The stories have been selected by Robin Malan (in a close collaboration with me) to introduce this extraordinarily rich terrain to a general audience, as well as those interested more specifically in southern African literature. Together, the stories offer the perspectives, complex and multi-faceted, of women from different race, class and regional backgrounds during a period of considerable political and social upheaval. The issues raised by the volume are in many ways universal, in others unique to the African sub-continent.

There has been a flourishing of published writing by women writers in recent years, particularly in South Africa. The short story, along with autobiography, has been a popular form. Consequently, a volume of this size cannot and does not claim to be comprehensive, nor does it claim to do justice to the diversity of subject matter and form in writing by southern African women, particularly as it does not include oral narratives or stories written in languages other than English. Like so many African writers, some of the authors in this volume have made a conscious choice to write in English, not their first language but that in which they have almost all studied at a tertiary level and in which they communicate in their daily lives. An exception to this is Gcina Mhlophe, who also performs and writes stories in Xhosa and in Zulu; while Sindiwe Magona has made Xhosa translations of some of her English originals.

What were our criteria for selection? Firstly, we deliberately focused on writing from and about the lives of women. However, these did not have to be explicitly feminist texts. Gcinaphi Dlamini's *Ethel, the sensible*, for example, exhibits ambivalence towards feminism. To complicate this picture, some stories which come across as unambiguously feminist, like *The collector of treasures* and *The De Wets come to Kloof Grange*, have been written by women who eschew the label. There are stories like Nadine Gordimer's *The ultimate safari*, Agnes Sam's *High heels* and Sheila Roberts's *I'd sell my horses* which, while they may describe the lives of women, have as their central focus a comment on broader cultural or political issues and relationships.

Secondly, we tried to draw on writing from as broad a range of geographical, political and social contexts as possible. So there are stories from Botswana, Namibia, South Africa, Swaziland and Zimbabwe. Most of the stories were written in post-colonial southern Africa, but have as their setting both colonial and Apartheid contexts. A number of recent stories deal with post-colonial Namibia, independent Zimbabwe and the 'new' South Africa.

We have chosen to sequence the stories chronologically in terms of the historical period in which each is set. Inasmuch as the larger political landscape impinges on the everyday lives of nearly all the women in these stories, the reader is taken through a myriad of responses to the sub-continent's history. There are stories which etch out landscapes of pain: tales of physical and emotional dislocation, violence and poverty; and then there are tales of love, intimacy and newly discovered paths beckoning freedom.

Another significant aspect of selection is that we have placed emerging voices like Gcinaphi Dlamini, Kaleni Hiyalwa and Jane Katjavivi alongside well-established figures such as Bessie Head, Nadine Gordimer and Doris Lessing. Our definition of southern African women extends to those who came to live in southern Africa from elsewhere, and to the many who went into exile, whether by choice or force of circumstance. In fact, over half of the writers in this volume have been in exile at some point, which in itself says something about how the political upheavals of the sub-continent have dislocated the lives of many people.

Aside from these considerations, we freely admit that the choices made are in many respects idiosyncratic and reflect our view of what constitutes a 'good read', rather than currently fashionable head-counting notions of representivity or political correctness. We wanted stories which are well-crafted, which engage with their social surroundings, and which lay bare the ironies, the contradictions and ruptures of everyday life. That nearly all of the stories fall into the category of realism is a reflection of the body of work by African writers as a whole. The more recent stories by Moira Crosbie Lovell and Dlamini possibly signal new trends in formal experimentation. Their humour and self-irony also contrast markedly with the seriousness of most of the other stories.

The sequencing by historical context debunks any simplistic notions of teleology with regard to the position of women. An example of this is in the treatment of sexual relations. In Head's *The collector of treasures*, ironically, male castration enables emotional and physical liberation for the rural uneducated female protagonist who has suffered her husband's ill-treatment for many years. In Yvonne Vera's *Independence Day* the freedom of the country is portrayed as an essentially male domain, symbolised by waiting for 'the prince' and celebrated with a 'beer and a woman' in 'style and triumph'. The woman's body is literally functional to the male desire to claim power – she has to open her legs at precisely midnight. However, the man has to pay for the privilege and the distancing effect used in the narration means that we are left in doubt as to who is the more colonised. In Dlamini's racy sketch *Ethel, the sensible* the modern, well-educated, independent woman is entrapped by the 'stifling convention of political correctness and gender sensitivity'. She considers reclaiming 'Barbie and friends' as her role models, to submit intellectually and sexually in a bid to 'play the game so well men will die defending her honour and sincerity'.

Through the dialogue thus established within these three fascinating stories, the question is raised as to what actually constitutes sexual liberation.

Another effect of the anthologising process, perhaps exaggerated by the preponderance of women writers in exile, is the emergence of a striking concern with the relationship between identity and home. In three of the stories women leave home, fleeing the identity it entails. In Gordimer's *No place like*, the title story of this anthology, the woman protagonist rejects the limitations of 'identity and place' symbolised by her passport and boarding pass. The narrator in Sindiwe Magona's *Flight* recalls her aunt's escape from rural entrapment and the constraints of being a new wife. From her example, the young girl learns 'about determination and the power of one's will'. In Farida Karodia's story *Crossmatch*, her protagonist can pursue a career and a relationship of her choice only by leaving the country.

In other stories, women have to find safe spaces in which to take refuge, to uncover a sense of self outside of the confines of home or school. In Mhlophe's autobiographical story *Transforming moments*, for example, the emerging young writer, conscious of the taunt of being 'Miss-ugly-top-of-the-class', finds a space of solitude and peace, where she gains the confidence necessary to discover her identity as a writer. In Crosbie Lovell's *Supermarket soliloquy* her narrator uses a supermarket for an allegorical exploration of her past.

In two of the stories by South African exile writers, the protagonists have become estranged from home. They discover that the codes in the 'new' South Africa have shifted, although not necessarily changed. In Elleke Boehmer's *Ginger* and Roberts's *I'd sell my horses* the white exiles are wary of commentary, as they feel their voices are muted by those whites who stayed, who did not take the 'chicken run'. Their reticence is contrasted with the confident judgements made by the South Africans, who themselves nevertheless suffer various forms of neurosis and alienation as they do or don't attempt to reconcile themselves to the new South Africa.

In Katjavivi's *Uerieta* and Lessing's *The De Wets come to Kloof Grange* the two British protagonists wrestle to come to terms with the concept of home and identity in Africa. Their struggles are portrayed in complex physical and emotional terms with very different effects. Katjavivi's protagonist engages with her social and physical environment whereas Mrs Gale in the Lessing story despises the people of the country and finds solace only in the landscape. The combination of the African mountains and the English garden which she maintains at great expense provides a refuge which sustains her in her preferred isolation.

Hiyalwa's *The baby's baby*, Vera's *Shelling peanuts,* and Gordimer's *The ultimate safari* all describe the lives of families who have suffered dislocation as a result of war or famine. In *The ultimate safari* the concepts of home and identity have been redefined by the physical, yet artificial, boundaries of state created by colonialism and maintained in post-colonial Africa. In all three stories it is women who are left behind to pick up the pieces and reconstruct a semblance of home.

Not surprisingly, given the historical context, there is a self-consciousness about racial or ethnic identity in all of the stories except those by Dlamini and Crosbie Lovell. However, the extent to which racial identity is foregrounded varies considerably and no easy generalisations are possible. With the exception of Gordimer, the white writers refer to relationships between black and white people rather obliquely. In the depictions by Head and Hiyalwa, colonial oppression and gender oppression are closely linked. Black men, themselves victims, are also agents of female oppression. Significantly, Head, unlike many other scholars and writers, does not ascribe patriarchal oppression solely to colonialism. She departs from her story to provide a documentary account of patriarchal oppression. She traces its origins to pre-colonial times. Then she describes how colonialism humiliated and

degraded men and disrupted family life. Finally, she shows
how men and women have had to rely on their own resources
after independence.

More often than not, tradition is depicted in the stories as
an oppressive force which defends boundaries of gender, race,
class, age and religion in the face of change. The notion of
warm, caring families and communities is often questioned,
as women find their personal and physical spaces violated
from within, often by other women. In their role as the primary
agents of socialisation, they are chiefly responsible for the
censorship of the behaviour of young girls. In Vera's *Shelling
peanuts* and Karodia's *Crossmatch* older women end up as the
defenders and custodians of the culture which oppresses
women. In Lessing's *The De Wets come to Kloof Grange* class
and ethnic prejudices act as barriers to any possibility of
breaking the mould which assigns women roles as wives and
mothers, silent and compliant.

The use of language in the stories is worth commenting
on. The linguistic richness of the region is captured in the
idiom of many of the stories. Sometimes the language of the
region is used for direct speech. In Magona's story the old
man's phonetically rendered cries contrast with the silence of
the woman whose graceful flight, as 'away she floated', is
described in the register of the fairy tale. In Zoë Wicomb's story
A clearing in the bush the social and identity politics surrounding
English and Afrikaans in the Cape is central to the story.

The volume begins with a woman fleeing her oppression
'riding the air – no part of her body making contact with the
ground' and ends with introspection in a supermarket from
which the protagonist exits 'Trolleyless. Trailing loo paper like
Lazarus'. Between these two stories a wealth of experience is
narrated with candour, anger, humour, warmth, bitterness and
irony. The challenge and the enjoyment for us lie in recognising
and appreciating the complexity of each story.

Rochelle Kapp

Flight

Sindiwe Magona

Cries of *'Khawulele! Wenk'umntu!'* shattered the stillness of the saucer-like village nestling in the valley, surrounded by green hills and scrub-dotted mountains.

Echoes bounced from hilltops, clashed mid-air, ricocheted and fell in jumbled noises that boomed, invading our ears and jamming out all other sounds.

weh weh weh khauu khauu khauu
leh leh leh leh tuu tuu tuu!

Like a powerful magnet, the commotion pulled us away from the rag dolls that had so occupied us but a moment before.

Iii-iiiWuu-uuuuu!
Mmbaa – mbeeehh-ni!
Qhaaa-wuu-lee-laani!

An old man: short, tight-curled springs of wool on his head making a greyish-white skull cap tottered past in what I saw as his earnest attempt at running. His left hand clasped the blanket loosely wrapped around his body; his right arm, from the shoulder, was stuck out as if from a toga. Thin, long, and bony, it swung back and front in time to his intended accelerated step. Held high in the hand, a *knobkerrie* jutted out and away from his body. Each time he shouted – *'Mbambeni!* – Catch her!' he stretched out the arm holding the *knobkerrie*, pointing the stick towards the mountain.

My eyes leapt to where he pointed. The mountain was playing a game of hide and seek with the sun. Or was it with the clouds? Anyway, half the mountain had disappeared. I threw my eyes towards the remaining half. There, distance-shrunk figures scurried, hurried, ran, and scrambled.

Ahead, a lone figure darted like a hare with a pack of dogs hard on its tail. The clouds were no idle players, I saw. They were the third party to this game; and they would make the telling difference.

Clearly, that day, I witnessed the birth of tears. The clouds wept and showered soft tears of mist onto the silent mountain. Would the fleeing figure gain the mist blanket in time? The sun smiled and the mist disappeared in a spray of long, hot, yellow needles, the children of the sun.

There she was, clearly, I saw her. Surely, her pursuers too could see her? – see her as I did?

My insides churned. A hot ball of fear curled inside my stomach. But the clouds, not to be outdone, wept. Thick, fat, dark-grey spears fell. Fast and hard they came. Thick, fat; safe for her to be enveloped in and lost to her pursuers.

'*Uye phi? Uye phi?* Where's she gone?'

Sounds of distress from those who were bent on her capture reached me. I held my breath as I strained with her, willing her to elude them, urging her on and on and on.

My last glimpse of her: blue German-print dress paled to a soft sky-blue by distance and lack of light … there she was, flitting here and there between boulders, her long new-wife-length dress making her seem without feet. As she hurried escaping, she appeared to me to be riding the air – no part of her body making contact with the ground.

Away she floated; the men plodded behind her.

I saw her waft into the wall of mist. I saw it close the crack she'd almost made gliding into it. Like a fish slicing into water, she'd but disturbed it. And it rearranged itself, accepting her into itself. And away from those who harried her.

I cannot remember her face at all. It was a long time ago and perhaps she had not tarried long with us. I don't know. But I remember her leaving. And that is because it taught me about determination, the power of one's will.

She was a young woman, a new wife. Her husband, my uncle, was away at work in one of the mines where all the men of the village went for a very long time. Later, much later, with great learning to aid me order my world, I would come to know the precise length of their stay – eleven months each year. However, this knowledge was light years away from me that fear-filled day long, long ago.

It must have been midday for the sun was well up and we children were already outside at play; that is, those of us too little to go to the one mud-walled, grass-thatched house called school.

I know I should've been sad at losing an aunt. I know she was a good *makoti*, cooked and cleaned well, and we children were saved from a lot of chores by her coming – new wives are worked like donkeys as initiation into their new status. I know I should have sympathised with my uncle who lost not only a wife but also the cattle, the *lobola*, he had given for her.

All I know, is the thrill I felt watching her escape into the thick grey cloud and mist.

The De Wets come to Kloof Grange
Doris Lessing

The veranda, which was lifted on stone pillars, jutted forward over the garden like a box in the theatre. Below were luxuriant masses of flowering shrubs, and creepers whose shiny leaves, like sequins, reflected light from a sky stained scarlet and purple and apple-green. This splendiferous sunset filled one half of the sky, fading gently through shades of mauve to a calm expanse of ruffling grey, blown over by tinted cloudlets; and in this still evening sky, just above a clump of darkening conifers, hung a small crystal moon.

There sat Major Gale and his wife, as they did every evening at this hour, side by side trimly in deck chairs, their sundowners on small tables at their elbows, critically watching, like connoisseurs, the pageant presented for them.

Major Gale said, with satisfaction: 'Good sunset tonight,' and they both turned their eyes to the vanquishing moon. The dusk drew veils across sky and garden; and punctually, as she did every day, Mrs Gale shook off nostalgia like a terrier shaking off water and rose, saying: 'Mosquitoes!' She drew her deck chair to the wall, where she neatly folded and stacked it.

'Here is the post,' she said, her voice quickening; and Major Gale went to the steps, waiting for the native who was hastening towards them through the tall shadowing bushes. He swung a sack from his back and handed it to Major Gale. A sour smell of raw meat rose from the sack. Major Gale said with the kindly contempt he used for his native servants: 'Did the spooks get you?' and laughed. The native who had panted the last mile of his ten-mile journey through a bush filled with unnameable phantoms, ghosts of ancestors, wraiths of tree and beast, put on a pantomime of fear and chattered and shivered for a moment like an ape, to amuse his master. Major Gale dismissed the boy. He ducked thankfully around the corner of the house to the back, where there were lights and companionship.

Mrs Gale lifted the sack and went into the front room. There she lit the oil lamp and called for the houseboy, to whom she handed the groceries and meat for removal. She took a fat bundle of letters from the very bottom of the sack and wrinkled her nose slightly: blood from the meat had stained them. She sorted the letters into two piles; and then husband and wife sat themselves down opposite each other to read their mail.

It was more than the ordinary farm living-room. There were koodoo horns branching out over the fireplace, and a bundle of *knobkerries* hanging on a nail; but on the floor were fine rugs, and the furniture was two hundred years old. The table was a pool of softly-reflected lights; it was polished by Mrs Gale herself every day before she set on it an earthenware crock filled with thorny red flowers. Africa and the English eighteenth century mingled in this room and were at peace.

From time to time Mrs Gale rose impatiently to attend to the lamp, which did not burn well. It was one of those terrifying paraffin things that have to be pumped with air to a whiter-hot flame from time to time, and which in any case emit a continuous soft hissing noise. Above the heads of the Gales a light cloud of flying insects wooed their fiery death and dropped one by one, plop, plop, plop to the table among the letters.

Mrs Gale took an envelope from her own heap and handed it to her husband. 'The assistant,' she remarked abstractedly, her eyes bent on what she held. She smiled tenderly as she read. The letter was from her oldest friend, a woman doctor in London, and they had written to each other every week for thirty years, ever since Mrs Gale came to exile in Southern

Rhodesia. She murmured half-aloud: 'Why, Betty's brother's daughter is going to study economics,' and though she had never met Betty's brother, let alone the daughter, the news seemed to please and excite her extraordinarily. The whole of the letter was about people she had never met and was not likely ever to meet – about the weather, about English politics. Indeed, there was not a sentence in it that would not have struck an outsider as having been written out of a sense of duty; but when Mrs Gale had finished reading it, she put it aside gently and sat smiling quietly: she had gone back half a century to her childhood.

Gradually sight returned to her eyes, and she saw her husband where previously she had sat looking through him. He appeared disturbed; there was something wrong about the letter from the assistant.

Major Gale was a tall and still military figure, even in his khaki bush-shirt and shorts. He changed twice a day. His shorts were creased sharp as folded paper, and the six pockets of his shirt were always buttoned up tight. His small head, with its polished surface of black hair, his tiny jaunty black moustache, his farmer's hands with their broken but clean nails – all these seemed to say that it was no easy matter not to let oneself go, not to let this damned disintegrating gaudy easy-going country get under one's skin. It wasn't easy, but he did it; he did it with the conscious effort that had slowed his movements and added the slightest touch of caricature to his appearance: one finds a man like Major Gale only in exile.

He rose from his chair and began pacing the room, while his wife watched him speculatively and waited for him to tell her what was the matter. When he stood up, there was something not quite right – what was it? Such a spruce and tailored man he was; but the disciplined shape of him was spoiled by a curious fatness and softness: the small rounded head was set on a thickening neck; the buttocks were fattening too, and quivered as he walked. Mrs Gale, as these facts assailed her, conscientiously excluded them: she had her own picture of her husband, and could not afford to have it destroyed.

At last he sighed, with a glance at her; and when she said: 'Well, dear?' he replied at once, 'The man has a wife.'

'Dear me!' she exclaimed, dismayed.

At once as if he had been waiting for her protest, he returned briskly: 'It will be nice for you to have another woman about the place.'

'Yes, I suppose it will,' she said humorously. At this most familiar note in her voice, he jerked his head up and said aggressively: 'You always complain I bury you alive.'

And so she did. Every so often, but not so often now, she allowed herself to overflow into a mood of gently humorous bitterness; but it had not carried conviction for many years; it was more, really, of an attention to him, like remembering to kiss him good night. In fact, she had learned to love her isolation, and she felt aggrieved that he did not know it.

'Well, but they can't come to the house. That I really couldn't put up with.' The plan had been for the new assistant – Major Gale's farming was becoming too successful and expanding for him to manage any longer by himself – to have the spare room and share the house with his employers.

'No, I suppose not, if there's a wife.' Major Gale sounded doubtful; it was clear he would not mind another family sharing with them. 'Perhaps they could have the old house?' he enquired at last.

'I'll see to it,' said Mrs Gale, removing the weight of worry off her husband's shoulders. Things he could manage: people bothered him. That they bothered her, too, now, was something she had become resigned to his not understanding. For she knew he was hardly conscious of her; nothing existed for him outside his farm. And this suited her well. During the early years of their marriage, with the four children growing up, there was always a little uneasiness between them, like an unpaid debt. Now they were friends and could forget each other. What a relief when he no longer 'loved' her! (That was how she put it.) Ah, that 'love' – she thought of it with a small humorous distaste. Growing old had its advantages.

When she said 'I'll see to it', he glanced at her, suddenly, directly; her tone had been a little too comforting and maternal. Normally his gaze wavered over her, not seeing her. Now he really observed her for a moment; he saw an elderly Englishwoman, as thin and dry as a stalk of maize in September, sitting poised over her letters, one hand touching them lovingly, gazing at him with her small flower-blue eyes. A look of guilt in them troubled him. He crossed to her and kissed her cheek. 'There!' she said, inclining her face with a sprightly, fidgety laugh. Overcome with embarrassment he stopped for a moment, then said determinedly: 'I shall go and have my bath.'

After his bath, from which he emerged pink and shining like an elderly baby, dressed in flannels and a blazer, they ate their dinner under the wheezing oil lamp and the cloud of flying insects. Immediately the meal was over he said: 'Bed,' and moved off. He was always in bed before eight and up by five. Once Mrs Gale had adapted herself to his routine. Now, with the four boys out sailing the seven seas in the navy, and nothing really to get her out of bed (her servants were perfectly trained), she slept until eight, when she joined her husband at breakfast. She refused to have that meal in bed; nor would she have dreamed of appearing in her dressing-gown. Even as things were she was guilty enough about sleeping those three daylight hours, and found it necessary to apologise for her slackness. So, when her husband had gone to bed she remained under the lamp, re-reading her letters, sewing, reading or simply dreaming about the past, the very distant past, when she had been Caroline Morgan, living near a small country town, a country squire's daughter. That was how she liked best to think of herself.

Tonight she soon turned down the lamp and stepped on to the veranda. Now the moon was a large, soft, yellow fruit caught in the top branches of the blue-gums. The garden was filled with glamour, and she let herself succumb to it. She passed quietly down the steps and beneath the trees, with one quick solicitous glance back at the bedroom window: her husband hated her to be out of the house by herself at night. She was on her way to the old house that lay half a mile distant over the veld.

Before the Gales had come to this farm, two brothers had it, South Africans by birth and upbringing. The houses had then been separated by a stretch of untouched bush, with not so much as a fence or a road between them; and in this state of guarded independence the two men had lived, both bachelors, both quite alone. The thought of them amused Mrs Gale. She could imagine them sending polite notes to each other, invitations to meals or to spend an evening. She imagined them loaning each other books by native bearer, meeting at a neutral point between their homes. She was amused, but she respected them for a feeling she could understand. She had made up all kinds of pretty ideas about these brothers, until one day she learned from a neighbour that in fact the two men had quarrelled continually, and had eventually gone bankrupt because they could not agree how the farm was to be run. After this discovery Mrs Gale ceased to think about them; a pleasant fancy had become a distasteful reality.

The first thing she did on arriving was to change the name of the farm from Kloof Nek to Kloof Grange, making a link with home. One of the houses was denuded of furniture and used as a storage space. It was a square, bare box of a place, stuck in the middle of the bare veld, and its shut windows flashed back light to the sun all day. But her own home had been added to and extended, and surrounded with verandas and fenced; inside the fence were two acres of garden, that she had created over years of toil. And what a garden! These were what she lived for: her flowering African shrubs, her vivid English lawns, her water-garden with the goldfish and water lilies. Not many people had such a garden.

She walked through it this evening under the moon, feeling herself grow lightheaded and insubstantial with the influence of the strange greenish light, and of the perfumes from the flowers. She touched the leaves with her fingers as she passed, bending her face to the roses. At the gate, under the hanging white trumpets of the moonflower she paused, and lingered for a while, looking over the space of empty veld between her and the other house. She did not like going outside her garden at night. She was not afraid of natives, no: she had contempt for women who were afraid, for she regarded Africans as rather pathetic children, and was very kind to them. She did not know what made her afraid. Therefore she took a deep breath, compressed her lips, and stepped carefully through the gate, shutting it behind her with a sharp click. The road before her was a glimmering white ribbon, the hard-crusted sand sending up a continuous small sparkle of light as she moved. On either side were sparse stumpy trees, and their shadows were deep and black. A nightjar cut across the stars with crooked trailing wings, and she set her mouth defiantly: why, this was only the road she walked over every afternoon, for her constitutional! These were the trees she had pleaded for, when her husband was wanting to have them cut for firewood: in a sense they were her trees. Deliberately slowing her steps, as a discipline, she moved through the pits of shadow, gaining each stretch of clear moonlight with relief, until she came to the house. It looked dead, a dead thing with staring eyes, with those blank windows gleaming pallidly back at the moon. Nonsense, she told herself. Nonsense. And she walked to the front door, unlocked it, and flashed her torch over the floor. Sacks of grain were piled to the rafters, and the brick floor was scattered with loose mealies. Mice scurried invisibly to safety and flocks of cockroaches blackened the walls. Standing in a patch of moonlight on the brick, so that she would not unwittingly walk into a spiderweb or a jutting sack, she drew in deep breaths of the sweetish smell of maize, and made a list in her head of what had to be done; she was a very capable woman.

Then something struck her: if the man had forgotten, when applying for the job, to mention a wife, he was quite capable of forgetting children too. If they had children it wouldn't do; no, it wouldn't. She simply couldn't put up with a tribe of children – for Afrikaners never had less than twelve – running wild over the beautiful garden and teasing her goldfish. Anger spurted in her. De Wet – the name was hard on her tongue. Her husband should not have agreed to take on an Afrikaner. Really, really, Caroline, she chided herself humorously, standing there in the deserted moonlit house, don't jump to conclusions, don't be unfair.

She decided to arrange the house for a man and his wife, ignoring the possibility of children. She would arrange things, in kindness, for a woman who might be unused to living in loneliness; she would be good to this woman; so she scolded herself, to make atonement for her short fit of pettiness. But when she tried to form a picture of this woman who was coming to share her life, at least to the extent of taking tea with her in the mornings, and swapping recipes (so she supposed), imagination failed her. She pictured a large Dutch frau, all homely comfort and sweating goodness, and was repulsed. For the first time the knowledge that she must soon, next week, take another woman into her life, came home to her; and she disliked it intensely.

Why must she? Her husband would not have to make a friend of the man. They would work together, that was all; but because they, the wives, were two women on an isolated farm, they would be expected to live in each other's pockets. All her instincts towards privacy, the distance which she had put between herself and other people, even her own husband, rebelled against it. And because she rebelled, rejecting this imaginary Dutch woman, to whom she felt so alien, she began to think of her friend Betty, as if it were she who would be coming to the farm.

Still thinking of her friend Betty she returned through the silent veld to her home, imagining them walking together over this road and talking as they had been used to do. The thought of Betty, who had turned into a shrewd, elderly woman doctor with kind eyes, sustained her through the frightening silences. At the gate she lifted her head to sniff the heavy perfume of the moonflowers, and became conscious that something else was invading her dream: it was a very bad smell, an odour of decay mingled with the odour of the flowers. Something had died on the veld, and the wind had changed and was bringing the smell towards the house. She made a mental note: I must send the boy in the morning to see what it is. Then the conflict between her thoughts of her friend and her own life presented itself sharply to her. You are a silly woman, Caroline, she said to herself. Three years before they had gone on holiday to England, and she had found she and Betty had nothing to say to each other. Their lives were so far apart, and had been for so long, that the weeks they spent together were an offering to a friendship that had died years before. She knew it very well, but tried not to think of it. It was necessary to her to have Betty remain, in imagination at least, as a counter-weight to her loneliness. Now she was being made to realise the truth. She resented that too, and somewhere the resentment was chalked up against Mrs De Wet, the Dutch woman who was going to invade her life with impertinent personal claims.

And next day, and the days following, she cleaned and swept and tidied the old house, not for Mrs De Wet, but for Betty. Otherwise she could not have gone through with it. And when it was all finished she walked through the rooms which she had furnished with things taken from her own home, and said to a visionary Betty (but Betty as she had been thirty years before): 'Well, what do you think of it?' The place was bare but clean now, and smelling of sunlight and air. The floors had coloured coconut matting over the brick; the beds, standing on opposite sides of the room, were covered with gaily striped counterpanes. There were vases of flowers everywhere. 'You would like living here,' Mrs Gale said to Betty, before locking the house up and returning to her own, feeling as if she had won a victory over herself.

The De Wets sent a wire saying they would arrive on Sunday after lunch. Mrs Gale noted with annoyance that this would spoil her rest, for she slept every day, through the afternoon heat. Major Gale, for whom every day was a working day (he hated idleness and found odd jobs to occupy him on Sundays), went off to a distant part of the farm to look at his cattle. Mrs Gale laid herself down on her bed with her eyes shut and listened for a car, all her nerves stretched. Flies buzzed drowsily over the window-panes; the breeze from the garden was warm and scented. Mrs Gale slept uncomfortably, warring all the afternoon with the knowledge that she should be awake. When she woke at four she was cross and tired, and there was still no sign of a car. She rose and dressed herself, taking a frock from the cupboard without looking to see what it was: her clothes were often fifteen years old. She brushed her hair absentmindedly; and then, recalled by a sense that she had not taken enough trouble, slipped a large gold locket round her neck, as a conscientious mark of welcome. Then she left a message with the houseboy that she would be in the garden and walked away from the veranda with a strong excitement growing in her. This excitement rose as she moved through the crowding shrubs under the walls, through the rose garden with its wide green lawns where water sprayed all the year round, and arrived at her favourite spot among the fountains and the pools of water lilies. Her water-garden was an extravagance, for the pumping of the water from the river cost a great deal of money.

She sat herself on a shaded bench; and on one side were the glittering plumes of the fountains, the roses, the lawns, the house, and beyond them the austere wind-bitten high veld; on the other, at her feet, the ground dropped hundreds of feet sharply to the river. It was a rocky shelf thrust forward over the gulf, and here she would sit for hours, leaning dizzily outwards, her short grey hair blown across her face, lost in adoration of the hills across the river. Not of the river itself, no, she thought of that with a sense of danger, for there, below her, in that green-crowded gully, were suddenly the tropics: palm trees, a slow brown river that eddied into reaches of marsh or curved round belts of reeds twelve feet high. There were crocodiles, and leopards came from the rocks to drink. Sitting there on her exposed shelf, a smell of sun-warmed green, of hot decaying water, of luxurious growth, an intoxicating heady smell rose in waves to her face. She had learned to ignore it, and to ignore the river, while she watched the hills. They were *her* hills: that was how she felt. For years she had sat here, hours every day, watching the cloud shadows move over them, watching them turn blue with distance or come close after rain so that she could see the exquisite brushwork of trees on the lower slopes. They were never the same half an hour together. Modulating light created them anew for her as she looked, thrusting one peak forwards and withdrawing another, moving them back so that they were hazed on a smoky horizon, crouched in sullen retreat; or raising them so that they towered into a brilliant cleansed sky. Sitting here, buffeted by winds, scorched by the sun or shivering with cold, she could challenge anything. They were her mountains; they were what she was; they had made her, had crystallised her loneliness into a strength, had sustained her and fed her.

And now she almost forgot the De Wets were coming, and were hours late. Almost, not quite. At last, understanding that the sun was setting (she could feel its warmth striking below her shoulders), her small irritation turned to anxiety. Something might have happened to them? They had taken the wrong road, perhaps? The car had broken down? And there was the Major, miles away with their own car, and so there was no means of looking for them. Perhaps she should send out natives, along the roads? If they had taken the wrong turning, to the river, they might be bogged in mud to the axles. Down there, in the swampy heat, they could be bitten by mosquitoes and then ...

Caroline, she said to herself severely (thus finally withdrawing from the mountains), don't let things worry you so. She stood up and shook herself, pushed the hair out of her face, and gripped her whipping skirts in a thick bunch. She stepped backwards away from the wind that raked the edges of the cliff, sighed a good-bye to her garden for that day, and returned to the house. There, outside the front door, was a car, an ancient jalopy bulging with luggage, its back doors tied with rope. And children! She could see a half-grown girl on the steps. No, really, it was too much. On the other side of the car stooped a tall, thin, fairheaded man, burnt as brown as toffee, looking for someone to come. He must be the father. She approached, adjusting her face to a smile, looking apprehensively about her for the children. The man slowly came forward, the girl after him. 'I expected you earlier,' began Mrs Gale briskly, looking reproachfully into the man's face. His eyes were cautious, blue, assessing. He looked her casually up and down, and seemed not to take her into account. 'Is Major Gale about?' he asked. 'I am Mrs Gale,' she replied. Then, again: 'I expected you earlier.' Really, four hours late, and not a word of apology!

'We started late,' he remarked. 'Where can I put our things?'

Mrs Gale swallowed her annoyance and said: 'I didn't know you had a family. I didn't make arrangements.'

'I wrote to the Major about my wife,' said De Wet. 'Didn't he get my letter?' He sounded offended.

Weakly Mrs Gale said: 'Your wife?' and looked in wonderment at the girl, who was smiling awkwardly behind her husband. It could be seen, looking at her more closely, that she might perhaps be eighteen. She was a small creature, with delicate brown legs and arms, a brush of dancing black curls, and large excited black eyes. She put both hands round her husband's arm, and said, giggling: 'I am Mrs De Wet.'

De Wet put her away from him, gently, but so that she pouted and said: 'We got married last week.'

'Last week,' said Mrs Gale, conscious of dislike.

The girl said, with an extraordinary mixture of effrontery and shyness: 'He met me in the cinema and we got married next day.' It seemed as if she were in some way offering herself to the older woman, offering something precious of herself.

'Really,' said Mrs Gale politely, glancing almost apprehensively at this man, this slow-moving, laconic, shrewd South African, who had behaved with such violence and folly. Distaste twisted her again.

Suddenly the man said, grasping the girl by the arm, and gently shaking her to and fro, in a sort of controlled exasperation: 'Thought I had better get myself a wife to cook for me, all this way out in the blue. No restaurants here, hey, Doodle?'

'Oh, Jack,' pouted the girl, giggling. 'All he thinks about is his stomach,' she said to Mrs Gale, as one girl to another, and then glanced with delicious fear up at her husband.

'Cooking is what I married you for,' he said, smiling down at her intimately.

There stood Mrs Gale opposite them, and she saw that they had forgotten her existence; and that it was only by the greatest effort of will that they did not kiss. 'Well,' she remarked dryly, 'this is a surprise.'

They fell apart, their faces changing. They became at once what they had been during the first moments: two hostile strangers. They looked at her across the barrier that seemed to shut the world away from them. They saw a middle-aged English lady, in a shapeless old-fashioned blue silk dress, with a gold locket sliding over a flat bosom, smiling at them coldly, her blue, misted eyes critically narrowed.

'I'll take you to your house,' she said energetically. 'I'll walk, and you go in the car – no, I walk it often.' Nothing would induce her to get into the bouncing rattle-trap that was bursting with luggage and half-suppressed intimacies.

As stiff as a twig she marched before them along the road, while the car jerked and ground along in bottom gear. She knew it was ridiculous; she could feel their eyes on her back, could feel their astonished amusement; but she could not help it.

When they reached the house, she unlocked it, showed them briefly what arrangements had been made, and left them. She walked back in a tumult of anger, caused mostly because of her picture of herself walking along that same road, meekly followed by the car, and refusing to do the only sensible thing, which was to get into it with them.

She sat on her veranda for half an hour, looking at the sunset sky without seeing it, and writhing with various emotions, none of which she classified. Eventually she called the houseboy, and gave him a note, asking the two to come to dinner. No sooner had the boy left, and was trotting off down the bushy path to the gate, than she called him back. 'I'll go myself,' she said. This was partly to prove that she made nothing of walking the half mile, and partly from contrition. After all, it was no crime to get married, and they seemed very fond of each other. That was how she put it.

When she came to the house, the front room was littered with luggage, paper, pots and pans. All the exquisite order she had created was destroyed. She could hear voices from the bedroom.

'But, Jack, I don't want you to. I want you to stay with me.' And then his voice, humorous, proud, slow, amorous: 'You'll do what I tell you, my girl. I've got to see the old man and find out what's cooking. I start work tomorrow, don't forget.'

'But, Jack ...' Then came sounds of scuffling, laughter and a sharp slap.

'Well,' said Mrs Gale, drawing in her breath. She knocked on the wood of the door, and all sound ceased. 'Come in,' came the girl's voice. Mrs Gale hesitated, then went into the bedroom.

Mrs De Wet was sitting in a bunch on the bed, her flowered frock spread around her, combing her hair. Mrs Gale noted that the two beds had already been pushed together. 'I've come to ask you to dinner,' she said briskly. 'You don't want to have to cook when you've just come.'

Their faces had already become bland and polite.

'Oh no, don't trouble, Mrs Gale,' said De Wet, awkwardly. 'We'll get ourselves something, don't worry.' He glanced at the girl, and his face softened. He said, unable to resist it: 'She'll get busy with the tin-opener in a minute, I expect. That's her idea of feeding a man.'

'Oh, Jack,' pouted his wife.

De Wet turned back to the washstand, and proceeded to swab lather on his face. Waving the brush at Mrs Gale, he said: 'Thanks all the same. But tell the Major I'll be over after dinner to talk things over.'

'Very well,' said Mrs Gale, 'just as you like.'

She walked away from the house. Now she felt rebuffed. After all, they might have had the politeness to come; yet she was pleased they hadn't; yet if they preferred making love to getting to know the people who were to be their close neighbours for what might be years, it was their own affair...

Mrs De Wet was saying, as she painted her toenails, with her knees drawn up to her chin, and the bottle of varnish gripped between her heels: 'Who the hell does she think she is, anyway? Surely she could give us a meal without making such a fuss when we've just come.'

'She came to ask us, didn't she?'

'Hoping we would say no.'

And Mrs Gale knew quite well that this was what they were thinking, and felt it was unjust. She would have liked them to come: the man wasn't a bad sort, in his way; a simple soul, but pleasant enough; as for the girl, she would have to learn, that was all. They should have come, it was their fault. Nevertheless she was filled with that discomfort that comes of having done a job badly. If she had behaved differently they would have come. She was cross throughout dinner; and that meal was not half finished when there was a knock on the door. De Wet stood there, apparently surprised they had not finished, from which it seemed that the couple had, after all, dined off sardines and bread and butter.

Major Gale left his meal and went out to the veranda to discuss business. Mrs Gale finished her dinner in state, and then joined the two men. Her husband rose politely at her coming, offered her a chair, sat down and forgot her presence. She listened to them talking for some two hours. Then she interjected a remark (a thing she never did, as a rule, for women get used to sitting silent when men discuss farming) and did not know herself what made her say what she did about the cattle; but when De Wet looked round absently as if to say she should mind her own business, and her husband remarked absently, 'Yes, dear,' when a Yes dear did not fit her remark at all, she got up angrily and went indoors. Well, let them talk, then, she did not mind.

As she undressed for bed, she decided she was tired, because of her broken sleep that afternoon. But she could not sleep then, either. She listened to the sound of the men's voices, drifting brokenly round the corner of the veranda. They seemed to be thoroughly enjoying themselves. It was after twelve when she heard De Wet say, in that slow facetious way of his: 'I'd better be getting home. I'll catch it hot, as it is.' And, with rage, Mrs Gale heard her husband laugh. He actually laughed. She realised that she herself had been planning an acid remark for when he came to the bedroom; so when he did enter, smelling of tobacco smoke, and grinning, and then proceeded to walk jauntily about the room in his underclothes, she said nothing, but noted that he was getting fat, in spite of all the hard work he did.

'Well, what do you think of the man?'

'He'll do very well indeed,' said Major Gale, with satisfaction. 'Very well. He knows his stuff all right. He's been doing mixed farming in the Transvaal for years.' After a moment he asked politely, as he got with a bounce into his own bed on the other side of the room: 'And what is she like?'

'I haven't seen much of her, have I? But she seems pleasant enough.' Mrs Gale spoke with measured detachment.

'Someone for you to talk to,' said Major Gale, turning himself over to sleep. 'You had better ask her over to tea.'

At this Mrs Gale sat straight up in her own bed with a jerk of annoyance. Someone for her to talk to, indeed! But she composed herself, said good night with her usual briskness, and lay awake. Next day she must certainly ask the girl to morning tea. It would be rude not to. Besides, that would leave the afternoon free for her garden and her mountains.

Next morning she sent a boy across with a note, which read: 'I shall be so pleased if you will join me for morning tea.' She signed it: Caroline Gale.

She went herself to the kitchen to cook scones and cakes. At eleven o'clock she was seated on the veranda in the green-dappled shade from the creepers, saying to herself that she believed she was in for a headache. Living as she did, in a long, timeless abstraction of growing things and mountains and silence, she had become very conscious of her body's responses to weather and to the slow advance of age. A small ache in her ankle when rain was due was like a cherished friend. Or she would sit with her eyes shut, in the shade, after a morning's pruning in the violent sun, feeling waves of pain flood back from her eyes to the back of her skull, and say with satisfaction: 'You deserve it, Caroline!' It was right she should pay for such pleasure with such pain.

At last she heard lagging footsteps up the path, and she opened her eyes reluctantly. There was the girl, preparing her face for a social occasion, walking primly through the bougainvillaea arches, in a flowered frock as vivid as her surroundings. Mrs Gale jumped to her feet and cried gaily: 'I am so glad you had time to come.' Mrs De Wet giggled irresistibly and said: 'But I had nothing else to do, had I?' Afterwards she said scornfully to her husband: 'She's nuts. She writes me letters with stuck-down envelopes when I'm five minutes away, and says Have I the time? What the hell else did she think I had to do?' And then, violently: 'She can't have anything to do. There was enough food to feed ten.'

'Wouldn't be a bad idea if you spent more time cooking,' said De Wet fondly.

The next day Mrs Gale gardened, feeling guilty all the time, because she could not bring herself to send over another note of invitation. After a few days, she invited the De Wets to dinner, and through the meal made polite conversation with the girl while the men lost themselves in cattle diseases. What could one talk to a girl like that about? Nothing! Her mind, as far as Mrs Gale was concerned, was a dark continent, which she had no inclination to explore. Mrs De Wet was not interested in recipes, and when Mrs Gale gave helpful advice about ordering clothes from England, which was so much cheaper than buying them in the local towns, the reply came that she had made all her own clothes since she was seven. After that there seemed nothing to say, for it was hardly possible to remark that these strapped sun-dresses and bright slacks were quite unsuitable for the farm, besides being foolish, since bare shoulders in this sun were dangerous. As for her shoes! She wore corded beach sandals which had already turned dust colour from the roads.

There were two more tea parties; then they were allowed to lapse. From time to time Mrs Gale wondered uneasily what on earth the poor child did with herself all day, and felt it was her duty to go and find out. But she did not.

One morning she was pricking seedlings into a tin when the houseboy came and said the little missus was on the veranda and she was sick.

At once dismay flooded Mrs Gale. She thought of a dozen tropical diseases, of which she had had unpleasant experience, and almost ran to the veranda. There was the girl, sitting screwed up in a chair, her face contorted, her eyes red, her whole body shuddering violently. 'Malaria,' thought Mrs Gale at once, noting that trembling.

'What is the trouble, my dear?' Her voice was kind. She put her hand on the girl's shoulder. Mrs De Wet turned and flung her arms around her hips, weeping, weeping, her small curly head buried in Mrs Gale's stomach. Holding herself stiffly away from this dismaying contact, Mrs Gale stroked her head and made soothing noises.

'Mrs Gale, Mrs Gale ...'

'What is it?'

'I can't stand it. I shall go mad. I simply can't stand it.'

Mrs Gale, seeing that this was not a physical illness, lifted her up, led her inside, laid her on her own bed, and fetched cologne and handkerchiefs. Mrs De Wet sobbed for a long while, clutching the older woman's hand, and then at last grew silent. Finally she sat up with a small rueful smile, and said pathetically: 'I am a fool.'

'But what *is* it, dear?'

'It isn't anything, really. I am so lonely. I wanted to get my mother up to stay with me, only Jack said there wasn't room, and he's quite right, only I got mad, because I thought he might at least have had my mother ...'

Mrs Gale felt guilt like a sword: she could have filled the place of this child's mother.

'And it isn't anything, Mrs Gale, not really. It's not that I'm not happy with Jack. I am, but I never see him. I'm not used to this kind of thing. I come from a family of thirteen counting my parents, and I simply can't stand it.'

Mrs Gale sat and listened, and thought of her own loneliness when she first began this sort of life.

'And then he comes in late, not till seven sometimes, and I know he can't help it, with the farm work and all that, and then he has supper and goes straight off to bed. I am not sleepy then. And then I get up sometimes and I walk along the road with my dog ...'

Mrs Gale remembered how, in the early days after her husband had finished with his brief and apologetic embraces, she used to rise with a sense of relief and steal to the front room, where she lighted the lamp again and sat writing letters, reading old ones, thinking of her friends and of herself as a girl. But that was before she had her first child. She thought: This girl should have a baby; and could not help glancing downwards at her stomach.

Mrs De Wet, who missed nothing, said resentfully: 'Jack says I should have a baby. That's all he says.' Then, since she had to include Mrs Gale in this resentment, she transformed herself all at once from a sobbing baby into a gauche but armoured young woman with whom Mrs Gale could have no contact. 'I am sorry,' she said formally. Then, with a grating humour: 'Thank you for letting me blow off steam.' She climbed off the bed, shook her skirts straight, and tossed her head. 'Thank you. I am a nuisance.' With painful brightness she added: 'So, that's how it goes. Who would be a woman, eh?'

Mrs Gale stiffened. 'You must come and see me whenever you are lonely,' she said, equally bright and false. It seemed to her incredible that this girl should come to her with all her defences down, and then suddenly shut her out with this facetious nonsense. But she felt more comfortable with the distance between them, she couldn't deny it.

'Oh, I will, Mrs Gale. Thank you so much for asking me.' She lingered for a moment, frowning at the brilliantly polished table in the front room, and then took her leave. Mrs Gale watched her go. She noted that at the gate the girl started whistling gaily, and smiled comically. Letting off steam! Well, she said to herself, well ... And she went back to her garden.

That afternoon she made a point of walking across to the other house. She would offer to show Mrs De Wet the garden. The two women returned together, Mrs Gale wondering if the girl regretted her emotional lapse of the morning. If so, she showed no signs of it. She broke into bright chatter when a topic mercifully occurred to her; in between were polite silences full of attention to what she seemed to hope Mrs Gale might say.

Mrs Gale was relying on the effect of her garden. They passed the house through the shrubs. There were the fountains, sending up their vivid showers of spray, there the cool mats of water lilies, under which the coloured fishes slipped, there the irises, sunk in green turf.

'This must cost a packet to keep up,' said Mrs De Wet. She stood at the edge of the pool, looking at her reflection dissolving among the broad green leaves, glanced obliquely up at Mrs Gale, and dabbed her exposed red toenails in the water.

Mrs Gale saw that she was thinking of herself as her husband's employer's wife. 'It does, rather,' she said dryly, remembering that the only quarrels she ever had with her husband were over the cost of pumping water. 'You are fond of gardens?' she asked. She could not imagine anyone not being fond of gardens.

Mrs De Wet said sullenly: 'My mother was always too busy having kids to have time for gardens. She had her last baby early this year.' An ancient and incommunicable resentment dulled her face. Mrs Gale, seeing that all this beauty and peace meant nothing to her companion that she would have it mean, said, playing her last card: 'Come and see my mountains.' She regretted the pronoun as soon as it was out – *so* exaggerated.

But when she had the girl safely on the rocky verge of the escarpment, she heard her say: 'There's my river.' She was leaning forward over the great gulf, and her voice was lifted with excitement. 'Look,' she was saying. 'Look, there is it.' She turned to Mrs Gale, laughing, her hair spun over her eyes in a fine iridescent rain, tossing her head back, clutching her skirts down, exhilarated by the tussle with the wind.

'Mind, you'll lose your balance.' Mrs Gale pulled her back. 'You have been down to the river, then?'

'I go there every morning.'

Mrs Gale was silent. The thing seemed preposterous. 'But it is four miles there and four back.'

'Oh, I'm used to walking.'

'But ...' Mrs Gale heard her own sour, expostulating voice and stopped herself. There was after all no logical reason why the girl should not go to the river. 'What do you do there?'

'I sit on the edge of a big rock and dangle my legs in the water, and I fish, sometimes. I caught a barbel last week. It tasted foul, but it was fun catching it. And I pick water lilies.'

'There are crocodiles,' said Mrs Gale sharply. The girl was wrong-headed; anyone was who could like that steamy bath of vapours, heat, smells and – what? It was an unpleasant place. 'A native girl was taken there last year, at the ford.'

'There couldn't be a crocodile where I go. The water is clear, right down. You can see right under the rocks. It is a lovely pool. There's a kingfisher, and water-birds, all colours. They are so pretty. And when you sit there and look, the sky is a long narrow slit. From there it looks quite far across the river to the other side, but really it isn't. And the trees crowding close make it narrower. Just think how many millions of years it must have taken for the water to wear down the rock so deep.'

'There's bilharzia, too.'

'Oh, bilharzia!'

'There's nothing funny about bilharzia. My husband had it. He had injections for six months before he was cured.'

The girl's face dulled. 'I'll be careful,' she said irrationally, turning away, holding her river and her long hot dreamy mornings away from Mrs Gale, like a secret.

'Look at the mountains,' said Mrs Gale, pointing. The girl glanced over the chasm at the foothills, then bent forward again, her face reverent. Through the mass of green below were glimpses of satiny brown. She breathed deeply: 'Isn't it a lovely smell?' she said.

'Let's go and have some tea,' said Mrs Gale. She felt cross and put out; she had no notion why. She could not help being brusque with the girl. And so at last they were quite silent together; and in silence they remained on that veranda above the beautiful garden, drinking their tea and wishing it was time for them to part.

Soon they saw the two husbands coming up the garden. Mrs De Wet's face lit up; and she sprang to her feet and was off down the path, running lightly. She caught her husband's arm and clung there. He put her away from him, gently. 'Hullo,' he remarked good-humouredly. 'Eating again?' And then he turned back to Major Gale and went on talking. The girl lagged up the path behind her husband like a sulky small girl, pulling at Mrs Gale's beloved roses and scattering crimson petals everywhere.

On the veranda the men sank at once into chairs, took large cups of tea, and continued talking as they drank thirstily. Mrs Gale listened and smiled. Crops, cattle, disease; weather, crops and cattle. Mrs De Wet perched on the veranda wall and swung her legs. Her face was petulant, her lips trembled, her eyes were full of tears. Mrs Gale was saying silently under her breath, with ironical pity, in which there was also cruelty: You'll get used to it, my dear; you'll get used to it. But she respected the girl, who had courage: walking to the river and back, wandering round the dusty flowerbeds in the starlight, trying to find peace – at least, she was trying to find it.

She said sharply, cutting into the men's conversation: 'Mr De Wet, did you know your wife spends her mornings at the river?'

The man looked at her vaguely, while he tried to gather the sense of her words: his mind was on the farm. 'Sure,' he said at last. 'Why not?'

'Aren't you afraid of bilharzia?'

He said laconically: 'If we were going to get it, we would have got it long ago. A drop of water can infect you, touching the skin.'

'Wouldn't it be wiser not to let the water touch you in the first place?' she enquired with deceptive mildness.

'Well, I told her. She wouldn't listen. It is too late now. Let her enjoy it.'

'But ...'

'About that red heifer,' said Major Gale, who had not been aware of any interruption.

'No,' said Mrs Gale sharply. 'You are not going to dismiss it like that.' She saw the three of them look at her in astonishment. 'Mr De Wet, have you ever thought what it means to a woman being alone all day, with not enough to do? It's enough to drive anyone crazy.'

Major Gale raised his eyebrows; he had not heard his wife speak like that for so long. As for De Wet, he said with a slack good-humour that sounded brutal: 'And what do you expect me to do about it?'

'You don't realise,' said Mrs Gale futilely, knowing perfectly well there was nothing he could do about it. 'You don't understand how it is.'

'She'll have a kid soon,' said De Wet. 'I hope so, at any rate. That will give her something to do.'

Anger raced through Mrs Gale like a flame along petrol. She was trembling. 'She might be that red heifer,' she said at last.

'What's the matter with having kids?' asked De Wet. 'Any objection?'

'You might ask me first,' said the girl bitterly.

Her husband blinked at her, comically bewildered. 'Hey, what is this?' he enquired. 'What have I done? You said you wanted to have kids. Wouldn't have married you otherwise.'

'I never said I didn't.'

'Talking about her as if she were ...'

'When, then?' Mrs Gale and the man were glaring at each other.

'There's more to women than having children,' said Mrs Gale at last, and flushed because of the ridiculousness of her words.

De Wet looked her up and down, up and down. 'I want kids,' he said at last. 'I want a large family. Make no mistake about that. And when I married her' – he jerked his head at his wife – 'I told her I wanted them. She can't turn round now and say I didn't.'

'Who is turning round and saying anything?' asked the girl, fine and haughty, staring away over the trees.

'Well, if no one is blaming anyone for anything,' asked Major Gale, jauntily twirling his little moustache, 'what is all this about?'

'God knows, I don't,' said De Wet angrily. He glanced sullenly at Mrs Gale. 'I didn't start it.'

Mrs Gale sat silent, trembling, feeling foolish, but so angry she could not speak. After a while she said to the girl: 'Shall we go inside, my dear?' The girl, reluctantly, and with a lingering backward look at her husband, rose and followed Mrs Gale. 'He didn't mean anything,' she said awkwardly, apologising for her husband to her husband's employer's wife. This room, with its fine old furniture, always made her apologetic. At this moment, De Wet stooped into the doorway and said: 'Come on, I am going home.'

'Is that an order?' asked the girl quickly, backing so that she came side by side with Mrs Gale: she even reached for the other woman's hand. Mrs Gale did not take it: this was going too far.

'What's got into you?' he said, exasperated. 'Are you coming or are you not?'

'I can't do anything else, can I?' she replied, and followed him from the house like a queen who has been insulted.

Major Gale came in after a few moments. 'Lovers' quarrel,' he said, laughing awkwardly. This phrase annoyed Mrs Gale. 'That man!' she exclaimed. 'That man!'

'Why, what's wrong with him?' She remained silent, pretending to arrange her flowers. This silly scene, with its hinterlands of emotion, made her furious. She was angry with herself, angry with her husband, and furious at that foolish couple who had succeeded in upsetting her and destroying her peace. At last she said: 'I am going to bed. I've such a headache, I can't think.'

'I'll bring you a tray, my dear,' said Major Gale, with a touch of exaggeration in his courtesy that annoyed her even more. 'I don't want anything, thank you,' she said, like a child, and marched off to the bedroom.

There she undressed and went to bed. She tried to read, found she was not following the sense of the words, put down the book, and blew out the light. Light streamed into the room from the moon; she could see the trees along the fence banked black against stars. From next door came the clatter of her husband's solitary meal.

Later she heard voices from the veranda. Soon her husband came into the room and said: 'De Wet is asking whether his wife has been here.'

'What!' exclaimed Mrs Gale, slowly assimilating the implications of this. 'Why, has she gone off somewhere?'

'She's not at home,' said the Major uncomfortably. For he always became uncomfortable and very polite when he had to deal with situations like this.

Mrs Gale sank back luxuriously on her pillow. 'Tell that fine young man that his wife often goes for long walks by herself when he's asleep. He probably hasn't noticed it.' Here she gave a deadly look at her husband. 'Just as I used to,' she could not prevent herself adding.

Major Gale fiddled with his moustache, and gave her a look which seemed to say: 'Oh lord, don't say we are going back to all that business again?' He went out, and she heard him saying: 'Your wife might have gone for a walk, perhaps?' Then the young man's voice: 'I know she does sometimes. I don't like her being out at night, but she just walks around the house. And she takes the dogs with her. Maybe she's gone farther this time – being upset, you know.'

'Yes, I know,' said Major Gale. Then they both laughed. The laughter was of a quite different quality from the sober responsibility of their tone a moment before: and Mrs Gale found herself sitting up in bed, muttering: 'How *dare* he?'

She got up and dressed herself. She was filled with premonitions of unpleasantness. In the main room her husband was sitting reading, and since he seldom read, it seemed he was also worried. Neither of them spoke. When she looked at the clock, she found it was just past nine o'clock.

After an hour of tension, they heard the footsteps they had been waiting for. There stood De Wet, worried sick, his face white, his eyes burning.

'We must get the boys out,' he said, speaking directly to Major Gale, and ignoring Mrs Gale.

'I am coming too,' she said.

'No, my dear,' said the Major cajolingly. 'You stay here.'

'You can't go running over the veld at this time of night,' said De Wet to Mrs Gale, very blunt and rude.

'I shall do as I please,' she returned.

The three of them stood on the veranda, waiting for the natives. Everything was drenched in moonlight. Soon they heard a growing clamour of voices from over a ridge, and a little while later the darkness there was lighted by flaring torches held high by invisible hands: it seemed as if the night were scattered with torches advancing of their own accord. Then a crowd of dark figures took shape under the broken lights. The farm natives, excited by the prospect of a night's chasing over the veld, were yelling as if they were after a small buck or hare.

Mrs Gale sickened. 'Is it necessary to have all these natives in it?' she asked. 'After all, have we even considered the possibilities? Where can a girl run *to* on a place like this?'

'That is the point,' said Major Gale frigidly.

'I can't bear to think of her being – pursued, like this, by a crowd of natives. It's horrible.'

'More horrible still if she has hurt herself and is waiting for help,' said De Wet. He ran off down the path, shouting to the natives and waving his arms. The Gales saw them separate into three bands, and soon there were three groups of lights jerking away in different directions through the hazy dark, and the yells and shouting came back to them on the wind.

Mrs Gale thought: She could have taken the road back to the station, in which case she could be caught by car, even now.

She commanded her husband: 'Take the car along the road and see.'

'That's an idea,' said the Major, and went off to the garage. She heard the car start off, and watched the rear light dwindle redly into the night.

But that was the least ugly of the possibilities. What if she had been so blind with anger, grief, or whatever emotion it was that had driven her away, that she had simply run off into the veld not knowing where she went? There were thousands of acres of trees, thick grass, gullies, *kopjes*. She might at this moment be lying with a broken arm or leg; she might be pushing her way through grass higher than her head, stumbling over roots and rocks. She might be screaming for help somewhere for fear of wild animals, for if she crossed the valley into the hills there were leopards, lions, wild dogs. Mrs Gale suddenly caught her breath in an agony of fear: the valley! What if she had mistaken her direction and walked over the edge of the escarpment in the dark? What if she had forded the river and been taken by a crocodile? There were so many things: she might even be caught in a game trap. Once, taking her walk, Mrs Gale herself had come across a tall sapling by the path where the spine and ribs of a large buck dangled, and on the ground were the pelvis and legs, fine eroded bones of an animal trapped and forgotten by its trapper. Anything might have happened. And worse than any of the actual physical dangers was the danger of falling a victim to fear: being alone on the veld, at night, knowing oneself lost: this was enough to send anyone off balance.

The silly little fool, the silly little fool: anger and pity and terror confused in Mrs Gale until she was walking crazily up and down her garden through the bushes, tearing blossoms and foliage to pieces in trembling fingers. She had no idea how time was passing; until Major Gale returned and said that he had taken the ten miles to the station at seven miles an hour, turning his lights into the bush this way and that. At the station everyone was in bed; but the police were standing on the alert for news.

It was long after twelve. As for De Wet and the bands of searching natives, there was no sign of them. They would be miles away by now.

'Go to bed,' said Major Gale at last.

'Don't be ridiculous,' she said. After a while she held out her hand to him, and said: 'One feels so helpless.'

There was nothing to say; they walked together under the stars, their minds filled with horrors. Later she made some tea and they drank it standing; to sit would have seemed heartless. They were so tired they could hardly move. Then they got their second wind and continued walking. That night Mrs Gale hated her garden, that highly-cultivated patch of luxuriant growth, stuck in the middle of a country that could do this sort of thing to you suddenly. It was all the fault of the country! In a civilised sort of place, the girl would have caught the train to her mother, and a wire would have put everything right. Here, she might have killed herself, simply because of a passing fit of despair. Mrs Gale began to get hysterical. She was weeping softly in the circle of her husband's arm by the time the sky lightened and the redness of dawn spread over the sky.

As the sun rose, De Wet returned over the veld. He said he had sent the natives back to their huts to sleep. They had found nothing. He stated that he also intended to sleep for an hour, and that he would be back on the job by eight. Major Gale nodded: he recognised this as a necessary discipline against collapse. But after the young man walked off across the veld towards his house, the two older people looked at each other and began to move after him. 'He must not be alone,' said Mrs Gale sensibly. 'I shall make him some tea and see that he drinks it.'

'He wants sleep,' said Major Gale. His own eyes were red and heavy.

'I'll put something in his tea,' said Mrs Gale. 'He won't know it is there.' Now she had something to do, she was much more cheerful. Planning De Wet's comfort, she watched him turn in at his gate and vanish inside the house: they were some two hundred yards behind.

Suddenly there was a shout, and then a commotion of screams and yelling. The Gales ran fast along the remaining distance and burst into the front room, white-faced and expecting the worst, in whatever form it might choose to present itself.

There was De Wet, his face livid with rage, bending over his wife, who was huddled on the floor and shielding her head with her arms, while he beat her shoulders with his closed fists.

Mrs Gale exclaimed: 'Beating your wife!'

De Wet flung the girl away from him, and staggered to his feet. 'She was here all the time,' he said, half in temper, half in sheer wonder. 'She was hiding under the bed. She told me. When I came in she was sitting on the bed and laughing at me.'

The girl beat her hands on the floor and said, laughing and crying together: 'Now you have to take some notice of me. Looking for me all night over the veld with your silly natives! You looked so stupid, running about like ants, looking for me.'

'My God,' said De Wet simply, giving up. He collapsed backwards into a chair and lay there, his eyes shut, his face twitching.

'So now you have to notice me,' she said defiantly, but beginning to look scared. 'I have to pretend to run away, but then you sit up and take notice.'

'Be quiet,' said De Wet, breathing heavily. 'Be quiet, if you don't want to get hurt bad.'

'Beating your wife,' said Mrs Gale. 'Savages behave better.'

'Caroline, my dear,' said Major Gale awkwardly. He moved towards the door.

'Take that woman out of here if you don't want me to beat her too,' said De Wet to Major Gale.

Mrs Gale was by now crying with fury. 'I'm not going,' she said. 'I'm not going. This poor child isn't safe with you.'

'But what was it all about?' said Major Gale, laying his hand kindly on the girl's shoulder. 'What was it, my dear? What did you have to do it for, and make us all so worried?'

She began to cry. 'Major Gale, I am sorry. I forgot myself. I got mad. I told him I was going to have a baby. I told him when I got back from your place. And all he said was: that's fine. That's the first of them, he said. He didn't love me, or say he was pleased, or nothing.'

'Dear Christ in hell,' said De Wet wearily, with the exasperation strong in his voice, 'what do you make me do these things for? Do you think I want to beat you? Did you think I wasn't pleased: I keep telling you I want kids, I love kids.'

. 'But you don't care about me,' she said, sobbing bitterly.

'Don't I?' he said helplessly.

'Beating your wife when she is pregnant,' said Mrs Gale. 'You ought to be ashamed of yourself.' She advanced on the young man with her own fists clenched, unconscious of what she was doing. 'You ought to be beaten yourself, that's what you need.'

Mrs De Wet heaved herself off the floor, rushed on Mrs Gale, pulled her back so that she nearly lost balance, and then flung herself on her husband. 'Jack,' she said, clinging to him desperately, 'I am sorry, I am so sorry, Jack.'

He put his arms round her. 'There,' he said simply, his voice thick with tiredness, 'don't cry. We got mixed up, that's all.'

Major Gale, who had caught and steadied his wife as she staggered back, said to her in a low voice: 'Come, Caroline. Come. Leave them to sort it out.'

'And what if he loses his temper again and decides to kill her this time?' demanded Mrs Gale, her voice shrill.

De Wet got to his feet, lifting his wife with him. 'Go away now, Mrs Major,' he said. 'Get out of here. You've done enough damage.'

'I've done enough damage?' she gasped. 'And what have I done?

'Oh nothing, nothing at all,' he said with ugly sarcasm. 'Nothing at all. But please go and leave my wife alone in future, Mrs Major.'

'Come, Caroline, *please*,' said Major Gale.

She allowed herself to be drawn out of the room. Her head was aching so that the vivid morning light invaded her eyes in a wave of pain. She swayed a little as she walked.

'Mrs Major,' she said, 'Mrs Major!'

'He was upset,' said her husband judiciously.

She snorted. Then, after a silence: 'So, it was all my fault.'

'He didn't say so.'

'I thought that was what he was saying. He behaves like a brute and then says it is my fault.'

'It was no one's fault,' said Major Gale, patting her vaguely on shoulders and back as they stumbled back home.

They reached the gate, and entered the garden, which was now musical with birds.

'A lovely morning,' remarked Major Gale.

'Next time you get an assistant,' she said finally, 'get people of our kind. These might be savages, the way they behave.'

And that was the last word she would ever say on the subject.

High heels

Agnes Sam

1

I'm playing in the street with boys when Lindi comes hobbling on the pavement towards me. She's wearing high heel shoes too big for her.

Lindi poses on the pavement with her hand on her hip, pushing her hip out like she's carrying a baby. Only she got no baby. She only got a big black handbag hanging on her arm. After a bit, she changes the bag round and poses with her other hip sticking out. All the time she's tossing her head about, looking to the boys, her eyes wide like she's surprised. Only they're busy playing cricket. They're not bothered about Lindi's high heel shoes.

After a bit she yells at me, 'Hey, Ruthie! What ya doing?' She throws her head my way, then looks to the boys again.

All the time I'm making like my eyes are shut, but I'm looking down at Lindi's high heel shoes. They're bright red with peep toes and shiny buckles. When I can't stand to look at Lindi's shoes any more I open my eyes wide, like I'm also surprised, and say, 'Can't you see?'

'I see ya standing in the street! Where it's dangerous!' she yells back at me.

I know what she means. She means I'm *spek en boontjies* – like when they let you play a game but you're not really playing. I stick out my tongue. She flashes her bum. She's wearing proper panties! Then she goes on posing on the pavement, sticking her arm out so her handbag swings about. I wish I could take my eyes off her shoes.

'Ya like my shoes?' She twirls round on the pavement. 'Sissie gave it me.'

'You don't walk right in high heel shoes,' I say. But I really want to say I wish I had a sister to give me her high heel shoes.

'Ya want to try 'em on?'

I'm on the pavement before Lindi closes her mouth. She jumps back. Then she stares down at my feet like she just thought of something.

'We the same size,' I say, forgetting the shoes are too big for both of us.

Then suddenly Lindi screams out loud so everyone in the street can hear, 'Ya feet are dirty!' and hobbles away, with her handbag swinging by her side.

'Lin-di-we!' I scream after her like she left me in a burning house. 'Lin-di-we! Come back here! My feet are clean! Lin-di-we!'

But she just sways down the street away from me, on her high heel shoes. Like she don't hear me. So I shout after her, 'I *wish* you fall flat on your face,' and I shut my eyes tight and scream, 'I wish! I wish!' Only she don't fall.

I'm really playing cricket in the street with the boys. I'm scouting at the top end. Say the ball comes too far behind the wicket, I must run and give it back to them. When I throw they don't get it.

Always I like to play bouncing ball when I get the ball. Till they chase me. Then I hide the ball inside   my underpants and sing, 'First say when's *my* turn to bat!' When they all shout together, 'You're last man!', only then I take the ball out, making sure they don't see I'm wearing Mattie's underpants, and toss it back to them.

Mostly I'm first man. Sometimes I'm first man and last man, if I cry when I'm out. Like today. Only now I'm getting tired waiting for the ball. I don't know how many runs the batsman got. I don't even know what number's batting. And I want to look at Hama's high heel shoes. I'm going in.

'Hey Ruthie! The game's not over.'

'I need a wee!' I say, squeezing my legs together.

Because I forget to go to the lav when I play outside they get into trouble if they don't remind me. So they shout, 'All right! All right! But make quick!'

I run inside.

Sh! Sh! Sh! The house is secret when they're outside. So full of sun. Like fairies dancing on the floor. The floorboards smell of new polish. Their door creaks. The planes swoop down at me. The net curtain huffs and puffs. Funny! I still don't reach the planes. Even standing on their beds. And I got a birthday coming.

Say you pull the bottom drawer out – Sh! – like baby's sleeping – you can stand on it. Their things aren't for girls. You know you mustn't touch. Just look. Poor grasshopper still can't get out. Worms still in a tangle. Marbles – ugh! – still too heavy. Coca-Cola bottle tops make a jingling sound if you shake them. I never saw this plane before. It feels too soft. It mustn't be wood. Oh-oh! Better go.

I shut the door – Sh! – and turn round in the passage. The curtain moved.

I see it for the first time. There's a door behind the curtain at the end of the passage. I never knew there's a door behind the curtain. And Hama's sandals are by the door. I knock and listen. 'Hama? … Hama?' It's quiet. Like someone's waiting for me to go away. I try the handle. It's locked.

I do a wee and come out.

The door's still there. I rattle the handle. It's still locked. I run outside to tell the boys. 'Hey! Come and look! I found a door! I found a door.' They're not bothered about a door. They want me to scout again. Oh-oh. Lindi's coming back from the shops.

'We also got a secret door,' she says.

'You never told me about no secret door before!' I say.

'Don't get cross 'cause I c'n keep a secret.'

'You know what's behind the door?' I ask.

She looks at me down her nose and says, 'Yeah! Don't look so surprised, Ruthie! Ya not smart like me.'

'Go on, then. You can tell me now. It's no secret no more.'

Lindi frowns for a bit, then she asks, 'Why *they* don't tell ya?', looking at the boys.

'Because I only just found the door, this minute!'

'Even so, betcha they don't tell ya.'

'Why?'

She laughs. 'Ya have to open it yerself.'

'But why?'

'What good's a door if ya don't open it?'

'Anyone can open a door!'

'I betcha anything, ya won't go through the door.'

'Anything?'

'Yeah!'

'*Any*-thing?'

'I said anything, baby girl.'

'Okay! I bet you your shoes.'

'I just got given these shoes!'

'You said anything, Lindi!'

'I got a handbag. Better than *this* one.'

'I don't want a handbag.'

'All right then! But … ya only got till … till yer birthday party. Then the bet's off!'

'Why?'

"Cause I'm invited to yer party, ain't I?'

'And so?'

'Well then … ya have until yer party to go through the secret door.'

'But why?'

'Then I c'n give ya the shoes for a present, silly baby girl. Else my Ma will buy ya a present, and ya won't get high heel shoes.'

I don't understand this Lindi. But I don't want to show she's smarter than me. So I ask Mattie how many days to my birthday. My birthday's on Sunday. It's Thursday today. Mattie says that makes three days. There's plenty of time. And it's easy-peasy. All I got to do is ask Hama to unlock the secret door.

2

I wait for Hama to come through the secret door. After a bit I'm tired of waiting and maybe Hama won't ever come back, so I look for the key. I look in Hama's apron hanging on the hook. In all the tins and jars on the kitchen dresser. In the pockets of Hama's jersey and in her coat ... Under Hama's pillow. In her handbag. I look everywhere. Even under Hama's bed. And in her shoes.

These shoes fit me – if you don't look behind. I can put my elbows on Hama's dressing table standing on the floor in high heel shoes. There's Hama's treasure. No one must touch Hama's things. I won't touch! It's all blue glass. Children mustn't touch glass. There's a tray, two candlesticks, a powder bowl, a trinket box, a scent bottle.

Say you lift the glass lid with two hands and move your hands to the side – and bring it down slow-ly – it don't break. It's easy as pie. Hama's jewels are all colours. I can just stand and look at them all day.

I know how to put a string of pearls over my head. Only the knot won't stay. Clip-on earrings are easy. Gold bangles slip off. Hama's new lipstick tastes like apricot jam. It gets on your teeth say you press too hard. Oh-oh – crayons don't break so easy. Rouge is hard. Like a paint box. You can make it wet – with scent – or – you can scrape it with your fingernails. Like so ... Powder don't stay in the bowl. It likes to fly around the room. And make you sneeze. Say I comb my hair, I look just like Hama. I can walk in Hama's shoes. Better than Lindi. And gold bangles don't slip off if you hold your hands up.

I go outside and stand on the stoep. The boys are still playing cricket.

'Hey Ruthie! C'mon scout for us.'
'*I'm* not Ruthie! Can't you see? I'm Hama!'
They look at me and laugh. 'Minnie Mouse! Minnie Mouse! Ruthie looks like Minnie Mouse.'
'Ba-daah!' They smash a window. Everyone's running away. Now I got the bat I'll be first man when they start again.

I shout to them, 'No need to hide! No need to hide! Hama's gone through the door! She's not coming back.'

But the whole street heard the window go 'ba-daah!' Everyone's coming out. Hama's come back through the door. She's standing on the stoep. I'm standing with the bat, but everyone knows it's not me made the window go 'ba-daah!'

Hama's calling 'Matthew ... Mark ... Paul ... Tho-maas! Come for prayers!' They don't come. Hama calls again. 'Matthew ... Mark ... Paul ... Tho-maas!'

They come out from their hiding places. One by one. I call to them, 'Cock-roa-ches! Cock-roa-ches!' They look cross with me.

'I never told Hama where you hiding! I can keep a secret!'

Then Hama sees me. She says, 'This child!' and she comes over and slaps me. She takes her jewels and shoes away. I'm left standing in the street with no shoes when Lindi comes hobbling on the pavement in her high heel shoes again. If I try to run inside she'll see I'm crying. So I turn the other way. Lucky for me Mark picks me up and says, 'Come in for the litany of the saints!' and carries me high on his shoulder where Lindi can't see my face.

The boys kneel in the front room with Hama. Only I can't keep my eyes closed. They pull faces at me when Hama isn't looking. I tiptoe outside. Now the curtain's moved back. I move the curtain and see the door still there. I come back into the front room and whisper to Hama, 'What's behind the secret door?' She puts her finger to her lips, 'Sshh!'

They finish prayers and we sit around the kitchen table. I ask everyone what's behind the door. Hama says there's nothing behind the door. Dada laughs and shakes his head.

We're having supper when Father O'Malley comes in.
Father O'Malley looks around the table and says he expects
one of us to be a priest. Hama quickly makes a sign of the
cross.

'Hama, we already said grace,' I say.

Dada coughs.

When I ask Father O'Malley what's behind the curtain,
Dada tells me to sshh! Hama says there's nothing there and
Mark takes me quickly from the table.

'I'm still eating!' I say.

'Father O'Malley wants some of your food,' Mark says.

Before I go to bed I try the handle of the door. It's still
locked. When I'm in bed Paul sits by me. Paul says behind
the secret door is a dark, dark room. In the dark, dark room
is a dark, dark bed. In the dark, dark bed is an old, old lady.
Mark comes in and says, 'Shut-up! Someone with a capital
"s" will have nightmares.' They begin to whisper. Then they
quarrel. They say it's a cupboard. It's a lavatory. It leads to a
secret tunnel.

They don't know what's behind the door. They say we'll
find out when we're grown up. Only I can't wait. I can't ever
walk without high heel shoes again.

I wake up late in the night. Everyone's sleeping. I tiptoe
through the house. The door's locked. Hama's slippers are
outside the door. And Hama isn't in her bed. 'Hama? Let me
see inside the room, just once? Please Hama. I'll be a good
girl.' I wait in the passage for her to come out. I wake up
back in my bed.

Then on Friday Tata and Pharti come for my birthday party.
I tell Tata to show me behind the door for a birthday present.
Hama says, 'No!'

Tata says to Hama, 'Let her see the room, Ma. Sunday's
her birthday.'

'She'll tell Father O'Malley.'

Tata says, 'It might do him good.'

Now I know Hama won't give me the key. And I can't give up looking for it. Suddenly Hama's scent is all over the dressing table. I wipe it up with the powder puff. And Hama's standing at the bedroom door. She says I won't get a present for my birthday. But I don't want Hama's present. Hama won't give me her high heel shoes.

Now Hama's arranging flowers and polishing the candlesticks on the altar at church. I'm playing five-stones on the paving in the aisle. Hama doesn't want to leave me at home.

I hear Hama talking. But there's only me in the church. I stop playing to ask Hama who she's talking to. Hama says she's scolding God for not looking after us in a strange country.

She puts out her arms to me. When she's holding me she cries. I think hard what to say to stop her crying, so I say, 'Hama, show me what's in the room.'

She says, 'Shoo! Go play!'

3

It's Saturday. I still haven't found the key. In the morning we go to a wedding with Tata and Pharti. I sit near the front and see the bridegroom put a gold ring on the bride's finger. They receive Holy Communion. When we go to the bride's home he fastens a *Tali* round her neck before Father O'Malley arrives. They bathe the bride in turmeric. Then they give her a glass of milk with sliced bananas before breakfast. No one knows what's a *Tali*. Even Father O'Malley doesn't know.

We come home from the wedding and Lindi calls round to tell me her Ma has gone to town to buy my present. I jump up and down on the stoep shouting, 'I don't want a present! I don't want a present! I want high heel shoes!'

'But today's Saturday. If Ma don't buy ya present today – what ya gonna do tomorrow? Ya won't have high heel shoes or a present.'

'You said the bet's on till my birthday. And my birthday's only tomorrow.'

She runs away shouting, 'Give up, Ruthie! Give up! Give up, Ruthie! Give up!'

I run into the house and pull all Hama's clothes out of the dressing table drawer. I throw the pillows on the floor. I feel in the powder bowl. I empty the trinket box on the bed. The necklace breaks. The pearls roll all over the floor. I crawl about on the floor to pick up the pearls quickly before someone comes. Hama and Tata are standing at the door. I have the trinket box in my hands. And the pearls are still on the floor.

I'm not getting a present from Hama. Lindi's Ma bought me a present I don't want. And I'm not even having a birthday party.

Tata is helping me pick up the pearls while I'm crying, Hama is folding away her clothes saying, 'No birthday party!' and Tata reminds Hama about the time she pulled the dressing table cloth and pulled everything down with it. Everything broke, Tata says, but Hama says it was an accident. But I keep thinking I don't want a birthday party. No one coming to my party will bring a pair of high heel shoes for me.

When the pearls are in the trinket box Tata fluffs up the pillows, he takes my hand and walks with my to the corner shop. We buy chocolate cake and a bottle of Oros and a box of strawberry ice cream. At home Tata is setting one half of the table, placing a cushion on a chair for me, putting a tea towel over his arm and pretending he is a waiter serving me. Halfway through our party no one has come to bring me a present and tears are still running down my cheeks and into my mouth, spoiling the taste of the ice cream.

So Tata takes my hand and leads me into the passage. Without even asking Hama, Tata moves the curtain. He reaches up above the door and finds the key. Tata unlocks the door, he removes his shoes, then he removes mine. I turn the handle and we go through the secret door.

I've gone through the door. It's a room. There's no sick lady anywhere. Just rugs all around the floor. Blue and black and cream and green and brown. There's a brown wooden box in the middle of the room. It's covered with flowers and leaves made of the same wood. On the box is a little oil lamp with a red chimney and little trays and vases made of brass and gold and silver. Tata lifts the red glass chimney from the lamp. He strikes a match. A yellow flame leaps up. He lights the lamp. Then he touches an orange stone. It has two hollows. Tata takes a handful of grey powder from one hollow and places it in the other. Then he strikes another match. Again a yellow flame leaps up. He puts the flame to the powder. Blue smoke curls up into the room.

Tata says, '*Saamberani.*'

The room begins to smell of strange flowers. Then Tata sits cross-legged on a red cushion. He taps the cushion next to him. I kneel on the cushion looking up at him. He joins his hands and he begins to sing softly. I can't understand what he says. I can only make out the word 'Hama'. But I like his singing. It's not like the singing in church.

I look around the room. In one corner is a picture of Jesus with a bleeding heart and a statue of his Hama. I leave the room quietly and run to tell Lindi I went through the door.

Lindi knows. She's been waiting at the front door and sees me coming through the secret door.

'But do ya know what's the secret?'

I think hard. 'It's a prayer room!'

'What's secret 'bout a prayer room?' she asks.

'I know! It's a secret prayer room!'

She claps her hands. 'Ya don't know, Ruthie. Ya don't know the secret! Ya can't have my high heel shoes.'

'Lin-di!' I scream at her. 'I went through the secret door. I won the bet.'

'What's a use of gwain through the door, if ya don't know the secret?'

Lindi and I are about to scrap when Father O'Malley arrives and I rush to show him the secret room. With his hand in mine, I pull him down the passage. Suddenly Lindi calls sharply to me. She runs down the passage, grabs my hand and pulls me back to the front door.

'Ruthie, think hard 'bout the secret and ya c'n have my shoes. Only – ya must know why it's a secret.'

So I sit down on the edge of the pavement with Lindi's high heel shoes just by my face and think real hard. What other secret is there? There must be another secret or why did no one want to tell me what was in the room? I've gone through the door and I can't even tell Lindi the secret. Hama needn't be afraid I'll tell Father O'Malley. I don't even know what to tell. I only know there's a secret prayer room in our house. And then I remember that Hama wants the secret kept from Father O'Malley.

'Father O'Malley mustn't know about the prayer room,' I whisper in Lindi's ear.

When I look at Lindi's face, she's gone all sulky. Without speaking she sits next to me on the pavement and pulls off her shoes. I take off my shoes, brush the soles of my feet and put out my hand for the high heel shoes when Lindi has another idea.

'Why?' she asks. 'Ya must know why. Why mustn't Father O'Malley know?'

I still don't know. I still don't know why Father O'Malley mustn't know. I drop my hand and start to cry.

'Ya not smart like me, Ruthie. Your Hama is a Christian and that's a Hindu prayer room, silly baby girl!'

And Lindi gives me her high heel shoes. I put on the high heel shoes and I can see Lindi wants to cry.

Then Lindi says, her face all sulky, 'If ya smart like me … ya'll tell me … I c'n have the present … my Ma bought for ya.'

I know I'm not smart like Lindi or why didn't I think of that?

While I stand up in my own high heel shoes, Lindi's running barefoot down the street to get my present from her Ma.

A clearing in the bush

Zoë Wicomb

Tamieta, leaning against the east-facing wall, rolls her shoulders and like a cat rubs against the bricks to relieve the itching of her back. Which must mean something ominous, such a sudden and terrible itch, and she muses on its meaning, on its persistence, the rebellious flesh seems to align itself with the arrangement of bricks now imprinted on her back. She longs for the hot press of the sun that will brand the pattern of narrow new bricks into her flesh, iron the itch out of existence. She will never get used to this Cape Town weather so cold and wet in winter. It's about time summer showed its face; there hasn't been any sunshine for days. As for the itch, who thinks of conditions of the flesh that have just disappeared? When it should be freshest in the memory, that is the time when we do not think of an itch at all.

'Ag, a person mustn't complain,' she mutters to herself. 'This is the first morning of spring and even if it's not going to last, there's enough warmth to be soaked up against this wall.'

If only she knew what the omen was, for it's no good disregarding these things; they'll catch up with you all the same. Now, if it had been yesterday – and did she not yesterday look up at a hesitant sun and toy with the idea of taking her coffee outside, to lean against this nice wall? – yes, if it had been yesterday then she would have been able to exclaim as Charlie's Springbok radio bleeped the news, 'This is so. An itch of the back early in the morning means there's going to be an assassination.'

And as she drains her coffee grounds into the rough grass she remembers. Beatrice's wool. She promised to get to Bellville South after work to get a couple of ounces from her lay-by at Wilton Wools. Perhaps it's not an omen but a reminder: the itch leading to the bricks leading to the pattern in Beatrice's nimble hands. Knit four, purl one, chanting earnestly as she clicks her bricks into place. And the wool cleverly chosen by Beatrice to build a jersey in the colours of bricks and mortar. Ooh that child of hers is now clever. She can do just about anything with her hands and also her head, of course, because if your hands can do good so must the head. That is what the Apostle says and quite right too since it's all part of the same person.

As Tamieta braces herself for the day of labour in the canteen, her eyes fall on the bricks of this nice new wall and to her surprise must admit that it is not the colour of bricks at all. Really these are a greyish-black, with iridescent blue lights admittedly, but certainly not brick-red or brick-brown. Well, at least it isn't just our people who get it wrong; as far as she can think, people just haven't noticed, or people in spite of the evidence just go on talking nonsense. But she castigates herself for having been duped by a false association. She ought to have seen the futility of a reminder so early in the day when there is no need to remember. And now at this very moment the itch returns with new virulence. Tamieta has never known her flesh threaten to break free of its containing skin; such an itch must have a marrow-deep meaning.

Raising her head in order to scratch more effectively, she sees the first student settling into a seat on the top floor of the library. She has never been in there, even though it is the block closest to the cafeteria. Here, along these paths linking the four buildings that the government has given specially for our people, this is where Beatrice will walk one day, flying in and out of glass doors in her baby-louis heels and a briefcase bulging under her arm. But her skirts will be a decent length, not creeping above the knees like a few of the girls have started wearing them.

She climbs the steps to the cafeteria kitchen just as Charlie's sing-song voice calls, 'Tamieta, the mutton is chopped.' He has a voice to match his swagger and her ears twitch for a note of mockery, for it is amazing how that boy persists in thinking of her as a plaasjapie. That's why he slips in handfuls of English words as if she can't understand. Let him go on thinking it's so special to come from District Six.

Tamieta's energetic leap up the steps makes me wriggle in my seat. Large and slothful I sit pressed in my carrell on the top floor of the library making no progress whatsoever with the essay on Tess of the D'Urbervilles which should have been handed in yesterday. Failure to do it will lose me the right to take the end-of-year examination yet I have been unable even to start the thing. At the very moment yesterday as I strained for an excuse, trembling at the thought of a visit to Retief's office somewhere along a carpeted corridor, a pet abdominal tapeworm hissed persuasively into the ear of its Greek host, whose trembling hand grew still for a second to aim a fatal shot at the Prime Minister. Today I arrived early and hid here on the top floor amongst large botanical tomes since a tapeworm cannot protect me for ever. Along the margin of this blank sheet of foolscap I have drawn triangles and parallelograms, clean geometrical lines. I have no talent for likenesses and it is Retief's I wish to capture in this margin, someone to whom I can address the wormy tangle of questions that wriggle out of reach each time I pick up my pen. The Parker pen, a solemn gift from Father, lies before me, capped, unco-operative. I read through Retief's notes once more. A pity in some respects that I did not get to see his room. James, who once was in the same position, except that his mother's illness offered a legitimate excuse, says that close up Retief's skin is not white at all, rather a liverish-yellow with fine red veins, and that his speaking voice is hardly recognisable to a student who only hears him lecture in the large theatre. And what, I wonder, would I have interrupted in that room? In that functional cubicle of new uncluttered design the rugby-playing Retief will barely be able to stretch his legs while he copies out in long hand the lecture notes of the correspondence university to which we are affiliated. Pressed against the door I would have said, through a plate glass of awe and fear, something, something credible, so that he would draw up his long legs in attentive sympathy and say in a strange voice, 'But there is absolutely nothing to worry about, of course I understand my dear Miss ... er ...'

I could say anything to him and it is a relief to know that it does not matter in the slightest how I deliver my lie, for he does not know me, doesn't know any of us, and will not recognise me the next day.

I uncap my pen and read through Retief's dictated lecture. His pigeon head bobs up and down in empathy with the bowed heads of students before him as he pecks at his words in clipped English. The novel, he says, is about Fate. Alarmingly simple, but not quite how it strikes me, although I cannot offer an alternative. The truth is that I do not always understand the complicated language, though of course I got the gist of the story, the interesting bits where things happen. But even then, I cannot be sure of what actually happens in The Chase.

Wessex spreads like a well-used map before me, worn and dim along the fold-lines, the lush Frome Valley and the hills so picture-green where Persephone skips sprinkling daisies and buttercups from her clutched apron, caring not two hoots about the ones that fall face down destined to die. The scuffed green strip is The Chase where God knows what happened. Seduced, my notes say. Can you be seduced by someone you hate? Can trees gnarled with age whisper ancient ecstasies and waves of darkness upon dark lap until the flesh melts? I do, of course, not know of these matters, but shudder for Tess.

Beyond these pale buildings gleaming ghostly in the young spring light there is a fringe of respectably tall Port Jackson and bluegum trees that marks the clearing of university buildings from the surrounding bush. These raggle-taggle sentinels stand to tin-soldierly attention and behind them the bush stretches for miles across the Cape Flats. Bushes, I imagine, that send out wayward limbs to weave into the tangled undergrowth, for I have never left the concrete paths of this campus. Even summer couples may step out arm in arm to flaunt their love under the fluffy yellow flower of the Port Jackson, but never, surely, do they venture beyond. Somewhere beyond the administration block where today the flag flies half mast, they say there is a station where the train stops four times daily on the way to and from the Cape Flats. Skollie-boys sit all day long on the deserted platform, for there is no ticket office, and dangle their legs above the rails while they puff at their dagga pils. But even from this height there is no visible path winding through the bush. The handful of students who use the train must daily beat like pioneers a path through the undergrowth.

Along the top of my page enclosing the essay title, 'Fate in Tess', I have now drawn an infantile line of train carriages. I cannot start writing. I have always been able to distinguish good from bad but the story confuses me and the lecture notes offer no help.

Murder is a sin which should outrage all decent and civilised people.

The library is beginning to fill up and a boy I vaguely recognise as a Science student passes twice, darting resentful looks at me. No doubt I am in the seat that he has come to think of as his very own. Perhaps I should leave. Perhaps he can't work for being in a strange seat.

Through the window I watch James in his canary-yellow jersey, his jacket tucked under his arm, trotting to the Arts block for the English lecture. I shall get the notes from him.

James is a good friend; he is not like other boys. It is the distant sound of the nine o'clock siren that makes my courage fountain and the opening sentence spill on to the page in fluent English: 'Before we can assess the role of fate in the novel we must consider the question of whether Tess is guilty or not, whether she has erred in losing her virginity, deceiving her husband and killing her lover.'

Exhausted by my bold effort I can go no further. Outside, the pathways are deserted. English I students are by now seated in their row, shoulders hunched over Retief's dictation. The surly boy walks past me once again with a large volume under his arm. The hatred in his lingering look is unmistakable. I pack up my things hurriedly and before I reach the door the boy leaps up from his exposed seat at a central table and lurches indecently into the carrell so that I blush for the warm imprint of my buttocks which has not yet risen from the thin upholstery. It should be more comfortable on the first floor where I usually work amongst familiar faces, but by the time I reach the bottom of the stairs a reckless thirst propels me out, right out of the library towards the cafeteria where Tamieta's coffee pots croon on the hot plate.

She mutters, 'It's not ready', and clatters the lids of her pots and turns on a fierce jet of water so that Charlie jumps out of the spray and shouts, 'Jeez-like Auntie man, that's mos not necessary man.'

He tilts his face for the gracious acceptance of an apology but Tamieta's head remains bent over the sink. He cannot bear the silence and by way of introduction hums an irenic tune.

'That ou in there,' pointing at the door that leads into the lecturers' dining room, 'that ou said just now that Verwoerd was the architect of this place,' Charlie offers.

'It's because you listen to other people's conversations that you forget the orders hey. You'll never get on in this canteen business if you don't keep your head. Never mind the artitex;

clever people's talk got nothing to do with you,' Tamieta
retorts.

Charlie laughs scornfully. He discards the professional
advice because he will not believe that a speaker could fail to
be flattered by an eavesdropper. So that recognising the root
of the error he will not mind being brought curry instead of
bredie. Besides, he, Charlie, had only got an order wrong once,
several weeks ago.

'I know you don't need architects in the platteland. Not if
you build your houses out of sticks and mud, but here in
Cape Town there are special big-shot people who make
drawings and plan out the buildings.' He speaks slowly, with
pedagogical patience. 'So that's what I mean; the Prime
Minister got even more important things to do and a lecturer
should know better. That ou must be from the Theology
School over there,' driving a thumb in the wrong direction.
'Those moffies know buggerall there.'

Tamieta's fingers are greedy beaks pecking into the pastry
bowl and she fixes her eyes on the miracle of merging resistant
fat and flour. She will not be provoked by this blasphemous
Slams who has just confirmed her doubts about the etymology
of his 'Jeez-like'. They know nothing of God and yes it is her
Christian duty to defend her God, but this Charlie is beyond
the pale. The Old Man will have to look after himself today.
She adds the liquid slowly, absorbed by the wonder of turning
her ingredients into an entirely new substance. But it will not
last. Her melktert to rival all tarts, perfectly round and risen,
will melt in so many mouths, and that will be the end of it.

'... just reading the Bible all day long makes them stupid,
those preacher chaps from the platteland ...' Charlie's voice
weaves through her thoughts. This boy will not stop until
she speaks out against his irreverence and Tamieta sighs,
weary with the demands of God. Even the bonuses have
strings attached. What, for instance, is the point of having a
Sabbath when you have to work like a slave all Saturday in

order to prepare for the day of rest? When she first started in service with Ounooi van Graan, my word how she had to work. All the vegetables peeled the night before, the mutton half roasted in the pot and the sousboontjies all but cooked. And now in her own home in Bosheuwel, working all Saturday afternoon to make Sunday the day of rest. Oh what would she give to spread out the chores and do the ironing on Sundays. Instead she has to keep a watchful eye on Beatrice whose hands itch for her knitting needles. She feels for the child as they sit after the service and the special Sunday dinner wondering what to do so that she would yawn and shut her eyes and pray for strength to hold out against the child's desire to make something durable. For knitting on a Sunday pierces God directly in the eyes. It is her sacred duty to keep that child out of the roasting fires of hell for, not being her own, she is doubly responsible.

It was on her first visit back to Kliprand that she found cousin Sofie merry with drink and the two-year-old toddler wandering about with bushy hair in which the lice frolicked shamelessly. Then she pinned the struggling child between her knees and fought each louse in turn. She plaited her hair in tight rows that challenged the most valiant louse, and with her scalp soaked in Blue-butter the little Beatrice beamed a beauty that is born out of cleanliness. And Tamieta knew that she, not unlike the Virgin Mary, had been chosen as the child's rightful mother. She who adored little ones would have a child without the clumsiness of pregnancy, the burden of birth and the tobacco-breathed attentions of men with damp fumbling hands. Sofie agreed, weeping for her own weakness, and found parents for the other two, so that the validity of choosing a child at one's convenience was endorsed by the disposal of those she could no longer care for.

Eight good years together testify to the wisdom of the arrangement. Beatrice loves the yearly visits to Kilprand where Ousie Sofie awaits them with armfuls of presents, not always the sort of thing a girl would want in Town, but so jolly is Sofie telling her fabulous stories with much noise and actions that they all scream with mirth. A honey mouth that cousin of hers has, full of wise talk which only gets a person into trouble. Just as well she has kept to the country; Cape Town would not agree with her.

Beatrice has brought nothing but good luck. After serving the terrible English family in Cape Town – they paid well but never talked to her, nor for that matter did they talk to each other except in hushed tones as if someone in the family had just died – came Tamieta's lucky break at the UCT canteen where she could hold her head up high and do a respectable job of cooking for people whose brains needed nourishing. She was the one who kept the kitchen spotless, who cooked without waste and whose clockwork was infallible; it was only right that she should be chosen to run the canteen at the new Coloured university. The first kitchen boy was quiet, eager to please, but this Charlie is a thorn in her flesh. Full of himself and no respect for his elders. Why should he want to go on about the pondokkies of country folk? She casts a resentful look at the girl just sitting there, waiting for her coffee with her nose in her blinking book. She too is from the country. Tamieta knows of her father who drives a motor car in the very next village, for who in Little Namaqualand does not know of Shenton? The girl speaks English but that need not prevent her from saying something educated and putting this Charlie in his place. She, Tamieta, will turn on him and say as she rolls the pastry, pliant under her rolling pin, strike him with a real English saying which will make that know-all face frown. She has not worked for English people without learning a thing or two. She has learned to value their weapon of silence, and she has memorised Madam's icy words to the man with the briefcase, 'Fools rush in where angels fear to tread.' Oh to see Charlie's puzzled look before he pretends to know exactly what it means. Her fingers stiffen as the boy rises with his board of chopped onions, but what if he were just to laugh at her if she said it now? If only she could leave him alone, but Tamieta calls out just as he is about to drop the onions into the pan. Curtly, 'It needs to be finer than that.' Charlie's onion tears stream down his face.

'See how you make me cry, Tamieta? This is the tears of all my young years, and I'll have none left for your wedding. They say you getting married, Tamieta, when is the happy day?'

He runs his hand over the mirror surface of his greased hair, asserting his superiority. This Charlie with his smooth hair and nose like a tent will find every opportunity to humiliate her. She ought to ask him to wash his hands. No one wants Brylcreem-flavoured bredie. But her legs ache and her back starts up again, the itching pores like so many seething hot springs, so that she really can't give a damn. The stove will tend to the germs. This is no ordinary itch.

Tamieta turns to Charlie. 'We must get a move on. All tomorrow's work has to be done this morning as well 'cause this afternoon is the memorial and the cafeteria will be closed.'

'Ooh-hoo,' the boy crows loudly, 'I'm going up Hanover Street to get the material for our Carnival uniforms. We start practising next week and this year the Silver Blades is going to walk off with all the prizes.'

'Sies,' Tamieta remonstrates, 'I don't know how you Slamse can put yourself on show like that for the white people to laugh at on New Year's Day.'

'Oh, you country people know nothing man, Tamieta man. The best part is when we come out at midnight in our costumes. Have you even been in the city for the midnight?'

Tamieta seals her face and maintains a scornful silence.

'No,' he continues, 'you won't have seen the lights all down Adderley Street, man, twinkling like home-made stars, man, like all the planets just jiving in the streets. Then all the bells start ringing and that's when we run out from the shadows with the black polish.'

His hips grind as he dances towards her, waving his spread palms. She cannot ignore him and when she retreats with her wooden spoon, Charlie grabs his knees with mirth and crows breathlessly, 'That's when we get all the whities and rub the black polish all over their faces.'

'I must be a baboon to listen to all this nonsense. Where will a white person allow a troop of coons to even touch their faces? I may be born in a pondok but I wasn't born yesterday, you know.'

"Strue, Tamieta, 'strue,' he begs her to believe him. 'It's been going on for years now, it's a tradition you know,' and taking up his chopping knife he adds soberly, 'I suppose the whities who come there know it's going to happen and come specially for the black polish, but perhaps there is, yes there must be, one or two who get the fright of their lives when we jump out from the shadows.'

Tamieta sets the cups out on the counter. She really can't be listening to this boy's nonsense and if he doesn't know that he's supposed to spend the afternoon at the ceremony, well then, that's his problem.

'Here,' she called to the Shenton girl, 'here, the coffee's ready.'

Midst these unlikely sounds of clattering cups and the regular fall of the knife, the bass of the bean soup and the sizzling onion smells the essay is going tolerably well. There are human voices in the background, the amicable hum of Tamieta and Charlie, harmonising with the kitchen sounds that will materialise into bean soup favoured by the students and bredie for the staff.

I have followed the opening thrust with two more paragraphs that wantonly move towards exonerating Tess. Retief's notes are no good to me. He will not be pleased. Things are going well until an ill-timed ten o'clock siren sounds, signalling a visit to the lavatory. Since the collapse of the beehive I have not found a satisfactory way of doing my hair although the curve of my flick-ups is crisp as ever. Fortunately one can always rely on Amami hairspray. I wet my fingers at the tap and tug at the crinkly hairshaft of an otherwise perfectly straight fringe. Cape Town with its damp and misty mornings is no good for the hair. Thank God there is no full-length mirror to taunt me although I have a feeling that the waistband of my skirt has slackened. After a final glance at the now stabilised fringe and a rewarding thumb between my blouse and waistband, I am ready to face coffee-break.

The boys who play klawerjas at the back of the room are already installed and they let out the customary wolf whistle as I re-enter the cafeteria. Fortunately my table is right at the front so that I do not have to endure the tribute for long. It is of course encouraging to know that a few moments before the mirror does pay dividends; that the absorption with a card game can be pierced by a pleasing female tread. My pulse quickens. Though I sit with my back to them I don't know what to do. There is no question of carrying on with the essay. These males have a sixth sense. Whilst being held by the game they somehow know when a girl moves and will not fail to pucker the lips and allow the hot draught of air to escape even as you bend to retrieve a sheet of paper from the floor. There must be some girls who never get whistled at but I don't think I know of any. We are all familiar with the scale of appreciation, from the festive tantara for the beauties to the single whiplash of a whistle for the barely attractive. Then there is the business of who is whistling at you, and since you cannot possibly look, since you drop your eyes demurely or stare coldly ahead, and while you shiver deliciously to the vibrations of the whistle there can be a nagging discomfort, an inexplicable lump that settles like a cork in the trachea. Should it be some awful country boy with faltering English and a feathered hat ... but such a contingency is covered by the supportive group whistle. You will never know the original admirer so it is best not to look, not to speak.

I am pleased to see James and tidy away my folder to make room for him. But he collects a cup of coffee, drops his bag at my table and with a dismissive hallo goes straight to the back where he joins the boys. Unusual for him but it really does not matter. I stretch my legs and with my heels draw in James's bag to support my calves. Perhaps I should take my folder out again and try to work, but there is no point; the others will be here soon. Instead I decide on another cup of coffee. It is not an extravagance; I shall not have one this afternoon. With my ten-cent piece I tap on the stainless-steel counter until I realise that the sound is not drowned by the rowdy klawerjas players. No one has whistled. Have I in spite of my narrowing waistline become one of those who does not merit a second look?

When Moira enters she stands for a moment framed in the doorway, blinking, for the sun has come out again. It is one of those just-spring days when the sun plays crazy kiss-catch games and the day revolves through all the seasons of the year. So Moira blinks in this darkness after the glare outside. The silence of her entry is unnerving. Moira has never moved in this room without a fanfare of whistles and an urgent drumming on the tables. She hesitates as if that exhalation of hot air is the only source of kinetic energy that will produce motion in her exquisite legs. Moira is indisputably beautiful. The smooth skin. The delicately sculpted form. The sleek brown hair.

But now her eyes are troubled, her hovering form uncertain, so that I wave at her and lo, the legs swing into mobility, the left foot falls securely on the floor and she propels herself expertly towards me. 'Coffee or tea,' I whisper loudly and point at the table where my folder lies. Like an automaton she changes direction and manoeuvres into a chair.

'What's going on in here? Where's James?' she asks.

James always sits with us. We have learned to make allowances for the filtered version of friendship that boys offer;

nevertheless his behaviour today is certainly treacherous. Why has he gone without explanation to join the dark tower of boys peering down on to the table at the back? It is clearly not the klawerjas game that holds their attention. Someone screened from our vision is talking quietly, then bangs a fist on the table. The voices grow more urgent. We watch James withdraw from the inner circle and perch on the back of a chair shaking his head, but he does not look across at us.

By now the cafeteria is full. There is a long queue for coffee. The boys drift instinctively to the back to join the dark bank of murmuring males while the girls settle with their coffees at separate tables. Moira is agitated. What can they be talking about? We listen carefully but the sounds remain unintelligible. The group is no longer cohesive. It is too large, so that sub-groups mutter in cacophony, someone laughs derisively and above the noise the sound of Mr Johnson's gravel voice, herding the stragglers back into the fold. He is the older student who in his youth had something to do with politics and now bears the bereaved look of someone who cannot accept the death of the movement.

'I think,' says Moira, 'we should go and join them. If they've got something important to discuss then it's bound to affect us so we ought to go and find out.'

'Oh no,' I remonstrate anxiously. I can only think of crossing the room in slow-motion, elephantine, as my lumbering thighs rub together. A deadly silence except for the nylon scratching of left pantihose against right, then right against left, before the ambiguous sound from the lungs of that bulwark rings plangent in my ears. I do not recognise this register; can a whistle be distorted by slow-motion? I fail to summon the old familiar sound, its pitch or timbre. Some day, I think wildly, there will be a machine to translate a whistle, print it out boldly as a single, unequivocal adjective: complimentary ... or ... derisive? A small compact machine to carry conveniently in the pocket which will absorb the sound as confidently as I have done. The meaning must lie there in the pitch, audible, measurable; otherwise, surely, we would never have considered it as anything other than a sound, an expression of time. How did we ever know with such certainty that it spelled admiration?

Moira is determined to go until I say, 'They will whistle as we approach.'

She slumps back in her chair and tugs listlessly at her skirt that has risen above the knee. In the seated position these shrinking hemlines assert a dubious freedom. We console ourselves that we might have risked it in last year's skirts and curl our toes newly released from the restrictive points of last year's shoes.

When James strides over he stands for a moment with one foot on the chair while he lights a cigarette and languidly savours the smoke before it curls out of his nostrils.

'Hey,' he teases as his eyes fall on my folder. 'Have you done that essay yet? Retief asked after you this morning.'

I have no desire to banter with him. Has it occurred to James that Retief has no idea who any of us are? James turns the chair around and sits astride it, spreading his legs freely. He does not read the resentment in our unyielding postures.

The day slips into mid-winter. The sky darkens and a brisk rain beats against the glass. The wind tugs at the building, at this new brick and glass box placed in a clearing in the bush, and seems to lift it clean off the ground.

'My word,' says James and treats us to a lecture on the properties of glass as building material. It is clear that he will nurse the apple of knowledge in his lap, polish its red curve abstractedly until we drool with anticipation. Only then will he offer us little lady-like bites, anxious for the seemly mastication of the fruit and discreet about his power to withdraw it altogether.

'Come on, what's all this about?' Moira asks, pointing to the table at the back.

'We're organising the action for this afternoon's memorial service. We must be sure nobody goes. If we ...'

'But no one would want to go,' I interrupt.

'The point is that there are too many cowards who don't want to but who are intimidated into going. Fear of reprisals is no small thing when there is a degree at stake, but if no one, and I mean not a soul, goes, then there'll be nothing to fear. Obviously we can't call a public meeting so it's up to every one of us to get round and speak to as many people as possible. Everyone must be reassured that no one will go. You two are going to Psychology next, aren't you? So make sure that you get there early and get the word around. I'll miss it and go to Afrikaans-Netherlands I instead. There'll be someone in every lecture room this morning and a couple of chaps are staying in here. Mr Johnson and others are going round the library. The idea is that every student must be spoken to before one o'clock.'

We nod. I had hoped to miss all my classes today in order to finish the essay. I shall have to think of something since Retief will certainly not accept it after today, especially not after the boycott of the service.

'Do you feel any sense of horror or shock or even distaste at the assassination?' I ask.

Moira taps her beautiful fingers on the table. James gets up. 'I'd better get along and speak to Sally's table over there,' he says.

'Well, do you?' I persist. 'Can you imagine being a member of his family or anyone close to him?'

'No,' she says. 'Do you think there's something wrong with us? Morally deficient?'

'Dunno. My father would call it inhuman, unchristian. It seems to me as if common humanity is harped on precisely so that we don't have to consider the crucial question of whether we can imagine being a particular human being. Or deal with the implications of the answer. All I can tell of the

human condition is that we can always surprise ourselves
with thoughts and feelings we never thought we had.'

Moira laughs. 'You're always ready with a mouthful of
words. I'm surprised that you have any trouble with knocking
off an essay.'

As we go off towards the Arts block we watch the gardeners
in their brown overalls putting out hundreds of chairs in the
square to accommodate all the students and staff. The chairs
are squashed between the flowerboxes where the spring-green
of foliage just peeps over the concrete. I try to think what
they are but cannot imagine flowers tumbling over that
concrete rim now lashed by the shadow of the wind-tossed flag.

Later I lean against the brick wall at the back of the cafeteria,
my knees drawn up and the folder resting on the plane of
my thighs. The soil is somewhat damp but I do not mind
since a luke-warm sun has travelled round to this wall.
Besides, there is nowhere else to go; the library as well as the
cafeteria is shut and I wouldn't like to sit in the deserted Arts
block.

A heavy silence hangs over the campus. The bush is still
as if the birds are paying their respects to the dead Verwoerd.
This freshly rinsed light won't last; such a stillness can only
precede the enervating sweep of the south-easterly wind. I
watch an ant wriggle her thorax along a blade of grass before
I turn to my watch to find that the minute arm has raced
ahead. The ceremony will start in fifteen minutes. It will
probably last an hour and before that my essay must be
finished and delivered. I read Retief's notes and start afresh.
This will have to be my final copy since there is no time to
develop ideas, let alone rephrase clumsy language. My
attempt to understand the morality of the novel has to be
abandoned. Retief will get what he wants, a reworking of his
notes, and I will earn a mark qualifying for the examination.

It is not easy to work in this eerie silence. The stillness of
the trees, the dark bush ahead inspire an unknown fear, a

terror as if my own eyes, dark and bold as a squirrel's, stare at me from the bush. I am alone. The lecturers settling into their mourning seats under the flag some three hundred yards away offer no reassurance. If only a bird would scream or an animal rush across the red carpet of Rooikrans pods along the fringe of the bush, this agitation would settle. When the tall Australian bluegums shiver in the first stir of air, I retrieve my restless fingers raking though the grass to attend to Tess, luscious-lipped Tess, branded guilty and betrayed once more on this page. Time's pincers tighten round my fingers as I press on. This essay, however short and imperfect, must be done before three o'clock.

I start at the sound of gravel crunched underfoot. Surely there is no one left. Students in the hostel would keep to their rooms; others have rushed off for the 1.30 bus, too anxious to hitch the customary lift to the residential areas. I get up cautiously, tiptoe to the edge of the wall and peer round to see a few young men in their Sunday suits filing from the Theology College towards the square. They walk in silence, their chins lifted in a militaristic display of courage. I have no doubt that they have been asked to support the boycott. But they will think their defiance heroic and stifle the unease by marching soldier-like to mourn the Prime Minister.

Their measured tread marks the short minutes that go on sounding long after they have disappeared. I scribble wildly these words that trip each other up so that the page is defaced by inches of crossed-out writing and full stops swelled by a refractory pen that shrinks before a new sentence. Just as I finish, the gilt braid of fleece overhead slips under cover of a brooding raincloud. There is no time to make a fair copy. It is nearly three o'clock and I do not have the courage to wait for a bus or a lift at the main entrance where tall, fleshy cacti with grotesque limbs mock the human form. With difficulty I slip the essay without an explanatory note under Retief's close-fitting door then brace myself for the bush, for I must find the path that leads to the little station and wait for the Cape Flats train.

Tamieta shifts in her seat and lifts her wrist to check again the ticking of her watch. If this thing should let her down, should wilfully speed up the day so that she is left running about like a headless chicken amongst her pots ... But she allows her wrist to drop in her lap; the unthinkable cannot be developed any further. And yet she has just fallen breathless in her chair, the first in the last row, only to find no one here. Not a soul. All the chairs in front of her are empty, except for the first two rows where the Boers sit in silence. Only two of the lecturers are women who, in their black wide-brimmed hats, are curious shapes in the distance.

Tamieta had no idea that the ceremony was for white people only. Oh, what should she do, and the shame of it flames in her chest. Wait until she is told to leave? Or pick up the bag of working clothes she has just tucked under her chair and stagger off? But a few heads had turned as she sat down; she has already been seen, and besides how can she trust these legs now that her knees are calcified with shame and fear? She longs for a catastrophe, an act of justice, something divine and unimaginable, for she cannot conceive of a flood or a zigzag of lightning that will have her tumbling in scuffed shoes with her smoking handbag somersaulting over or entwined with the people at the front. There is no decent image of a credible demise to be summoned in the company of these mourners, so she fishes instead in her handbag for the handkerchief soaked in reviving scent. Californian Poppy, the bottle says, a sample that Beatrice has written away for and which arrived in the post with the picture on the label hardly discernible as a flower, just a red splodge, and as she inhales the soothing fragrance her mind clears into a sharp memory of the supervisor. Mr Grats said distinctly as he checked the last consignment of plates, 'Tomorrow is the ceremony, so close up straight after lunch. It won't last more than an hour so you still have an afternoon off.'

Unambiguous words. Mr Grats is a man who always speaks plainly. Besides, they would not have put the chairs out if Coloureds were not allowed, and her new-found security is confirmed by the arrival of the first students. She recognises the young men from the seminary, the future Dutch Reformed or rather Mission Church ministers, and her chest swells with relief which she interprets as pride in her people. They slip noiselessly into the third row but there are only eleven and they have no effect on the great expanse between her and the front.

Tamieta looks at her watch. It is five minutes past two. She would not expect students to be late for such an important ceremony; why should they want to keep Coloured time on an occasion like this and put her to shame? Where is everybody? And she sniffs, sniffs at the comforter impregnated with Californian Poppy.

The rector strides across from the Administration block in his grand cloak. He bellows like a bull preparing to storm the empty chairs.

'Ladies and gentlemen, let those of us who abhor violence, those of us who have a vision beyond darkness and savagery, weep today for the tragic death of our Prime Minister ...'

He is speaking to her ... Ladies and gentlemen ... that includes her, Tamieta, and what can be wrong with that? Why should she not be called a lady? She who has always conducted herself according to God's word? Whose lips have never parted for a drop of liquor or the whorish cigarette? And who has worked dutifully all her life? Yes, it is only right that she should be called a lady. And fancy it coming from the rector. Unless he hasn't seen her, or doesn't see her as part of the gathering. Does the group of strangers backed by the dark-suited Theology students form a bulwark, an edifice before which she must lower her eyes? How could she,

Tamieta Snewe, with her slow heavy thighs scale such heights?

'... these empty chairs are a sign of the barbarism, the immense task that lies ahead of the educator ...'

Should she move closer to the front? As his anger gives way to grief, she can no longer hear what he says. In Tamieta's ears the red locusts rattle among the mealies on the farm and the dry-throated wind croaks a heart-broken tale of treachery through the cracks of the door. She must wait, simply wait for these people to finish. Never, not even on a Sunday afternoon, has she known time to drag its feet so sluggishly. If she could pull out of her plastic bag a starched cap and apron and whip round smilingly after the last amen with a tray of coffee, perhaps then she could sit through the service in comfort. And the hot shame creeps up from her chest to the crown of her head. The straw hat pinned to the mattress of hair released from its braids for the occasion (for she certainly does not wear a doekie to church like a country woman) smoulders with shame for such a starched cap long since left behind.

So many years since the young Mieta carried water from the well, the zinc bucket balanced on her head, her slender neck taut and not a drop, never a drop of water spilled. Then she rolled her doekie into a wreath to fit the bottom of the bucket and protect her head from its cutting edge. So they swaggered back, the girls in the evening light when the sun melted orange in an indigo sky, laughing, jostling each other, heads held high and never a hand needed to steady the buckets.

If only there were other women working on the campus she would have known, someone would have told her. As for that godless boy, Charlie, he knew all right, even betrayed himself with all that nonsense about the carnival while she sniffed for his treachery in quite the wrong direction. Of course he knew all along that she would be the only person there.

And at this moment as he stands in Hanover Street with the pink and green satins flowing through his fingers, he sniggers at the thought of her, a country woman, sitting alone amongst white people, foolishly singing hymns. And he'll run triumphant fingers through his silky hair – but that is precisely when the Jewish draper will say, 'Hey you, I don't want Brylcreem on my materials, hey. I think you'd better go now.' And that will teach Charlie; that will show him that hair isn't everything in the world.

The words of the hymn do not leave her mouth. A thin sound escapes her parted lips but the words remain printed in a book, written in uneven letters on her school slate. Will the wind turn and toss her trembling hum southward into the ear of the dominee who will look up sternly and thunder, 'Sing up aia, sing up'?

Oh, how her throat grows wind-dry as the strips of biltong beef hung out on the farm in the evening breeze. The longing for a large mug of coffee tugs at her palate. Coffee with a generous spoonful of condensed milk, thick and sweet to give her strength. How much longer will she have to sit here and wait for time to pass? This time designated by strangers to mourn a man with a large head? For that was what the newspaper showed, a man with the large head of a bulldog, and Tamieta, allowing herself the unknown luxury of irreverence, passes a damp tongue over her parched lips.

She will watch the plants in the concrete flowerbox by her side. She does not know what they are called but she will watch these leaves grow, expand before her very eyes. By keeping an eye trained on one leaf – and she selects a healthy shoot resting on the rim – she will witness the miracle of growth. She has had enough of things creeping up on her, catching her unawares, offering unthinkable surprises. No, she will travel closely with the passage of time and see a bud thicken under her vigilant eye.

It is time to rise for prayer, and as she reminds herself to keep her lowered eyes fixed on the chosen leaf the plastic bag under her chair falls over and the overall, her old blue turban and the comfy slippers roll out for all the world to see. But all the eyes are shut so that she picks up her things calmly and places them back in the bag. Just in time for the last respectful silence. The heads hang in grief. Tamieta's neck aches. Tonight Beatrice will free the knotted tendons with her nimble fingers. She does not have the strength to go into town for the wool, but Beatrice will understand. Tamieta is the first to slip out of her seat, no point in lingering when the rain is about to fall, and with her handbag swinging daintily in the crook of her right arm and the parcel of clothes tucked under her left, she marches chin up into the bush, to the deserted station where the skollie-boys dangle their feet from the platform all day long.

No place like

Nadine Gordimer

The relief of being down, out, and on the ground after hours in the plane was brought up short for them by the airport building: dirty, full of up-ended chairs like a closed restaurant. *Transit? Transit?* Some of them started off on a stairway but were shooed back exasperatedly in a language they didn't understand. The African heat in the place had been cooped up for days and nights; somebody tried to open one of the windows but again there were remonstrations from the uniformed man and the girl in her white gloves and leopard-skin pillbox hat. The windows were sealed, anyway, for the air-conditioning that wasn't working; the offender shrugged. The spokesman that every group of travellers produces made himself responsible for a complaint; at the same time some of those sheep who can't resist a hole in a fence had found a glass door unlocked on the far side of the transit lounge – they were leaking to an open passage-way: grass, bougainvillaea trained like standard roses, a road glimpsed there! But the uniformed man raced to round them up and a cleaner trailing his broom was summoned to bolt the door.

The woman in beige trousers had come very slowly across the tarmac, putting her feet down on this particular earth once more, and she was walking even more slowly round the dirty hall. Her coat dragged from the crook of her elbow, her shoulder was weighed by the strap of a bag that wouldn't zip over a package of duty-free European liquor, her bright silk shirt opened dark mouths of wet when she lifted her arms. Fellow-glances of indignance or the seasoned superiority of a sense of humour found no answer in her. As her pace brought her into the path of the black cleaner, the two faces matched perfect indifference: his, for whom the distance from which these people came had no existence because he had been nowhere outside the two miles he walked from his village to the airport; hers, for whom the distance had no existence because she has been everywhere and arrived back.

Another black man, struggling into a white jacket as he unlocked wooden shutters, opened the bar, and the businessmen with their hard-top briefcases moved over to the row of stools. Men who had got talking to unattached women – not much promise in that now; the last leg of the journey was ahead – carried them glasses of gaudy synthetic fruit juice. The Consul who had wanted to buy her a drink with dinner on the plane had found himself a girl in red boots with a small daughter in identical red boots. The child waddled away and flirtation took the form of the two of them hurrying after to scoop it up, laughing. There was a patient queue of ladies in cardigans waiting to get into the lavatories. She passed – once, twice, three times in her slow rounds – a woman who was stitching *petit-point*. The third time she made out that the subject was a spaniel dog with orange-and-black-streaked ears. Beside the needlewoman was a husband of a species as easily identifiable as the breed of dog – an American, because of the length of bootlace, slotted through some emblem or badge, worn in place of a tie. He sighed and his wife looked up over her glasses as if he had made a threatening move.

The woman in the beige trousers got rid of her chit for Light Refreshment in an ashtray but she had still the plastic card that was her authority to board the plane again. She tried to put it in the pocket of the coat but she couldn't reach, so she had to hold the card in her teeth while she unharnessed herself from the shoulder-bag and the coat. She wedged the card into the bag beside the liquor packages, leaving it to protrude a little so that it would be easy to produce when the time came. But it slipped down inside the bag and she had to unpack the whole thing – the hairbrush full of her own hair, dead, shed; yesterday's newspaper from a foreign town; the book whose jacket tore on the bag's zip as it came out; wads of pink paper handkerchiefs, gloves for a cold climate, the quota of duty-free cigarettes, the Swiss pocket-knife that you couldn't buy back home, the wallet of travel documents. There at the bottom was the shiny card. Without it, you couldn't board the plane again. With it, you were committed to go on to the end of the journey, just as the passport bearing your name committed you to a certain identity and place. It was one of the nervous tics of travel to feel for the reassurance of that shiny card. She had wandered to the revolving stand of paperbacks and came back to make sure where she had put the card: yes, it was there. It was not a bit of paper; shiny plastic, you couldn't tear it up – indestructible, it looked, of course they use them over and over again. *Tropic of Capricorn, Kamasutra, Something of Value.* The stand revolved and brought round the same books, yet one turned it again in case there should be a book that had escaped notice, a book you'd been wanting to read all your life. If one were to find such a thing, here and now, on this last stage, this last stop ... She felt strong hope, the excitation of weariness and tedium perhaps. They came round – *Something of Value, Kamasutra, Tropic of Capricorn.*

She went to the seat where she had left her things and loaded up again, the coat, the shoulder-bag bearing down. Somebody had fallen asleep, mouth open, bottom fly-button undone, an Austrian hat with plaited cord and feather cutting into his damp brow. How long had they been in this place? What time was it where she had left? (Some airports had a whole series of clock-faces showing what time it was everywhere.) Was it still yesterday, there? – Or tomorrow. And where was she going? She thought, I shall find out when I get there.

A pair of curio vendors had unpacked their wares in a corner. People stood about in a final agony of indecision: What

would he do with a thing like that? Will she appreciate it, I
mean? A woman repeated as she must have done in bazaars
and shops and market-places all over the world, I've seen
them for half the price ... But this was the last stop of all, the
last chance *to take back something.* How else stake a claim? The
last place of all the other places of the world.

Bone bracelets lay in a collapsed spiral of overlapping
circles. Elephant hair ones fell into the pattern of the Olympic
symbol. There were the ivory paper-knives and the little
pictures of palm trees, huts and dancers on black paper. The
vendor, squatting in the posture that derives from the
necessity of the legless beggar to sit that way and has become
as much a mark of the street professional, in such towns as
the one that must be somewhere behind the airport, as the
hard-top briefcase was of the international businessman
drinking beer at the bar, importuned her with the obligation
to buy. To refuse was to upset the ordination of roles. He was
there to sell 'ivory' bracelets and 'African' art; they – these
people shut up for him in the building – had been brought
there to buy. He had a right to be angry. But she shook her
head, she shook her head, while he tried out his few words
of German and French (*bon marché, billig*) as if it could only
be a matter of finding the right cue to get her to play the part
assigned to her. He seemed to threaten, in his own tongue,
finally, his head in its white skullcap hunched between jutting
knees. But she was looking again at the glass case full of
tropical butterflies under the President's picture. The picture
was vivid, and new; a general successful in a coup only
months ago, in full dress uniform, splendid as the dark one
among the Magi. The butterflies, relic of some colonial
conservationist society, were beginning to fall away from their
pins in grey crumbs and gauzy fragments. But there was one
big as a bat and brilliantly emblazoned as the general:
something in the soil and air, in whatever existed out there –
whatever 'out there' there was – that caused nature and
culture to imitate each other ...?

If it were possible to take a great butterfly. Not take back; just take. But she had the Swiss knife and the bottles, of course. The plastic card. It would see her onto the plane once more. Once the plastic card was handed over, nowhere to go but across the tarmac and up the stairway into the belly of the plane, no turning back past the air hostess in her leopard-skin pillbox, past the barrier. It wasn't allowed; against regulations. The plastic card would send her to the plane, the plane would arrive at the end of the journey, the Swiss knife would be handed over for a kiss, the bottles would be exchanged for an embrace – she was shaking her head at the curio vendor (he had actually got up from his knees and come after her, waving his pictures), *no thanks, no thanks.* But he wouldn't give up and she had to move away, to walk up and down once more in the hot, enclosed course dictated by people's feet, the up-ended chairs and tables, the little shored-up piles of hand-luggage. The Consul was swinging the child in red boots by its hands, in an arc. It was half-whimpering, half-laughing, yelling to be let down, but the larger version of the same model, the mother, was laughing in a way to make her small breasts shake for the Consul, and to convey to everyone how marvellous such a distinguished man was with children.

There was a gritty crackle and then the announcement in careful, African-accented English, of the departure of the flight. A kind of concerted shuffle went up like a sigh: at last! The red-booted mother was telling her child it was silly to cry, the Consul was gathering their things together, the woman was winding the orange thread for her needlework rapidly round a spool, the sleepers woke and the beer-drinkers threw the last of their foreign small change on the bar counter. No queue outside the Ladies' now and the woman in the beige trousers knew there was plenty of time before the second call. She went in and, once more, unharnessed herself among crumpled paper towels and spilt powder. She tipped all the soap containers in turn until she found one that wasn't empty; she washed her hands thoroughly in hot and then cold water and put her wet palms on the back of her neck, under her hair. She went to one of the row of mirrors and looked at what she saw there a moment, and then took out from under the liquor bottles, the Swiss knife and the documents, the hairbrush. It was full of hair; a web of dead hairs that bound the bristles together so that they could not go through a head of live hair. She raked her fingers slowly through the bristles and was aware of a young Indian woman at the next mirror, moving quickly and efficiently about an elaborate toilet. The Indian back-combed the black, smooth hair cut in Western style to hang on her shoulders, painted her eyes, shook her ringed hands dry rather than use the paper towels, sprayed French perfume while she extended her neck, repleated the green and silver sari that left bare a small roll of lavender-grey flesh between waist and *choli*.

This is the final call for all passengers.

The hair from the brush was no-colour, matted and coated with fluff. Twisted round the forefinger (like the orange thread for the spaniel's ears) it became a fibrous tunnel, dusty and obscene. She didn't want the Indian girl to be confronted with it and hid it in her palm while she went over to the dustbin. But the Indian girl saw only herself, watching her reflection appraisingly as she turned and swept out.

The brush went easily through the living hair, now. Again and again, until it was quite smooth and fell, as if it had a memory, as if it were cloth that had been folded and ironed a certain way, along the lines in which it had been arranged by professional hands in another hemisphere. A latecomer rushed into one of lavatories, sounded the flush and hurried out, plastic card in hand.

The woman in beige trousers had put on lipstick and run a nail-file under her nails. Her bag was neatly packed. She dropped a coin in the saucer set out, like an offering for some humble household god, for the absent attendant. The African voice was urging all passengers to proceed immediately through Gate B. The voice had some difficulty with *l*'s, pronouncing them more like *r*'s; a pleasant, reasoning voice, asking only for everyone to present the boarding pass, avoid delay, come quietly.

She went into one of the lavatories marked 'Western-type toilet' that bolted automatically as the door shut, a patent device ensuring privacy; there was no penny to pay. She had the coat and bag with her and arranged them, the coat folded and balanced on the bag, on the cleanest part of the floor. She thought what she remembered thinking so many times before: not much time, I'll have to hurry. That was what the plastic card was for – surety for not being left behind, never. She had it stuck in the neck of the shirt now, in the absence of a convenient pocket; it felt cool and wafer-stiff as she put it there but had quickly taken on the warmth of her body. Some tidy soul determined to keep up Western-type standards had closed the lid and she sat down as if on a bench – the heat and the weight of the paraphernalia she had been carrying about were suddenly exhausting. She thought she would smoke a cigarette; there was no time for that. But the need for a cigarette hollowed out a deep sigh within her and she got the pack carefully out of the pocket of her coat without disturbing the arrangement on the floor. All passengers delaying the departure of the flight were urged to proceed immediately through Gate B. Some of the words were lost over the echoing intercommunication system and at times the only thing that could be made out was the repetition, Gate B, a vital fact from which all grammatical contexts could fall away without rendering the message unintelligible. Gate B. If you remembered, if you knew Gate B, the key to mastery of the whole procedure remained intact with you. Gate B was the converse of the open sesame; it would keep you, passing safely through it, in the known, the familiar, and inescapable, safe from caves of treasure and shadow. *Immediately. Gate B. Gate B.*

She could sense from the different quality of the atmosphere outside the door, and the doors beyond it, that the hall was emptying now. They were trailing, humping along under their burdens – the *petit-point*, the child in red boots – to the gate where the girl in the leopard-skin pillbox collected their shiny cards.

She took hers out. She looked around the cell as one looks around for a place to set down a vase of flowers or a note that mustn't blow away. It would not flush down the outlet; plastic doesn't disintegrate in water. As she had idly noticed before, it wouldn't easily tear up. She was not at all agitated; she was simply looking for somewhere to dispose of it, now. She heard the voice (was there a shade of hurt embarrassment in the rolling *r*-shaped *l*'s) appealing to the passenger who was holding up flight so-and-so to please ... She noticed for the first time that there was actually a tiny window, with the sort of pane that tilts outwards from the bottom, just above the cistern. She stood on the seat-lid and tried to see out, just managing to post the shiny card like a letter through the slot.

Gate B, the voice offered, *Gate B*. But to pass through Gate B you had to have a card, without a card Gate B had no place in the procedure. She could not manage to see anything at all, straining precariously from up there, through the tiny window; there was no knowing at all where the card had fallen. But as she half-jumped, half-clambered down again, for a second the changed angle of her vision brought into sight something like a head – the top of a huge untidy palm tree, up in the sky, rearing perhaps between buildings or above shacks and muddy or dusty streets where there were donkeys, bicycles and barefoot people. She saw it only for that second but it was so very clear, she saw even that it was an old palm tree, the fronds rasping and sharpening against each other. And there was a crow – she was sure she had seen the black flap of a resident crow.

She sat down again. The cigarette had made a brown aureole round itself on the cistern. In the corner what she had thought was a date-pit was a dead cockroach. She flicked the dead cigarette butt at it. Heel-taps clattered into the outer room, an African voice said, Who is there? Please, are you there? She did not hold her breath or try to keep particularly still. There was no one there. All the lavatory doors were rattled in turn. There was a high-strung pause, as if the owner of the heels didn't know what to do next. Then the heels rang away again and the door of the Ladies' swung to with the heavy sound of fanned air.

There were bursts of commotion without, reaching her muffledly where she sat. The calm grew longer. Soon the intermittent commotion would cease; the jets must be breathing fire by now, the belts fastened and the cigarettes extinguished, although the air-conditioning wouldn't be working properly yet, on the ground, and they would be patiently sweating. They couldn't wait forever, when they were so nearly there. The plane would be beginning to trundle like a huge perambulator, it would be turning, winking, shuddering in summoned power.

Take off. It was perfectly still and quiet in the cell. She thought of the great butterfly; of the general with his beautiful markings of braid and medals. Take off.

So that was the sort of place it was: crows in old dusty palm trees, crows picking the carrion in open gutters, legless beggars threatening in an unknown tongue. Not Gate B, but some other gate. Suppose she were to climb out that window, would they ask her for her papers and put her in some other cell, at the general's pleasure? The general had no reason to trust anybody who did not take Gate B. No sound at all, now. The lavatories were given over to their own internal rumblings; the cistern gulped now and then. She was quite sure, at last, that flight so-and-so had followed its course; was gone. She lit another cigarette. She did not think at all about what to do next, not at all; if she had been inclined to think that, she would not have been sitting wherever it was she was. The butterfly, no doubt, was extinct and the general would dislike strangers; the explanations (everything has an explanation) would formulate themselves, in her absence, when the plane reached its destination. The duty-free liquor could be poured down the lavatory, but there remained the problem of the Swiss pocket-knife. And yet – through the forbidden doorway: grass, bougainvillaea trained like standard roses, a road glimpsed there!

The collector of treasures

Bessie Head

The long-term central state prison in the south was a whole day's journey away from the villages of the northern part of the country. They had left the village of Puleng at about nine that morning and all day long the police truck droned as it sped southwards on the wide, dusty cross-country track-road. The everyday world of ploughed fields, grazing cattle, and vast expanses of bush and forest seemed indifferent to the hungry eyes of the prisoner who gazed out at them through the wire mesh grating at the back of the police truck. At some point during the journey, the prisoner seemed to strike at some ultimate source of pain and loneliness within her being and, overcome by it, she slowly crumpled forward in a wasted heap, oblivious to everything but her pain. Sunset swept by, then dusk, then dark and still the truck droned on, impersonally, uncaring.

At first, faintly on the horizon, the orange glow of the city lights of the new independence town of Gaborone appeared like an astonishing phantom in the overwhelming darkness of the bush, until the truck struck tarred roads, neon lights, shops and cinemas, and made the bush a phantom amidst a blaze of light. All this passed untimed, unwatched by the crumpled prisoner; she did not stir as the truck finally droned to a halt outside the prison gates. The torchlight struck the side of her face like an agonising blow. Thinking she was asleep, the policeman called out briskly:

'You must awaken now. We have arrived.'

He struggled with the lock in the dark and pulled open the grating. She crawled painfully forward, in silence.

Together, they walked up a short flight of stairs and waited a while as the man tapped lightly, several times, on the heavy iron prison door. The night-duty attendant opened the door a crack, peered out and then opened the door a little wider for them to enter. He quietly and casually led the way to a small office, looked at his colleague and asked: 'What do we have here?'

'It's the husband murder case from Puleng village,' the other replied, handing over a file.

The attendant took the file and sat down at a table on which lay open a large record book. In a big, bold scrawl he recorded the details: Dikeledi Mokopi. Charge: Manslaughter. Sentence: Life. A night-duty wardress appeared and led the prisoner away to a side cubicle, where she was asked to undress.

'Have you any money on you?' the wardress queried, handing her a plain, green cotton dress which was the prison uniform. The prisoner silently shook her head.

'So, you have killed your husband, have you?' the wardress remarked, with a flicker of humour. 'You'll be in good company. We have four other women here for the same crime. It's becoming the fashion these days. Come with me,' and she led the way along a corridor, turned left and stopped at an iron gate which she opened with a key, waited for the prisoner to walk in ahead of her and then locked it with the key again. They entered a small, immensely high-walled courtyard. On one side were toilets, showers, and a cupboard. On the other, an empty concrete quadrangle. The wardress walked to the cupboard, unlocked it and took out a thick roll of clean-smelling blankets which she handed to the prisoner. At the lower end of the walled courtyard was a heavy iron door which led to the cell. The wardress walked up to this door, banged on it loudly and called out: 'I say, will you women in there light your candle?'

A voice within called out: 'All right,' and they could hear the scratching of a match. The wardress again inserted a key, opened the door and watched for a while as the prisoner spread out her blankets on the floor. The four women prisoners already confined in the cell sat up briefly, and stared silently at their new companion. As the door was locked, they all greeted her quietly and one of the women asked: 'Where do you come from?'

'Puleng,' the newcomer replied, and seemingly satisfied with that, the light was blown out and the women lay down to continue their interrupted sleep. And as though she had reached the end of her destination, the new prisoner too fell into a deep sleep as soon as she had pulled her blankets about her.

The breakfast gong sounded at six the next morning. The women stirred themselves for their daily routine. They stood up, shook out their blankets and rolled them up into neat bundles. The day-duty wardress rattled the key in the lock and let them out into the small concrete courtyard so that they could perform their morning toilet. Then, with a loud clatter of pails and plates, two male prisoners appeared at the gate with breakfast. The men handed each woman a plate of porridge and a mug of black tea and they settled themselves on the concrete floor to eat. They turned and looked at their new companion and one of the women, a spokesman for the group, said kindly:

'You should take care. The tea has no sugar in it. What we usually do is scoop the sugar off the porridge and put it into the tea.'

The woman, Dikeledi, looked up and smiled. She had experienced such terror during the awaiting-trial period that she looked more like a skeleton than a human being. The skin creaked tautly over her cheeks. The other woman smiled, but after her own fashion. Her face permanently wore a look of cynical, whimsical humour. She had a full, plump figure. She introduced herself and her companions: 'My name is Kebonye. Then that's Otsetswe, Galeboe, and Monwana. What may your name be?'

'Dikeledi Mokopi.'

'How is it that you have such a tragic name?' Kebonye observed. 'Why did your parents have to name you *tears*?'

'My father passed away at that time and it is my mother's tears that I am named after,' Dikeledi said, then added: 'She herself passed away six years later and I was brought up by my uncle.'

Kebonye shook her head sympathetically, slowly raising a spoonful of porridge to her mouth. That swallowed, she asked next:

'And what may your crime be?'

'I have killed my husband.'

'We are all here for the same crime,' Kebonye said, then with her cynical smile asked: 'Do you feel any sorrow about the crime?'

'Not really,' the other woman replied.

'How did you kill him?'

'I cut off all his special parts with a knife,' Dikeledi said.

'I did it with a razor,' Kebonye said. She sighed and added: 'I have had a troubled life.'

A little silence followed while they all busied themselves with their food, then Kebonye continued musingly:

'Our men do not think that we need tenderness and care. You know, my husband used to kick me between the legs when he wanted that. I once aborted with a child, due to this treatment. I could see that there was no way to appeal to him if I felt ill, so I once said to him that if he liked he could keep some other woman as well because I couldn't manage to satisfy all his needs. Well, he was an education-officer and each year he used to suspend about seventeen male teachers for making schoolgirls pregnant, but he used to do the same. The last time it happened the parents of the girl were very angry and came to report the matter to me. I told them: "You leave it to me. I have seen enough." And so I killed him.'

They sat in silence and completed their meal, then they took their plates and cups to rinse them in the wash-room.

The wardress produced some pails and a broom. Their sleeping-quarters had to be flushed out with water; there was not a speck of dirt anywhere, but that was prison routine. All that was left was an inspection by the director of the prison. Here again Kebonye turned to the newcomer and warned:

'You must be careful when the chief comes to inspect. He is mad about one thing – attention! Stand up straight! Hands at your sides! If this is not done you should see how he stands there and curses. He does not mind anything but that. He is mad about that.'

Inspection over, the women were taken through a number of gates to an open, sunny yard, fenced in by high barbed wire where they did their daily work. The prison was a rehabilitation centre where the prisoners produced goods which were sold in the prison store; the women produced garments of cloth and wool; the men did carpentry, shoe-making, brick-making, and vegetable production.

Dikeledi had a number of skills – she could knit, sew, and weave baskets. All the women at present were busy knitting woollen garments; some were learners and did their work slowly and painstakingly. They looked at Dikeledi with interest as she took a ball of wool and a pair of knitting needles and rapidly cast on stitches. She had soft, caressing, almost boneless, hands of strange power – work of a beautiful design grew from those hands. By mid-morning she had completed the front part of a jersey, and they all stopped to admire the pattern she had invented in her own head.

'You are a gifted person,' Kebonye remarked, admiringly.

'All my friends say so,' Dikeledi replied smiling. 'You know, I am a woman whose thatch does not leak. Whenever my friends wanted to thatch their huts, I was there. They would never do it without me. I was always busy and employed because it was with these hands that I fed and reared my children. My husband left me after four years of marriage but I managed well enough to feed those mouths.

If people did not pay me in money for my work, they paid me with gifts of food.'

'It's not so bad here,' Kebonye said. 'We get a little money saved for us out of the sale of our work, and if you work like that you can still produce money for your children. How many children do you have?'

'I have three sons.'

'Are they in good care?'

'Yes.'

'I like lunch,' Kebonye said, oddly turning the conversation. 'It is the best meal of the day. We get samp and meat and vegetables.'

So the day passed pleasantly enough with chatter and work and at sunset the women were once more taken back to the cell for lock-up time. They unrolled their blankets and prepared their beds, and with the candle lit continued to talk a while longer. Just as they were about to retire for the night, Dikeledi nodded to her newfound friend, Kebonye:

'Thank you for all your kindness to me,' she said, softly.

'We must help each other,' Kebonye relied, with her amused, cynical smile. 'This is a terrible world. There is only misery here.'

And so the woman Dikeledi began phase three of a life that had been ashen in its loneliness and unhappiness. And yet she had always found gold amidst the ash, deep loves that had joined her heart to the hearts of others. She smiled tenderly at Kebonye because she knew already that she had found another such love. She was the collector of such treasures.

There were really only two kinds of men in the society. The one kind created such misery and chaos that he could be broadly damned as evil. If one watched the village dogs chasing a bitch on heat, they usually moved around in packs of four or five. As the mating progressed one dog would attempt to gain dominance over the festivities and oust all

the others from the bitch's vulva. The rest of the hapless dogs
would stand around yapping and snapping in its face while
the top dog indulged in a continuous spurt of orgasms, day
and night until he was exhausted. No doubt, during that
Herculean feat, the dog imagined he was the only penis in
the world and that there had to be a scramble for it. That kind
of man lived near the animal level and behaved just the same.
Like the dogs and bulls and donkeys, he also accepted no
responsibility for the young he procreated and, like the dogs
and bulls and donkeys, he also made females abort. Since
that kind of man was in the majority in the society, he needed
a little analysing as he was responsible for the complete
breakdown of family life. He could be analysed over three
time-spans. In the old days, before the colonial invasion of
Africa, he was a man who lived by the traditions and taboos
outlined for all the people by the forefathers of the tribe. He
had little individual freedom to assess whether these
traditions were compassionate or not – they demanded that
he comply and obey the rules, without thought. But when
the laws of the ancestors are examined, they appear on the
whole to have been vast, external disciplines for the good of
the society as a whole, with little attention given to individual
preferences and needs. The ancestors made so many errors
and one of the most bitter-making things was that they
relegated to men a superior position in the tribe, while women
were regarded, in a congenital sense, as being an inferior form
of human life. To this day, women still suffered from all the
calamities that befall an inferior form of human life. The
colonial era and the period of migratory mining labour to
South Africa was a further affliction visited on this man. It
broke the hold of the ancestors. It broke the old, traditional
form of family life and for long periods a man was separated
from his wife and children while he worked for a pittance in
another land in order to raise the money to pay his British
Colonial poll-tax. British Colonialism scarcely enriched his

life. He then became the 'boy' of the white man and a machine-tool of the South African mines. African independence seemed merely one more affliction on top of the afflictions that had visited this man's life. Independence suddenly and dramatically changed the pattern of colonial subservience. More jobs became available under the new government's localisation programme and salaries sky-rocketed at the same time. It provided the first occasion for family life of a new order, above the childlike discipline of custom, the degradation of colonialism. Men and women, in order to survive, had to turn inwards to their own resources. It was the man who arrived at this turning point, a broken wreck with no inner resources at all. It was as though he was hideous to himself and in an effort to flee his own inner emptiness, he spun away from himself in a dizzy kind of death dance of wild destruction and dissipation.

One such man was Garesego Mokopi, the husband of Dikeledi. For four years prior to independence, he had worked as a clerk in the district administration service, at a steady salary of R50.00 a month. Soon after independence his salary shot up to R200.00 per month. Even during his lean days he had had a taste for womanising and drink; now he had the resources for a real spree. He was not seen at home again and lived and slept around the village, from woman to woman. He left his wife and three sons – Banabothe, the eldest, aged four; Inalame, aged three; and the youngest, Motsomi, aged one – to their own resources. Perhaps he did so because she was the boring, semi-literate traditional sort, and there were a lot of exciting new women around. Independence produced marvels indeed.

There was another kind of man in the society with the power to create himself anew. He turned all his resources, both emotional and material, towards his family life and he went on and on with his own quiet rhythm, like a river. He was a poem of tenderness.

One such man was Paul Thebolo and he and his wife, Kenalepe, and their three children, came to live in the village of Puleng in 1966, the year of independence. Paul Thebolo had been offered the principalship of a primary school in the village. They were allocated an empty field beside the yard of Dikeledi Mokopi, for their new home.

Neighbours are the centre of the universe to each other. They help each other at all times and mutually loan each other's goods. Dikeledi Mokopi kept an interested eye on the yard of her new neighbours. At first, only the man appeared with some workmen to erect the fence, which was set up with incredible speed and efficiency. The man impressed her immediately when she went round to introduce herself and find out a little about the newcomers. He was tall, large-boned, slow-moving. He was so peaceful as a person that the sunlight and shadow played all kinds of tricks with his eyes, making it difficult to determine their exact colour. When he stood still and looked reflective, the sunlight liked to creep into his eyes and nestle there; so sometimes his eyes were the colour of shade, and sometimes light brown.

He turned and smiled at her in a friendly way when she introduced herself and explained that he and his wife were on transfer from the village of Bobonong. His wife and children were living with relatives in the village until the yard was prepared. He was in a hurry to settle down as the school term would start in a month's time. They were, he said, going to erect two mud huts first and later he intended setting up a small house of bricks. His wife would be coming around in a few days with some women to erect the mud walls of the huts.

'I would like to offer my help too,' Dikeledi said. 'If work always starts early in the morning and there are about six of us, we can get both walls erected in a week. If you want one of the huts done in woman's thatch, all my friends know that I am a woman whose thatch does not leak.'

The man smilingly replied that he would impart all this information to his wife, then he added charmingly that he thought she would like his wife when they met. His wife was a very friendly person; everyone liked her.

Dikeledi walked back to her own yard with a high heart. She had few callers. None of her relatives called for fear that since her husband had left her she would become dependent on them for many things. The people who called did business with her; they wanted her to make dresses for their children or knit jerseys for the winter time and at times when she had no orders at all, she made baskets which she sold. In these ways she supported herself and the three children but she was lonely for true friends.

All turned out as the husband said – he had a lovely wife. She was fairly tall and thin with a bright, vivacious manner. She made no effort to conceal that normally, and every day, she was a very happy person. And all turned out as Dikeledi had said. The work-party of six women erected the mud walls of the huts in one week; two weeks later, the thatch was complete. The Thebolo family moved into their new abode and Dikeledi Mokopi moved into one of the most prosperous and happy periods of her life. Her life took a big, wide upward curve. Her relationship with the Thebolo family was more than the usual friendly exchange of neighbours. It was rich and creative.

It was not long before the two women had going one of those deep, affectionate, sharing-everything kind of friendships that only women know how to have. It seemed that Kenalepe wanted endless amounts of dresses made for herself and her three little girls. Since Dikeledi would not accept cash for these services – she protested about the many benefits she received from her good neighbours – Paul Thebolo arranged that she be paid in household goods for these services so that for some years Dikeledi was always assured of her basic household needs – the full bag of corn, sugar, tea, powdered milk, and cooking oil. Kenalepe was also the kind of woman who made the whole world spin around her; her attractive personality attracted a whole range of women to her yard and also a whole range of customers for her dressmaking friend, Dikeledi. Eventually, Dikeledi became swamped with work, was forced to buy a second sewing-machine and employ a helper. The two women did everything together – they were forever together at weddings, funerals, and parties in the village. In their leisure hours they freely discussed all their intimate affairs with each other, so that each knew thoroughly the details of the other's life.

'You are a lucky someone,' Dikeledi remarked one day, wistfully. 'Not everyone has the gift of a husband like Paul.'

'Oh yes,' Kenalepe said happily, 'He is an honest somebody.' She knew a little of Dikeledi's list of woes and queried: 'But why did you marry a man like Garesego? I looked carefully at him when you pointed him out to me near the shops the other day and I could see at one glance that he is a butterfly.'

'I think I mostly wanted to get out of my uncle's yard,' Dikeledi replied. 'I never liked my uncle. Rich as he was, he was a hard man and very selfish. I was only a servant there and pushed about. I went there when I was six years old when my mother died, and it was not a happy life. All his children despised me because I was their servant. Uncle paid for my education for six years, then he said I must leave school. I longed for more because, as you know, education opens up the world for one. Garesego was a friend of my uncle and he was the only man who proposed for me. They discussed it between themselves and then my uncle said: "You'd better marry Garesego because you're just hanging around here like a chain on my neck." I agreed, just to get away from that terrible man. Garesego said at that time that he'd rather be married to my sort than the educated kind because those women were stubborn and wanted to lay down the rules for men. Really, I did not ever protest when he started running about. You know what the other women do. They chase after the man from one hut to another and beat up the girlfriends. The man just runs into another hut, that's all. So you don't really win. I wasn't going to do anything like that. I am satisfied I have children. They are a blessing to me.'

'Oh, it isn't enough,' her friend said, shaking her head in deep sympathy. 'I am amazed at how life imparts its gifts. Some people get too much. Others get nothing at all. I have always been lucky in life. One day my parents will visit – they live in the south – and you'll see the fuss they make over me. Paul is just the same. He takes care of everything so that I never have a day of worry …

The man, Paul, attracted as wide a range of male friends as his wife. They had guests every evening; illiterate men who wanted him to fill in tax forms or write letters for them, or his own colleagues who wanted to debate the political issues of the day – there was always something new happening every day now that the country had independence. The two women sat on the edge of these debates and listened with fascinated ears, but they never participated. The following day they would chew over the debates with wise, earnest expressions.

'Men's minds travel widely and boldly,' Kenalepe would comment. 'It makes me shiver the way they freely criticise our new government. Did you hear what Petros said last night? He said he knew all those bastards and they were just a lot of crooks who would pull a lot of dirty tricks. Oh dear! I shivered so much when he said that. The way they talk about the government makes you feel in your bones that this is not a safe world to be in, not like the old days when we didn't have governments. And Lentswe said that ten per cent of the population in England really control all the wealth of the country, while the rest live at starvation level. And he said communism would sort all this out. I gathered from the way they discussed this matter that our government is not in favour of communism. I trembled so much when this became clear to me ...' She paused and laughed proudly. 'I've heard Paul say this several times: "The British only ruled us for eighty years." I wonder why Paul is so fond of saying that?'

And so a completely new world opened up for Dikeledi. It was so impossibly rich and happy that, as the days went by, she immersed herself more deeply in it and quite overlooked the barrenness of her own life. But it hung there like a nagging ache in the mind of her friend, Kenalepe.

'You ought to find another man,' she urged one day, when they had one of their personal discussions. 'It's not good for a woman to live alone.'

'And who would that be?' Dikeledi asked, disillusioned. 'I'd only be bringing trouble into my life whereas now it is all in order. I have my eldest son at school and I can manage to pay the school fees. That's all I really care about.'

'I mean,' said Kenalepe, 'we are also here to make love and enjoy it.'

'Oh I never really cared for it,' the other replied. 'When you experience the worst of it, it just puts you off altogether.'

'What do you mean by that?' Kenalepe asked, wide-eyed.

'I mean it was just jump on and jump off and I used to wonder what it was all about. I developed a dislike for it.'

'You mean Garesego was like that!' Kenalepe said, flabbergasted. 'Why, that's just like a cock hopping from hen to hen. I wonder what he is doing with all those women. I'm sure they are just after his money and so they flatter him ...' She paused and then added earnestly: 'That's really all the more reason you should find another man. Oh, if you knew what it was really like, you would long for it, I can tell you! I sometimes think I enjoy that side of life far too much. Paul knows a lot about all that. And he always has some new trick with which to surprise me. He has a certain way of smiling when he has thought up something new and I shiver a little and say to myself: "Ha, what is Paul going to do tonight!"'

Kenalepe paused and smiled at her friend, slyly.

'I can loan Paul to you if you like,' she said, then raised one hand to block the protest on her friend's face. 'I would do it because I have never had a friend like you in my life before whom I trust so much. Paul had other girls, you know, before he married me, so it's not such an uncommon thing to him. Besides, we used to make love long before we got married and I never got pregnant. He takes care of that side too. I wouldn't mind loaning him because I am expecting another child and I don't feel so well these days ...'

Dikeledi stared at the ground for a long moment, then she looked up at her friend with tears in her eyes.

'I cannot accept such a gift from you,' she said, deeply moved. 'But if you are ill I will wash for you and cook for you.'

Not put off by her friend's refusal of her generous offer, Kenalepe mentioned the discussion to her husband that very night. He was so taken off-guard by the unexpectedness of the subject that at first he looked slightly astonished, and burst out into loud laughter and for such a lengthy time that he seemed unable to stop.

'Why are you laughing like that?' Kenalepe asked, surprised.

He laughed a bit more, then suddenly turned very serious and thoughtful and was lost in his own thoughts for some time. When she asked him what he was thinking he merely replied: 'I don't want to tell you everything. I want to keep some of my secrets to myself.'

The next day Kenalepe reported this to her friend.

'Now whatever does he mean by that? I want to keep some of my secrets to myself?'

'I think,' Dikeledi said smiling, 'I think he has a conceit about being a good man. Also, when someone loves someone too much, it hurts them to say so. They'd rather keep silent.'

Shortly after this Kenalepe had a miscarriage and had to be admitted to hospital for a minor operation. Dikeledi kept her promise 'to wash and cook' for her friend. She ran both their homes, fed the children and kept everything in order. Also, people complained about the poorness of the hospital diet and each day she scoured the village for eggs and chicken, cooked them, and took them to Kenalepe every day at the lunch-hour.

One evening Dikeledi ran into a snag with her routine. She had just dished up supper for the Thebolo children when a customer came around with an urgent request for an alteration on a wedding dress. The wedding was to take place the next day. She left the children seated around the fire eating and returned to her own house. An hour later, her own children asleep and settled, she thought she would check the Thebolo yard to see if all was well there. She entered the children's hut and noted that they had put themselves to bed and were fast asleep. Their supper plates lay scattered and unwashed around the fire. The hut which Paul and Kenalepe shared was in darkness. It meant that Paul had not yet returned from his usual evening visit to his wife. Dikeledi collected the plates and washed them, then poured the dirty dishwater on the still-glowing embers of the outdoor fire. She piled the plates one on top of the other and carried them to the third additional hut which was used as a kitchen. Just then Paul Thebolo entered the yard, noted the lamp and movement in the kitchen hut and walked over to it. He paused at the open door.

'What are you doing now, Mma-Banabothe?' he asked, addressing her affectionately in the customary way by the name of her eldest son, Banabothe.

'I know quite well what I am doing,' Dikeledi replied happily. She turned around to say that it was not a good thing to leave dirty dishes standing overnight but her mouth flew open in surprise. Two soft pools of cool liquid light were in his eyes and something infinitely sweet passed between them; it was too beautiful to be love.

'You are a very good woman, Mma-Banabothe,' he said softly.

It was the truth and the gift was offered like a nugget of gold. Only men like Paul Thebolo could offer such gifts. She took it and stored another treasure in her heart. She bowed her knee in the traditional curtsey and walked quietly away to her own home.

Eight years passed for Dikeledi in a quiet rhythm of work and friendship with the Thebolos. The crisis came with the eldest son, Banabothe. He had to take his primary school leaving examination at the end of the year. This serious event sobered him up considerably as like all boys he was very fond of playtime. He brought his books home and told his mother that he would like to study in the evenings. He would like to pass with a 'Grade A' to please her. With a flushed and proud face Dikeledi mentioned this to her friend, Kenalepe.

'Banabothe is studying every night now,' she said. 'He never really cared for studies. I am so pleased about this that I bought him a spare lamp and removed him from the children's hut to my own hut where things will be peaceful for him. We both sit up late at night now. I sew on buttons and fix hems and he does his studies ...'

She also opened a savings account at the post office in order to have some standby money to pay the fees for his secondary education. They were rather high – R85.00. But in spite of all her hoarding of odd cents, towards the end of the year, she was short on R20.00 to cover the fees. Midway during the Christmas school holidays the results were announced. Banabothe passed with a 'Grade A'. His mother was almost hysterical in her joy at his achievement. But what to do? The two youngest sons had already started primary school and she would never manage to cover all their fees from her resources. She decided to remind Garesego Mokopi that he was the father of the children. She had not seen him in eight years except as a passer-by in the village. Sometimes he waved but he had never talked to her or enquired about her life or that of the children. It did not matter. She was a lower form of human life. Then this unpleasant something turned up at his office one day, just as he was about to leave for lunch. She had heard from village gossip that he had eventually settled down with a married woman who had a brood of children of her own. He had ousted her husband, in a typical village sensation of brawls, curses, and abuse. Most probably the husband did not care because there were always arms outstretched towards a man, as long as he looked like a man. The attraction of this particular woman for Garesego Mokopi, so her former lovers said with a snicker, was that she went in for heady forms of love-making like biting and scratching.

Garesego Mokopi walked out of his office and looked irritably at the ghost from his past, his wife. She obviously wanted to talk to him and he walked towards her, looking at his watch all the while. Like all the new 'success men', he had developed a paunch, his eyes were blood-shot, his face was bloated, and the odour of the beer and sex from the previous night clung faintly around him. He indicated with his eyes that they should move around to the back of the office block where they could talk in privacy.

'You must hurry with whatever you want to say,' he said impatiently. 'The lunch-hour is very short and I have to be back at the office by two.'

Not to him could she talk of the pride she felt in Banabothe's achievement, so she said simply and quietly: 'Garesego, I beg you to help me pay Banabothe's fees for secondary school. He has passed with a "Grade A" and, as you know, the school fees must be produced on the first day of school or else he will be turned away. I have struggled to save money the whole year but I am short by R20.00.'

She handed him her post office savings book, which he took, glanced at and handed back to her. Then he smiled, a smirky know-all smile, and thought he was delivering her a blow in the face.

'Why don't you ask Paul Thebolo for the money?' he said. 'Everyone knows he's keeping two homes and that you are his spare. Everyone knows about that full bag of corn he delivers to your home every six months so why can't he pay the school fees as well?'

She neither denied this, nor confirmed it. The blow glanced off her face which she raised slightly, in pride. Then she walked away.

As was their habit, the two women got together that afternoon and Dikeledi reported this conversation with her husband to Kenalepe, who tossed back her head in anger and said fiercely: 'The filthy pig himself! He thinks every man is like him, does he? I shall report this matter to Paul, then he'll see something.'

And indeed Garesego did see something but it was just up his alley. He was a female prostitute in his innermost being and, like all professional prostitutes, he enjoyed publicity and sensation – it promoted his cause. He smiled genially and expansively when a madly angry Paul Thebolo came up to the door of his house where he lived with his concubine. Garesego had been through a lot of these dramas over those eight years and he almost knew by rote the dialogue that would follow.

'You bastard!' Paul Thebolo spat out. 'Your wife isn't my concubine, do you hear?'

'Then why are you keeping her in food?' Garesego drawled. 'Men only do that for women they fuck! They never do it for nothing.'

Paul Thebolo rested one hand against the wall, half dizzy with anger, and he said tensely: 'You defile life, Garesego Mokopi. There's nothing else in your world but defilement. Mma-Banabothe makes clothes for my wife and children and she will never accept money from me so how else must I pay her?'

'It only proves the story both ways,' the other replied, vilely. 'Women do that for men who fuck them.'

Paul Thebolo shot out the other hand, punched him soundly in one grinning eye and walked away. Who could hide a livid, swollen eye? To every surprised enquiry, he replied with an injured air:

'It was done by my wife's lover, Paul Thebolo.'

It certainly brought the attention of the whole village upon him, which was all he really wanted. Those kinds of men were the bottom rung of government. They secretly hungered to be the President with all eyes on them. He worked up the sensation a little further. He announced that he would pay the school fees of the child of his concubine, who was also to enter secondary school, but not the school fees of his own child, Banabothe. People half liked the smear on Paul Thebolo; he was too good to be true. They delighted in making him a part of the general dirt of the village, so they turned on Garesego and scolded: 'Your wife might be getting things from Paul Thebolo but it's beyond the purse of any man to pay the school fees of his own children as well as the school fees of another man's children. Banabothe wouldn't be there had you not procreated him, Garesego, so it is your duty to care for him. Besides, it's your fault if your wife takes another man. You left her alone all these years.'

So that story was lived with for two weeks, mostly because people wanted to say that Paul Thebolo was a part of life too and as uncertain of his morals as they were. But the story took such a dramatic turn that it made all the men shudder with horror. It was some weeks before they could find the courage to go to bed with women; they preferred to do something else.

Garesego's obscene thought processes were his own undoing. He really believed that another man had a stake in his hen-pen and, like any cock, his hair was up about it. He thought he'd walk in and re-establish his own claim to it and so, after two weeks, once the swelling in his eye had died down, he espied Banabothe in the village and asked him to take a note to his mother. He said the child should bring a reply. The note read: 'Dear Mother, I am coming home again so that we may settle our differences. Will you prepare a meal for me and some hot water that I might take a bath. Gare.'

Dikeledi took the note, read it and shook with rage. All its overtones were clear to her. He was coming home for some sex. They had had no differences. They had not even talked to each another.

'Banabothe,' she said. 'Will you play nearby? I want to think a bit then I will send you to your father with the reply.'

Her thought processes were not very clear to her. There was something she could not immediately touch upon. Her life had become holy to her during all those years she had struggled to maintain herself and the children. She had filled her life with treasures of kindness and love she had gathered from others and it was all this that she wanted to protect from defilement by an evil man. Her first panic-stricken thought was to gather up the children and flee the village. But where to go? Garesego did not want a divorce, she had left him to approach her about the matter, she had desisted from taking any other man. She turned her thoughts this way and that and could find no way out except to face him. If she wrote back, don't you dare put foot in this yard I don't want to see you, he would ignore it. Black women didn't have that kind of power. A thoughtful, brooding look came over her face. At last, at peace with herself, she went into her hut and wrote a reply: 'Sir, I shall prepare everything as you have said. Dikeledi.'

It was about midday when Banabothe sped back with the reply to his father. All afternoon Dikeledi busied herself making preparations for the appearance of her husband at sunset. At one point Kenalepe approached the yard and looked around in amazement at the massive preparations, the large iron water pot full of water with a fire burning under it, the extra cooking pots on the fire. Only later Kenalepe brought the knife into focus. But it was only a vague blur, a large kitchen knife used to cut meat and Dikeledi knelt at a grinding-stone and sharpened it slowly and methodically. What was in focus then was the final and tragic expression on the upturned face of her friend. It threw her into confusion and blocked their usual free and easy feminine chatter. When Dikeledi said: 'I am making some preparations for Garesego. He is coming home tonight,' Kenalepe beat a hasty retreat to her own home, terrified. They knew they were involved because when she mentioned this to Paul he was distracted and uneasy for the rest of the day. He kept on doing upside-down sort of things, not replying to questions, absent-mindedly leaving a cup of tea until it got quite cold, and every now and again he stood up and paced about, lost in his own thoughts. So deep was their sense of disturbance that towards evening they no longer made a pretence of talking. They just sat in silence in their hut. Then, at about nine o'clock, they heard those wild and agonised bellows. They both rushed out together to the yard of Dikeledi Mokopi.

He came home at sunset and found everything ready for him as he had requested, and he settled himself down to enjoy a man's life. He had brought a pack of beer along and sat outdoors slowly savouring it while every now and then his eye swept over the Thebolo yard. Only the woman and children moved about the yard. The man was out of sight. Garesego smiled to himself, pleased that he could crow as loud as he liked with no answering challenge.

A basin of warm water was placed before him to wash his hands and then Dikeledi served him his meal. At a separate distance she also served the children and then instructed them to wash and prepare for bed. She noted that Garesego displayed no interest in the children whatsoever. He was entirely wrapped up in himself and thought only of himself and his own comfort. Any tenderness he offered the children might have broken her and swerved her mind away from the deed she had carefully planned all that afternoon. She was beneath his regard and notice too for when she eventually brought her own plate of food and sat near him, he never once glanced at her face. He drank his beer and cast his glance every now and again at the Thebolo yard. Not once did the man of the yard appear until it became too dark to distinguish anything any more. He was completely satisfied with that. He could repeat the performance every day until he broke the mettle of the other cock again and forced him into angry abuse. He liked that sort of thing.

'Garesego, do you think you could help me with Banabothe's school fees?' Dikeledi asked at one point.

'Oh, I'll think about it,' he replied casually.

She stood up and carried buckets of water into the hut, which she poured into a large tin bath that he might bathe himself, then while he took his bath she busied herself tidying up and completing the last of the household chores. Those done, she entered the children's hut. They played hard during the day and they had already fallen asleep with exhaustion. She knelt down near their sleeping mats and stared at them for a long while, with an extremely tender expression. Then she blew out their lamp and walked to her own hut. Garesego lay sprawled across the bed in such a manner that indicated he only thought of himself and did not intend sharing the bed with anyone else. Satiated with food and drink, he had fallen into a deep, heavy sleep the moment his head touched the pillow. His concubine had no doubt taught him that the correct way for a man to go to bed was naked. So he lay, unguarded and defenceless, sprawled across the bed on his back.

The bath made a loud clatter as Dikeledi removed it from the room, but still he slept on, lost to the world. She re-entered the hut and closed the door. Then she bent down and reached for the knife under the bed which she had merely concealed with a cloth. With the precision and skill of her hard-working hands, she grasped hold of his genitals and cut them off with one stroke. In doing so, she slit the main artery which ran on the inside of the groin. A massive spurt of blood arched its way across the bed. And Garesego bellowed. He bellowed his anguish. Then all was silent. She stood and watched his death anguish with an intent and brooding look, missing not one detail of it. A knock on the door stirred her out of her reverie. It was the boy, Banabothe. She opened the door and stared at him, speechless. He was trembling violently.

'Mother,' he said, in a terrified whisper. 'Didn't I hear father cry?'

'I have killed him,' she said, waving her hand in the air with a gesture that said – well, that's that. Then she added sharply: 'Banabothe, go and call the police.'

He turned and fled into the night. A second pair of footsteps followed hard on his heels. It was Kenalepe running back to her own yard, half out of her mind with fear. Out of the dark Paul Thebolo stepped towards the hut and entered it. He took in every detail and then he turned and looked at Dikeledi with such a tortured expression that for a time words failed him. At last he said: 'You don't have to worry about the children, Mma-Banabothe. I'll take them as my own and give them all a secondary school education.'

Shelling peanuts

Yvonne Vera

'Take cover! Take cover!'

The small boys run through the streets and the yards carrying AK-rifles. They shoot through the hedges and yell as they drop to the ground, then rise again to confront each other. They contort their faces, making them as diabolical as possible. They want to look mean and merciless. They imitate the rut-a-tut sound of bursting fire. The girls watch and laugh gleefully as the boys roll themselves on the ground and hide behind tall grasses and imaginary protective rocks.

'You are cheating. I said "Take cover!" but you kept on running. You don't know how to play this game. If I say "Take cover!" you must lie down and hide. It means I am going to shoot at the enemy or else the enemy is going to shoot.'

'We should start again. We need more people to make the game exciting. Let us call the girls to join us, then we can have two teams.'

'Girls don't know how to fight and they cry if you push them. I don't think we should call the girls into our team.'

'Not all girls cry if you push them. Rebecca doesn't cry. Let's call her, then there will be four of us.'

'My mother told me that some women have also gone to fight and that they hold big guns and fight beside the men. I have seen pictures of dead women who have been killed by the soldiers in The African Times. My uncle shows them to us. This means we must call the girls to join us.'

'Okay then. But let us decide first how we are going to play the game. You two are going to be the soldiers and I will be the rebel with Rebecca. You must first of all tell us your demands, then we will refuse. You must then go away and we will start fighting. If we shoot and you haven't said "Take cover" then you are captured. We must also wear banana leaves as helmets and paint our faces. What are your demands?'

'We want more money. We want to know why you cannot make enough money in your machine to give to everyone?'

The mother watched from where she sat under a shade, listening to the boys argue and decide. Her cheeks shivered slightly, though her eyes were dry of tears. She held her knitting needles tightly together between her outstretched legs. A basket of unshelled peanuts rested on one side of the mat. She watched her daughter Rebecca join the boys in the fight for territory, and was disturbed. Was it possible the daughter and the father were at this moment carrying out the same act? They had never met. The father and the daughter.

'Take cover! Take cover!' the daughter shouted. The woman was in an agony of recollection. She put the needles aside, picked up the basket of peanuts, and folded her legs under her. The shade had shifted a little and she got up to move her mat to the other side of the tree.

'You're dead! You're dead!' The children's voices pierced the air. They dived into the hedge, raising small clouds of dust behind them, their bare feet protruding beneath the shadows.

The woman thought about the face that she remembered, scanning in her mind the broad shoulders, the muscular arms, and she was afraid. A young man not much older than herself, then. What would she do now that she was carrying his child? He said he couldn't stay, as he had already made plans to leave. He had not thought that their circumstances would change, that a baby would be on the way.

'I shot you! You're dead ... stop cheating!' Rebecca shouted indignantly. The young boy only laughed, then turned rapidly around in mock anger, his brow contorted, firing a chain of bullets towards her. The mother heard the shrieking voice of her daughter, then the pleading tones of the father whose memory was awakened.

'We shall start all over when I return,' he had told her.

'When you return?' she echoed. 'Will you return?'

He looked away to his trousers, which were torn at the knees.

'Those who have no jobs have to leave. There is a job out there.' In his mind he meant no place in particular, only a piece of battleground in the bush, where he could claim some territory.

'What shall I do,' she asked, seeking his eyes, 'on my own?'

He did not answer. Perhaps he was ashamed of what he could not do for her.

'Take cover! Take cover!' The children's guns sent metallic fire over the rooftops.

'We shall wipe you out!' the daughter shouted.

The mother, disturbed, could not bear her daughter's determined voice. She wanted to call her and send her to the shops, or give her some woman's duty in the house. She saw the daughter's legs disappearing behind the tree under which she sought shade, and saw a small boy run after her, clutching a hand grenade.

'Surrender,' the little boy said as the two struggled behind the tree. The mother closed her eyes in search of the missing face.

The man, standing up, was about to leave but kept looking at the woman, whom he was seeing for the last time. Perhaps she would say or do something to make him stay. Not only today, but for good. But what could she say? Everything had come to her already decided. She could not reshape what had come to her complete, already out of reach. Only something of the man was left with her, and she had to nurture it, inside her. The man stared again at the woman, wanting to touch her for the last time, but he wanted her to come forward, to give herself. She would not do it, however, and he left.

The dead ones got up and walked. In the noonday heat the children ran around in circles, tiring of their game. They were laughing at each other and at the silliness of their sport. The mother had shelled the peanuts into a small basket, which she secured steadily with her knees. Each of the children withdrew into his own world, lying under the shade of the green hedge and recovering his energy.

'You're dead! You're dead!' The children mocked the collapse of their fantastic visions, as the game drew to an end, and the mother welcomed the quiet that followed their play.

The mother knew that if they invented another game, they would all jump up in enthusiasm, if it pleased them to do so. She called Rebecca, and sent her inside the house with the shelled peanuts.

Transforming moments

Gcina Mhlophe

I was seventeen years old and feeling very unsure of myself. With my schoolwork I was doing exceptionally well and most teachers at the high school loved me – or they seemed to. My essays were the example of good work and they would be read to the whole class. I was probably proud of myself even though I didn't really give it any serious thought. Somehow it did not do much for my confidence or give me any self-love. I thought I was very ugly and the fact that my hair was so hard to manage did not make things easier. I used to describe it as dry grass in winter. And after a while I stopped combing it. I'd wash it and dry it, get dressed in my black skirt and white shirt which were not as nice as other girls', and I'd be on my way to school. To top it all, I had knock-knees and big feet! I was just ugly and awkward – I hated myself. And, my God, I sat in the front desk – Miss-ugly-top-of-the-class.

Our school was one of the biggest high schools in the Eastern Cape and we had a great school choir that simply collected trophies. I remember Bulelwa's voice every time I think of our choir. I used to close my eyes and enjoy listening to her sing. I don't know how many times I wished I had a tape recorder so I could tape her and be sure to listen to her all my life. And I must say I felt great on those rare afternoons when Bulelwa would come and study with me under the black wattle tree near the teachers' cottages. I loved that spot. And I also remember that Bulelwa stood by me when some girls in our dormitory would tease me about boys. They knew I was not very interested in boys and they would go on ... But who would want to go out with her, she doesn't even try to look good!

I remember this good-looking boy from Port Elizabeth who played rugby, it was half through the year and he still did not have a girlfriend. He was the star of our rugby team. I knew his name and I'd heard lots about how good he was but I didn't really know him – I was not one to go to the sports field. I was forever buried in my books. I read all the prescribed books for my year and then I read any other book or newspaper or magazine. I read love stories by Barbara Cartland, Catherine Cookson, I read James Baldwin ... I read so much you'd think that was the only thing that kept me alive. By the time the teacher came to certain books I had long finished them and I wished we'd move on to something I didn't know. Boys in my class did not like me very much – except when they needed help with schoolwork.

In the girls' dormitory my bed was at the far corner from the entrance, far enough from the Matron too. So, long after the lights were switched off, my deep voice would be heard droning away, doing what we had termed 'coughing' – I used to 'cough' out chapters and chapters of our set books and history to my classmates who'd left it till too late to do their schoolwork and the big test was on Monday or so. While I helped them out, it also helped me to do the 'coughing', it also helped to revive my memory, because I had read the book and then carried on to read others that had nothing particular to do with the syllabus. Some girls were forced to be my part-time friends for this reason. But then came one day when we were rehearsing a new school play and the boy from Port Elizabeth·walked up to me and told me that he loved me and wished I'd try to love him too.

Well, I thought he was crazy! What did a good-looking boy like that want with me – and besides I went to that school to study, not to sleep with boys! I told him so. He tried to convince me that he did not particularly mean to rush things – I did not have to sleep with him, he just liked me and he wanted to be my boyfriend. He said he really wanted to spend

time with me and we could have good times together talking
and reading if that's what I wanted. I asked him to please
leave me alone.

Well, the boy didn't leave me alone but many girls did.
They thought he was too good for me, they claimed he was a
city boy and should therefore go for a city girl. There were
many remarks too that I was ugly and did not have any
fashionable clothes. Many girls looked the other way when I
walked past or towards them and many unkind remarks were
whispered behind my back. At first it annoyed me – I told
whoever would listen that I didn't want anything to do with
the handsome city boy – they could have him. But the hostility
got worse and the boy continued to follow me. And then I
began to find it funny. I looked at the girls who hated me and
I wondered what would happen if I decided to accept the
rugby star as my boyfriend. Sometimes I laughed alone as I
imagined what they could be whispering about me. Then I
thought well, he's not blind, he can see that I'm ugly, he can
see I don't have any fashionable clothes, he can see I read too
much – I thought fine, I'll go out with him. He had chosen an
unsuitable girl and set the whole school on fire. My English
teacher thought it was really funny – he congratulated me
for causing such a stir! It turned out that Sizwe was a lovely
person and we'd become quite good friends by the time he
left the school at the end of that year.

I carried on with my schoolwork and continued to please
my sister in Johannesburg – she was the one to pay for my
education. I could imagine her face glowing when she
received my good results and I wished I could see her then. I
was doing my Standard 9 and we'd just come back for the
second semester after the winter holidays. Life was all right,
everything was going the same as it always had. I am not
quite sure how it started but as time went on I had the feeling
that the minister liked me. But then, maybe I don't have to
explain such a lot. I think everyone has somebody in their

lives who seems to like them – just like that. Sure, I was always well-behaved in church and I was one of the three girls who cut and arranged flowers for the church vases every Sunday morning. I had been kicked out of the school choir because my voice was too deep and I was impatiently told to sing tenor with the boys or leave. Everybody had laughed and I got the general feeling that my voice was not too good. I left. That also added to my Miss-ugly-top-of-the-class image. But the minister insisted that I be in the church choir despite my protestations that my voice was ugly. He said my voice was strong and resonant – not ugly. That's the first time I heard the word 'resonant', and I liked it, so I joined the church choir.

Then there was this Friday afternoon, a group of lazy girls was walking back from school. The winter sun seemed as lazy as we were. We had just walked past the minister's house when a young boy ran up to us. He said the minister wanted to see me. I went with him and I was about to walk into the kitchen when the minister himself came out and gave me fast instructions that I must go and get my weekend bag packed because he was going to visit his family and I was coming with him. I stood there at the top of the stairs open-mouthed, unable to move or speak. He looked at me and laughed out loud. He told me we had less than an hour to go, so I should run. Without a word I turned and took the five steps in one big jump. Running at top speed, clutching my books tightly to my chest – I realised that I was not alone in the world – everyone was staring at me. I tried to pull myself together and put a hand across my lips to hide the big grin.

Once in my dormitory I did not know what to take or leave, I was not exactly used to going on weekends. I quickly got out of my school uniform and into my best dress. I ran to the bathroom to wet my hair a little so I could try to comb it. It was too painful but I sort of tugged and patted it down with my hand. When I thought it felt better I went and got my plastic bag with the few necessities for the weekend. Then I realised I had forgotten my nightie. I jumped to get it from under my pillow. People were following me around but too proud to ask what was going on and I was not going to say a word till they asked.

Nosisa grabbed me by the arm as I was just walking out the door – 'Aren't you going to tell us where you are going?!'

That opened it up for everyone to ask me questions all at the same time.

'I am going with Father Fikeni to visit his family for the weekend, he said I must run.' With that I pulled my arm free and walked quickly out of the gate.

The drive to Tsolo was relaxing, with the sun setting ahead of us and me dreaming away in the back seat. The minister and his wife sat in front and they seemed to be at peace with themselves. Mrs Fikeni was a beautiful lady who did not talk too much. Many times in church I would look at her and wish that some angel would come into the church and ask me what I wanted. I knew exactly what I would ask for – I wanted to be as beautiful as the minister's wife.

That night we went to bed at about ten-ish after the evening prayer. I fell asleep very quickly, maybe I was too tired from all my excitement. But then I was still excited when I woke up the next morning, to realise that no bell rang for me to wake up or to go to the dining hall and to go to school ... I had a shower and went to help out in the kitchen. I liked the fact that I was not treated like some special guest who couldn't even do the dishes with them. I felt very much at home.

We were all sitting, on t he verandah drinking some tea, a short while after breakfast, and I was sitting next to the minister's wife. She was knitting a huge jersey with red and blue stripes. It looked so big I doubted it was hers, but she said yes it was – she just liked it that way, long and big like a coat. I was sitting there just staring at her fast-moving hands, and to look at her face was something else. It was as relaxed and beautiful as ever. She hardly looked at her knitting except when she ran out of wool or when she had to change colour. We were sitting like that when the minister stood up and stretched his arms and said that it was time to go. Time to go where? I half-heartedly wondered, but I carried on looking at the knitting hands. When he did not move I looked up, maybe I was feeling his eyes on me. He said maybe I should go with him. He said he had a surprise for me. I looked around at the eyes around me, but none seemed to give me a clue. I stood up and followed him inside the house. He sort of explained that he was going to this meeting and he thought I'd like to see what goes on in such meetings. I did not know what to say – so I smiled and got ready to go.

The meeting was held at a nearby village and it was at the chief's place. It was very well attended – looking at all the people sitting on the grass, on rocks or wooden stools near the cattle kraal, I decided the whole village – everyone – was there. We were late but no one seemed to be that concerned – they made space for us to sit while the speaker carried on and the people listened. I remember that he was saying something about cattle being allowed to go into the mealie fields at the same time, something like all the people should come to an agreement and this should happen after everyone has finished reaping their crops. It was somewhere along those lines and more people participated in the discussion that followed, but my problem was that I didn't have much to do with it all. I sat there quietly trying to be as interested as I could. And then this man, tall with big shoulders and a very dark face, he stood up with a leap – his eyes flashing this way and that, like he was on the alert for something. He wore this beautifully made dark red hat with some beads and a long black feather on it. He had more beads around his neck and waist. Then he had this leather skirt – the front part just above the knees and the back much longer and flowing behind. Also he had this strong-looking short stick and then the tip was made longer by a white oxtail attached to it. He was holding it in one hand and in the other he was holding a biggish red, almost blanket-like cloth – thrown casually over his arm. Everyone sat up expectantly when the man stood up. The minister looked at me with a big smile. I think the look in his eyes told me: 'This is it now – enjoy1'

The brightly dressed man started by singing the praises of the chief's family and then about the chief's achievements, about the village people, great heroes of the past and of the present. His use of language was pure and flowing – and so were his movements. He leapt forward and hit the ground with his oxtail stick, hardly making a sound – he had some people unconsciously imitating him. He would be praising the one minute, and the next he was reflective and critical. I had heard of *imbongi* – a praise poet – but I'd never dreamt that I'd see one in action. I was staring open-mouthed; even today looking back, I still don't know exactly how to describe the feeling I had right then. I only remember that when the man had finished and people moved forward to congratulate him, I knew I was too tired to even clap my hands or join in the ululation and whistles ... I just sat there and in my dreamy mind saw myself in a kind of similar attire, doing what I had just seen the man do. I made my decision there and then that I was also a praise poet. That was a beautiful moment, to think of myself as such. I shook a few people's hands and the minister introduced me to the chief, who thanked him for coming and laughingly asked what I was doing at such a meeting. And then the poet came to greet Father Fikeni. After their longish chat I was introduced to him as a very good student – during which time I was frozen and dumb from disbelief and God knows what else. To feel the poet's hot, sweaty hand holding mine I felt baptised as a poet too. I think I wanted to say something clever but all I could do at the moment was smile and fidget with my buttonholes. He went on to talk with other people who called him Cira.

It was Monday afternoon and I was lying on my stomach at my favourite corner under the black wattle trees when I wrote my first poem. I've never had a child, but the great feeling that swept over me was too overwhelming for words, maybe that's how people feel when they have their first baby, I don't know *. I sat up and read it out loud. I liked the sound of my own voice – I liked to hear the poem. I put the paper down and ran my fingers on my face to feel my features – the smile that wouldn't leave my face, my nose, my cheekbones, my eyes, my ears – everything just felt fine. My voice sounded like it was a special voice made especially to recite poems – with dignity. Resonant – was that it? That's the day I fell in love with myself – everything about me was just perfect.

I collected my books and the towel I was lying on, stood up and stretched my limbs – I felt tall and fit. I felt like jumping and laughing until I could not laugh any more. I wanted tomorrow to come so I could go buy myself a new notebook to write my poems in. A woman praise poet – I'd never heard of one, but what did it matter? – I could be the first one. I knew Father Fikeni would agree with me. I couldn't wait to see his face when I read him my poem. Across the fence a big red cock flapped its wings and crowed loudly at me, in agreement too!

---

* Gcina Mhlophe writes: 'On the 11th of July 1996 I had a lovable little girl. I named her Nomakhwezi, "girl of the morning star". I discovered waves of love in my heart that I did not even suspect were there.'

Independence Day

Yvonne Vera

'Move back! Move back!' the policemen shouted.

Today they were lining the main street in the city to see the Prince who had come from England to give their country back to them. At midnight.

The woman took shelter in the green space in her head, and waited. The children, released early from school, were standing along a stretch of empty road, books held above their heads casting inky shadows on their faces. The sun shone brightly on the tarred road. A policeman stood on the broad yellow centre line, his starched cap exploring the distance. Policemen in heavy brown boots and khaki uniforms, holding guns and batons, told the children to move back. The Prince from England would not like to be crowded upon.

On the other side of the road women were dancing and singing traditional songs, under the towering gum tree. Sweat poured down their faces as they welcomed the future. The policemen with guns and batons told them to move to the back of the crowd or line up with the rest of the people. One gave them tiny flags to wave, a new flag for a new nation. While waiting for the Prince, sent by his mother the Queen, the woman held a branch from a jacaranda bush over her tired face, and stayed shielded in the green space in her head.

A limousine came down the street that was lined with exploding purple jacarandas. Children broke into screams, thinking it was the very important person who had come all the way from England to give them back their country. The woman watched the car drive up, and then heard the excitement die down. This was not the moment. It was just another car.

'We shall not know which car the Prince is in when he finally drives by,' a man said. 'For security reasons. But we have to wave at all the cars as they drive by. One of them has the Prince.'

'You mean we shall not see the Prince?' the woman asked, perplexed. She had woken up very early, to see the man who had the power to give them back their country. She heard the sound of sirens, and saw policemen rush by on motorbikes, followed by several cars moving slowly behind.

'Stay back! Stay back!' the policemen shouted to the excited students who extended their arms and waved their tiny flags in front of the stream of passing vehicles.

'Which car has the Prince?' asked the woman.

'Certainly not the first or the second one, for security reasons,' the man answered. 'And certainly not the last, it's too obvious.'

It must be the third then. The woman looked hard through the heavily tinted windows, but saw nothing. Still, everyone waved and shouted. They saw only their own excited faces, intercepted among reflections of purple jacaranda blooms. Along that very road the Prince surely had passed. If they had not seen him, maybe he had seen them. 'Did you see the Prince?' they asked each other on the way home. Later, some of them would see him at the stadium, at midnight. The woman would not go.

The man kept one arm around the woman, while with the other he held a bottle of cold beer. He had the television on, and insisted that he would watch the Independence celebrations first. He had already given her the money, and she kept it knotted in a yellow handkerchief which she had tied on the strap of her bra. The stadium, usually reserved for soccer matches, was filled to capacity. First there was traditional dancing in the middle of the stadium. The woman withdrew into the safe space in her mind, and watched the pictures go by on the screen.

The new Prime Minister gave a long speech, and people clapped and shouted. They raised their fists in jubilation. The new Prime Minister spoke into a microphone. The women continued dancing while the Prime Minister was speaking. The people waved their flags when they were told everything would be changing soon. Jobs and more money. Land and education. Wealth and food. The woman saw the Prince sitting quietly, dressed in spotless white clothing. They said his mother could not come. But in these matters he was as important as his mother. The new Prime Minister said something about the Prince, and everyone cheered.

The man watching the screen went to the kitchen for another beer. He was going to celebrate Independence properly: with cold beer and a woman. Now it was ten minutes to midnight. She must take her clothes off. The screen flashed the ticking minutes. The Prince and the new Prime Minister walked to the large flagpole in the middle of the stadium. The old flag was flapping in the air, the new one was hanging below. The man pushed the woman onto the floor. He was going into the new era in style and triumph. She opened her legs. It was midnight, and the new flag went up. The magic time of change. Green, yellow, white. Food, wealth, reconciliation.

When he was through he sent her home. When he awoke he preferred the whole house to himself. They had met under the jacarandas, waiting for the English Prince.

In the morning she saw miniature flags caught along the hedge: the old flag and the new.

The ultimate safari

Nadine Gordimer

The African Adventure Lives On... You can do it!
The ultimate safari or expedition
with leaders who know Africa.

—TRAVEL ADVERTISEMENT,
Observer, LONDON, 27/11/88

That night our mother went to the shop and she didn't come back. Ever. What happened? I don't know. My father also had gone away one day and never came back; but he was fighting in the war. We were in the war, too, but we were children, we were like our grandmother and grandfather, we didn't have guns. The people my father was fighting – the bandits, they are called by our government – ran all over the place and we ran away from them like chickens chased by dogs. We didn't know where to go. Our mother went to the shop because someone said you could get some oil for cooking. We were happy because we hadn't tasted oil for a long time; perhaps she got the oil and someone knocked her down in the dark and took that oil from her. Perhaps she met 'the bandits. If you meet them, they will kill you. Twice they came to our village and we ran and hid in the bush and when they'd gone we came back and found they had taken everything; but the third time they came back there was nothing to take, no oil, no food, so they burned the thatch and the roofs of our houses fell in. My mother found some pieces of tin and we put those up over part of the house. We were waiting there for her that night she never came back.

We were frightened to go out, even to do our business, because the bandits did come. Not into our house – without a roof it must have looked as if there was no one in it, everything gone – but all through the village. We heard people screaming and running. We were afraid even to run, without our mother to tell us where. I am the middle one, the girl, and my little brother clung against my stomach with his arms round my neck and his legs round my waist like a baby monkey to its mother. All night my first-born brother kept in his hand a broken piece of wood from one of our burnt house-poles. It was to save himself if the bandits found him.

We stayed there all day. Waiting for her. I don't know what day it was; there was no school, no church any more in our village, so you didn't know whether it was a Sunday or a Monday.

When the sun was going down, our grandmother and grandfather came. Someone from our village had told them we children were alone, our mother had not come back. I say 'grandmother' before 'grandfather' because it's like that: our grandmother is big and strong, not yet old, and our grandfather is small, you don't know where he is, in his loose trousers, he smiles but he hasn't heard what you're saying, and his hair looks as if he'd left it full of soap-suds. Our grandmother took us – me, the baby, my first-born brother, our grandfather – back to her house and we were all afraid (except the baby, asleep on our grandmother's back) of meeting the bandits on the way. We waited a long time at our grandmother's place. Perhaps it was a month. We were hungry. Our mother never came. While we were waiting for her to fetch us our grandmother had no food for us, no food for our grandfather and herself. A woman with milk in her breasts gave us some for my little brother, although at our house he used to eat porridge, same as we did. Our grandmother took us to look for wild spinach but everyone else in her village did the same and there wasn't a leaf left.

Our grandfather, walking a little behind some young men, went to look for our mother but didn't find her. Our grandmother cried with other women and I sang the hymns with them. They brought a little food – some beans – but after two days there was nothing again. Our grandfather used to have three sheep and a cow and a vegetable garden but the bandits had long ago taken the sheep and the cow, because they were hungry, too; and when planting time came our grandfather had no seed to plant.

So they decided – our grandmother did; our grandfather made little noises and rocked from side to side, but she took no notice – we would go away. We children were pleased. We wanted to go away from where our mother wasn't and where we were hungry. We wanted to go where there were no bandits and there was food. We were glad to think there must be such a place; away.

Our grandmother gave her church clothes to someone in exchange for some dried mealies and she boiled them and tied them in a rag. We took them with us when we went and she thought we would get water from the rivers but we didn't come to any river and we got so thirsty we had to turn back. Not all the way to our grandparents' place but to a village were there was a pump. She opened the basket where she carried some clothes and the mealies and she sold her shoes to buy a big plastic container of water. I said, Gogo, how will you go to church now even without shoes, but she said we had a long journey and too much to carry. At that village we met other people who were also going away. We joined them because they seemed to know where that was better than we did.

To get there we had to go through the Kruger Park. We knew about the Kruger Park. A kind of whole country of animals – elephants, lions, jackals, hyenas, hippos, crocodiles, all kinds of animals. We had some of them in our own country, before the war (our grandfather remembers; we children weren't born yet) but the bandits kill the elephants and sell their tusks, and the bandits and our soldiers have eaten all the buck. There was a man in our village without legs – a crocodile took them off, in our river; but all the same our country is a country of people, not animals. We knew about the Kruger Park because some of our men used to leave home to work there in the places where white people come to stay and look at the animals.

So we started to go away again. There were women and other children like me who had to carry the small ones on their backs when the women got tired. A man led us into the Kruger Park; are we there yet, are we there yet, I kept asking our grandmother. Not yet, the man said, when she asked him for me. He told us we had to take a long way to get round the fence, which he explained would kill you, roast off your skin the moment you touched it, like the wires high up on poles that give electric light in our towns. I've seen that sign of a head without eyes or skin or hair on an iron box at the mission hospital we used to have before it was blown up.

When I asked the next time, they said we'd been walking in the Kruger Park for an hour. But it looked just like the bush we'd been walking through all day, and we hadn't seen any animals except the monkeys and birds which live around us at home, and a tortoise that, of course, couldn't get away from us. My first-born brother and the other boys brought it to the man so it could be killed and we could cook and eat it. He let it go because he told us we could not make a fire; all the time we were in the Park we must not make a fire because the smoke would show we were there. Police, wardens, would come and send us back where we came from. He said we must move like animals among the animals, away from the roads, away from the white people's camps. And at that moment I heard – I'm sure I was the first to hear – cracking branches and the sound of something parting grasses and I almost squealed because I thought it was the police, wardens – the people he was telling us to look out for – who had found us already. And it was an elephant, and another elephant, and more elephants, big blots of dark moved wherever you looked between the trees. They were curling their trunks around the red leaves of the Mopane trees and stuffing them into their mouths. The babies leant against their mothers. The almost grown-up ones wrestled like my first-born brother with his friends – only they used trunks instead of arms. I was so interested I forgot to be afraid. The man said we should just stand still and be quiet while the elephants passed. They passed very slowly because elephants are too big to need to run from anyone.

The buck ran from us. They jumped so high they seemed to fly. The warthogs stopped dead, when they heard us, and swerved off the way a boy in our village used to zigzag on the bicycle his father had brought back from the mines. We followed the animals to where they drank. When they had gone, we went to their water-holes. We were never thirsty without finding water, but the animals ate, ate all the time. Whenever you saw them they were eating, grass, trees, roots. And there was nothing for us. The mealies were finished. The only food we could eat was what the baboons ate, dry little figs full of ants that grow along the branches of the trees at the rivers. It was hard to be like the animals.

When it was very hot during the day we would find lions lying asleep. They were the colour of the grass and we didn't see them at first but the man did, and he led us back and a long way round where they slept. I wanted to lie down like the lions. My little brother was getting thin but he was very heavy. When our grandmother looked for me, to put him on my back, I tried not to see. My first-born brother stopped talking; and when we rested he had to be shaken to get up again, as if he was just like our grandfather, he couldn't hear. I saw flies crawling on our grandmother's face and she didn't brush them off; I was frightened. I picked a palm leaf and chased them.

We walked at night as well as by day. We could see the fires where the white people were cooking in the camps and we could smell the smoke and the meat. We watched the hyenas with their backs that slope as if they're ashamed, slipping through the bush after the smell. If one turned its head, you saw it had big brown shining eyes like our own, when we looked at each other in the dark. The wind brought voices in our own language from the compounds where the people who work in the camps live. A woman among us wanted to go to them at night and ask them to help us. They can give us the food from the dustbins, she said, she started wailing and our grandmother had to grab her and put a hand over her mouth. The man who led us had told us that we must keep out of the way of our people who worked at the Kruger Park; if they helped us they would lose their work. If they saw us, all they could do was pretend we were not there; they had seen only animals.

Sometimes we stopped to sleep for a little while at night. We slept close together. I don't know which night it was – because we were walking, walking, any time, all the time – we heard the lions very near. Not groaning loudly the way they did far off. Panting, like we do when we run, but it's a different kind of panting: you can hear they're not running, they're waiting, somewhere near. We all rolled closer together, on top of each other, the ones on the edge fighting to get into the middle. I was squashed against a woman who smelled bad because she was afraid but I was glad to hold tight on to her. I prayed to God to make the lions take someone on the edge and go. I shut my eyes not to see the tree from which a lion might jump right into the middle of us, where I was. The man who led us jumped up instead, and beat on the tree with a dead branch. He had taught us never to make a sound but he shouted. He shouted at the lions like a drunk man shouting at nobody, in our village. The lions went away. We heard them groaning, shouting back at him from far off.

We were tired, so tired. My first-born brother and the man had to lift our grandfather from stone to stone when we found places to cross the rivers. Our grandmother is strong but her feet were bleeding. We could not carry the basket on our heads any longer, we couldn't carry anything except my little brother. We left our things under a bush. As long as our bodies get there, our grandmother said. Then we ate some wild fruit we didn't know from home and our stomachs ran. We were in the grass called elephant grass because it is nearly as tall as an elephant, that day we had those pains, and our grandfather couldn't just get down in front of people like my little brother, he went off into the grass to be on his own. We had to keep up, the man who led us always kept telling us, we must catch up, but we asked him to wait for our grandfather.

So everyone waited for our grandfather to catch up. But he didn't. It was the middle of the day; insects were singing in our ears and we couldn't hear him moving through the grass. We couldn't see him because the grass was so high and he was so small. But he must have been somewhere there inside his loose trousers and his shirt that was torn and our grandmother couldn't sew because she had no cotton. We knew he couldn't have gone far because he was weak and slow. We all went to look for him, but in groups, so we too wouldn't be hidden from each other in that grass. It got into our eyes and noses; we called him softly but the noise of the insects must have filled the little space left for hearing in his ears. We looked and looked but we couldn't find him. We stayed in that long grass all night. In my sleep I found him curled round in a place he had tramped down for himself, like the places we'd seen where the buck hide their babies.

When I woke up he still wasn't anywhere. So we looked again, and by now there were paths we'd made by going through the grass many times, it would be easy for him to find us if we couldn't find him. All that day we just sat and waited. Everything is very quiet when the sun is on your head, inside your head, even if you lie, like the animals, under the trees. I lay on my back and saw those ugly birds with hooked beaks and plucked necks flying round and round above us. We had passed them often where they were feeding on the bones of dead animals, nothing was ever left there for us to eat. Round and round, high up and then lower down and then high up again. I saw their necks poking to this side and that. Flying round and round. I saw our grandmother, who sat up all the time with my little brother on her lap, was seeing them, too.

In the afternoon the man who led us came to our grandmother and told her the other people must move on. He said, If their children don't eat soon they will die.

Our grandmother said nothing.

I'll bring you water before we go, he told her.

Our grandmother looked at us, me, my first-born brother, and my little brother on her lap. We watched the other people getting up to leave. I didn't believe the grass would be empty, all around us, where they had been. That we would be alone in this place, the Kruger Park, the police or the animals would find us. Tears came out of my eyes and nose onto my hands but our grandmother took no notice. She got up, with her feet apart the way she puts them when she is going to lift firewood, at home in our village, she swung my little brother onto her back, tied him in her cloth – the top of her dress was torn and her big breasts were showing but there was nothing in them for him. She said, Come.

So we left the place with the long grass. Left behind. We went with the others and the man who led us. We started to go away, again.

There's a very big tent, bigger than a church or a school, tied down to the ground. I didn't understand that was what it would be, when we got there, away. I saw a thing like that

the time our mother took us to the town because she heard
our soldiers were there and she wanted to ask them if they
knew where our father was. In that tent, people were praying
and singing. This one is blue and white like that one but it's
not for praying and singing, we live in it with other people
who've come from our country. Sister from the clinic says
we're two hundred without counting the babies, and we have
new babies, some were born on the way through the Kruger
Park.

Inside, even when the sun is bright it's dark and there's a
kind of whole village in there. Instead of houses each family
has a little place closed off with sacks or cardboard from boxes
– whatever we can find – to show the other families it's yours
and they shouldn't come in even though there's no door and
no windows and no thatch, so that if you're standing up and
you're not a small child you can see into everybody's house.
Some people have even made paint from ground rocks and
drawn designs on the sacks.

Of course, there really is a roof – the tent is the roof, far,
high up. It's like a sky. It's like a mountain and we're inside
it; through the cracks paths of dust lead down, so thick you
think you could climb them. The tent keeps off the rain
overhead but the water comes in at the sides and in the little
streets between our places – you can only move along them
one person at a time – the small kids like my little brother
play in the mud. You have to step over them. My little brother
doesn't play. Our grandmother takes him to the clinic when
the doctor comes on Mondays. Sister says there's something
wrong with his head, she thinks it's because we didn't have
enough food at home. Because of the war. Because our father
wasn't there. And then because he was so hungry in the
Kruger Park. He likes just to lie about on our grandmother
all day, on her lap or against her somewhere, and he looks at
us and looks at us. He wants to ask something but you can
see he can't. If I tickle him he may just smile. The clinic gives

us special powder to make into porridge for him and perhaps one day he'll be all right.

When we arrived we were like him – my first-born brother and I. I can hardly remember. The people who live in the village near the tent took us to the clinic, it's where you have to sign that you've come – away, through the Kruger Park. We sat on the grass and everything was muddled. One sister was pretty with her hair straightened and beautiful high-heeled shoes and she brought us the special powder. She said we must mix it with water and drink it slowly. We tore the packets open with our teeth and licked it all up, it stuck round my mouth and I sucked it from my lips and fingers. Some other children who had walked with us vomited. But I only felt everything in my belly moving, the stuff going down and around like a snake, and hiccups hurt me. Another Sister called us to stand in line on the verandah of the clinic but we couldn't. We sat all over the place there, falling against each other; the Sisters helped each of us up by the arm and then stuck a needle in it. Other needles drew our blood into tiny bottles. This was against sickness, but I didn't understand, every time my eyes dropped closed I thought I was walking, the grass was long, I saw the elephants, I didn't know we were away.

But our grandmother was still strong, she could still stand up, she knows how to write and she signed for us. Our grandmother got us this place in the tent against one of the sides, it's the best kind of place there because although the rain comes in, we can lift the flap when the weather is good and then the sun shines on us, the smells in the tent go out. Our grandmother knows a woman here who showed her where there is good grass for sleeping mats, and our grandmother made some for us. Once every month the food truck comes to the clinic. Our grandmother takes along one of the cards she signed and when it has been punched we get a sack of mealie meal. There are wheelbarrows to take it back to the tent; my first-born brother does this for her and then he and the other boys have races, steering the empty wheelbarrows back to the clinic. Sometimes he's lucky and a man who's bought beer in the village gives him money to deliver it – though that's not allowed, you're supposed to take that wheelbarrow straight back to the Sisters. He buys a cold drink and shares it with me if I catch him. On another day, every month, the church leaves a pile of old clothes in the clinic yard. Our grandmother has another card to get punched, and then we can choose something: I have two dresses, two pants and a jersey, so I can go to school.

The people in the village have let us join their school. I was surprised to find they speak our language; our grandmother told me, That's why they allow us to stay on their land. Long ago, in the time of our fathers, there was no fence that kills you, there was no Kruger Park between them and us, we were the same people under our own king, right from our village we left to this place we've come to.

Now that we've been in the tent for so long – I have turned eleven and my little brother is nearly three although he is so small, only his head is big, he's not come right in it yet – some people have dug up the bare ground around the tent and planted beans and mealies and cabbage. The old men weave branches to put up fences round their gardens. No one is allowed to look for work in the towns but some of the women have found work in the village and can buy things. Our grandmother, because she's still strong, finds work where people are building houses – in this village the people build nice houses with bricks and cement, not mud like we used to have at our home. Our grandmother carries bricks for these people and fetches baskets of stones on her head. And so she has money to buy sugar and tea and milk and soap. The store gave her a calendar she has hung up on our flap of the tent. I am clever at school and she collected advertising paper people throw away outside the store and covered my schoolbooks with it. She makes my first-born brother and me do our homework every afternoon before it gets dark because there is no room except to lie down, close together, just as we did in the Kruger Park, in our place in the tent, and candles are expensive. Our grandmother hasn't been able to buy herself a pair of shoes for church yet, but she has bought black school shoes and polish to clean them with for my first-born brother and me. Every morning, when people are getting up in the tent, the babies are crying, people are pushing each other at the taps outside and some children are already pulling the crusts of porridge off the pots we ate from last night, my first-born brother and I clean our shoes. Our grandmother makes us sit on our mats with our legs straight out so she can look carefully at our shoes to make sure we have done it properly. No other children in the tent have real school shoes. When we three look at them it's as if we are in a real house again, with no war, no away.

Some white people came to take photographs of our people living in the tent – they said they were making a film, I've never seen what that is though I know about it. A white woman squeezed into our space and asked our grandmother questions which were told us in our language by someone who understands the white woman's.

How long have you been living like this?

She means here? our grandmother said. In this tent, two years and one month.

And what do you hope for the future?

Nothing. I'm here.

But for your children?

I want them to learn so that they can get good jobs and money.

Do you hope to go back to Mozambique – to your own country?

I will not go back.

But when the war is over – you won't be allowed to stay here? Don't you want to go home?

I didn't think our grandmother wanted to speak again. I didn't think she was going to answer the white woman. The white woman put her head on one side and smiled at us.

Our grandmother looked away from her and spoke – There is nothing. No home.

Why does our grandmother say that? Why? I'll go back. I'll go back through that Kruger Park. After the war, if there are no bandits any more, our mother may be waiting for us. And maybe when we left our grandfather, he was only left behind, he found his way somehow, slowly, through the Kruger Park, and he'll be there. They'll be home, and I'll remember them.

The baby's baby

Kaleni Hiyalwa

'Pregnant? By who?' demanded Neumbo, principal of the Kwanza Sul School. 'I am asking who impregnated you.'
Silence.
'I say who did it?' the principal demanded angrily.
Silence.
'You are not answering? – Okay! Okay! I am sending you to the administrator. Maybe you will be able to explain better,' Principal Neumbo told the young schoolgirl, Shekupe, who was standing like a soldier at attention in front of him.
'Bazooka!' the principal called out for the messenger.
'Yesh, Comradi!' Bazooka replied.
'Come quickly!' the principal said. Principal Neumbo scribbled a note and pushed it into Bazooka's hand. 'Take it to Commander Kalubena and tell him to take action as soon as possible,' Principal Neumbo instructed.
'Yesh Comradi Principal!' Bazooka responded respectfully with a salute.
'Take her along! She is part of the letter,' Principal Neumbo explained. Bazooka and Shekupe walked like hungry lions who feared to miss their prey if they did not walk fast enough.
A group of pupils stared after Shekupe and Bazooka until they were swallowed up by trees. The pupils looked at each other and laughed. Surprisingly, no one commented or said anything to follow up their laughter.
The way to the administration camp passed through a big coffee farm. On their way, Shekupe thought bitterly of her pregnancy. 'Look at me, dear girl. I should have been proud of myself. Now that I have broken *ondjeva* – beads worn exclusively by girls around their waists. I should have kept

to myself. Oh! Gods of my forefathers! Why can't you come?
Just a magic spell and there will be nothing in my stomach.
Oh! Help me. Let there be a magic spell. I am too young to be
pregnant. Why did I do it? ... Why? ... Oh, God!'

Shekupe said 'God' too loudly. Bazooka turned and saw
tears streaming from her eyes. She had forgotten that she
was walking with someone.

'Why are you crying, Comradi?' Bazooka asked Shekupe
with surprise. 'Oh! No ... no ... no! Don't cry!'

Shekupe stopped crying and glared at him. With a big
lump in her throat, she burst out: 'Mind your own business!
Just have a little sense to mind your own business!'

'Oh ... Comradi, are you annoyed with me? I did not do
anything to make you angry like that,' he complained. 'Mind
you, comredish don't insult each other,' he reminded her. 'I
am sorry, if I have offended you.'

'Keep going!' she shouted. 'I don't need your foolish
apologies,' she snapped as she burned with anger. They
stopped quarrelling as they came near the main office at the
administration camp.

'Comradi Command!' Bazooka called.

'Yes, Comrade, come in!' Comrade Kalubena said,
inspecting Bazooka and Shekupe from head to toe as they
entered his office. Both Bazooka and Shekupe stood at
attention and gave a pioneer salute to Comrade Kalubena.

Just as they were about to stand at ease, the commander
glimpsed Bazooka's feet. He saw that he stood like the
Angolans in the Portuguese prisons. It was told that Angolans
were beaten on their ankles so much that the feet faced
sideways. At that time, a man who served a prison sentence
in Angola walked as if each foot led him in a different
direction. Those who saw them said they walked like crabs.

'Bazooka! ... What is wrong?' the officer asked with an
authoritative voice as if he was a commanding officer at the
battlefield.

Bazooka shook like a cloth under pressure of a strong wind. 'Nothing wrong, Comradi!' he answered.

'Why are your feet like that? Answer me, why are your feet like that?' asked the commander.

'No ... nothing, Comradi,' he said, as if he was pleading with the commander not to ask him any further question.

'Remove your boots!' Comrade Kalubena ordered.

'Pilishi, Comradi Commanda, here is a letter for you,' Bazooka said as he handed the letter to Comrade Kalubena.

'Thank you! But do what I told you to do.'

'Yeshi, yeshi!' Bazooka replied. He sat down and started to remove his heavy military boots carefully as if there was an egg hidden under his feet which he was afraid to break. Bazooka twisted his face while removing them and then there he was, with his feet almost rotten. The stench hit both the commander's and Shekupe's noses.

Shekupe looked at Bazooka with hatred. All this had developed in her because of the letter he carried. She hoped that the commander would follow up Bazooka's case and forget about hers. 'Time, hold on! Be kind to me. How am I going to tell him? I am only a child. What is he going to do to me? Beat me? Insult me? Or is he only going to yell at me? Which one is better? Shekupe, have courage, girl! After all, I am not pregnant. It was only Principal who told me that I am pregnant. Pregnant? Oh, God! I do not know what it is all about, after all.'

Comrade Kalubena was a very tough man. Handsome enough but frightening with his muscular body. One could think he could only hold your neck once and twist it like that of a chicken. But some who knew him well also said that he was a man of kindness and soft at heart like a woman. They explained that Commander Kalubena only pretended to be serious so that he could do his work effectively.

He ripped the letter open and began to read carefully. Every word he read brought a different expression on his face.

'What? You?' Commander Kalubena looked up at Shekupe in disbelief. 'How old are you?'

Shekupe swallowed, hoping to wet her throat. Unfortunately her mouth was deadly dry. Only a heavy lump seemed to stand in her throat. If she tried to let a word out of her mouth, all other words would be translated into tears. 'Shekupe girl, how old am I? I know but I have forgotten. Oh, Lord of Lords, help me to remember,' she thought.

'I am asking you. How old are you?' The commander repeated his question, still looking at Shekupe.

'I ... I ... I ... I am ...' Shekupe stammered.

'You are what?' Comrade Kalubena demanded.

'Shekupe!' she said in total confusion.

'I asked your age, not your name,' the commander corrected.

'Thirteen,' Shekupe said and burst into tears. Shekupe stood facing the commander. She pleaded with her eyes and heart. She sincerely did. Words could not come out. They were squeezed in by the lump in her throat. 'I am thirteen years old, Comrade Commander,' she said, crying bitterly.

'Why, then, did you do that?' Comrade Kalubena asked with pity in his voice.

Shekupe did not say anything. She only looked at him with her eyes full of tears. She thought she cried blood instead of pure tears. Her heart felt as if it was torn into four parts. Comrade Kalubena moved two steps towards her.

'Comrade Commander, I did not do it,' she shouted, and continued to cry bitterly. People who were in the queue outside waiting to see Comrade Kalubena were puzzled when they heard Shekupe crying. It had never happened before that Commander Kalubena had harmed anybody. A crowd moved to peep through the window.

As she saw the people by the window, Shekupe shouted for help. She needed help from all the comrades outside. They should come in, all, and carry her away. 'Comrades!

Kind comrades! Do not reject me. I did not do it,' Shekupe shouted.

Comrade Kalubena went outside and told everybody to go away from the window. He assured them that there was nothing foul going on and everything was normal. 'She is only a child,' he concluded. Comrade Kalubena came back to his office and told Shekupe to calm down.

'Yes, I am listening, my girl,' the commander said with a more relaxed voice. There was a long silence.

'But I did not do it, Comrade Commander,' Shekupe said between sobs. Commander Kalubena stared at Shekupe, in deep thought, without seeing her or even hearing what she had just said to him. Both Bazooka and Shekupe looked at the commander for a long while and wondered whether he had gone to sleep with his eyes open.

'All right! The two of you are going back to where you came from,' Comrade Commander finally said.

Bazooka was putting on his boots. He squeezed his face, showing that he was in pain.

'Aah – yes! I forgot. Show me your feet,' Comrade Kalubena said, while helping Bazooka to stand. This time, Bazooka did not show a sign of pain as he was afraid of the commander. 'What is this?' Commander Kalubena asked Bazooka.

'I … I have jigger, Comradi,' he said, shivering.

'What? Couldn't you have gone to the hospital before it became as serious as this?' the commander asked. Bazooka did not answer, though he opened his mouth twice in an attempt to answer and did not succeed. It was not only Bazooka who had rotten feet because of 'jigger' but many other schoolchildren and some older people in the resettlement. Because of the pains, many of them were afraid to remove it from their feet.

Commander Kalubena took a pen and a paper and wrote a letter to Principal Neumbo.

Dear Cde Neumbo:
Please see to it that Bazooka is treated. And do not forget
to tell the pioneer commander to inspect all the kids, and
check whether they are infected with 'jigger'.
Take Shekupe to the hospital for a check up. I am sure
health facilities are available.
Your comrade in the struggle
Kalubena

As they walked back to the school, Shekupe's thoughts went
back to when this problem started.

It all began one evening. The moon was full, the sky clear
and all the stars above twinkled. Traditionally when the moon
shone, all the smart girls got to their feet to see to it that culture
was not lost. Namibian girls, in resettlements, gathered at
night under the moon to sing and dance. The voices were
more beautiful than those of nightingales. Their songs
combined the legend of their heroic struggle with the social
provocations between girls and boys.

That evening, a convoy arrived in the resettlement from
Luanda. There were four trailers, vehicles all filled with sacks
of provisions. Two trailers were full of fish and the other ones
full of different kinds of foodstuffs. Everyone was jubilant.
The old women and men received the message with joy when
they heard that the convoy had arrived safely from the capital.
Whenever the convoy came, everyone went to bed with his
heart satisfied and happy. All knew that there would be
enough food to eat in the coming weeks.

But what was more important was that there was someone
somewhere who cared about the refugees in the camps.

In Angola, the political unrest made it difficult for vehicles
to move about freely. SWAPO convoys had to be guarded by
soldiers against UNITA attacks. That day, the convoy arrived
in Kwanza Sul so early that there was enough time for the
drivers and soldiers to look around. One of them noticed
pretty Shekupe.

Shekupe was an orphan. Her mother, Naita, died when she was only five years old. Her mother had been killed in the Kassinga massacre, in front of Shekupe's eyes. According to an eyewitness, Naita got up at dawn as usual to prepare her children for classes. She was just returning from the bathroom with Shekupe when she saw jets planting bombshells in the crowd of the people at the morning parade. Before she could make up her mind of what was happening, a bayonet was struck into her back.

Hundreds of people were left dead in the Kassinga massacre. The innocent children, women and old people were wiped out like flies and buried in a mass grave.

Shekupe was a survivor. She was found lying under the dead body of her mother, unconscious. Treated and discharged, Shekupe was sent to the NEC at Kwanza Sul.

A few years later, Shekupe was just writing her form three end-of-year examinations when she received a hand-delivered letter from the front. It read:

Comrade Shekupe
Sorry to inform you of the death of your father. He had fallen on 2nd September when the gallants clashed in a battle, at the western front with the enemy – South African Battalions. He is a symbol of freedom. He left a gap which cannot be filled. God bless you!
Your comrade in arms
Nakupanya

Shekupe did not cry. Not even a single teardrop from those big beautiful eyes. It was said that she inherited her mother's beauty. Naita was a woman everyone admired. All Naita's features were perfect despite the deplorable conditions under which she lived.

Since the day she received the letter from the front, Shekupe's life was never the same again. She did not know any uncle or relative on either side. There had not been time for her parents to tell her anything concerning families both at home and abroad. She was too young to understand things when she was parted with the father and when her mother was killed.

Shekupe became a very active member of the SWAPO Pioneer Movement. She worked hard. At the age of nine, she thought of becoming a soldier. She wanted revenge with those who killed her parents. And now that she was told that she was pregnant, how was she going to make her dreams and aspirations come true?

Later at the hospital, Shekupe sat waiting for her test result. All the time she thought of it, she felt chilled. She kept shifting from one side of the bench to the other. Her heart leapt into her throat. She wished that the earth could open to swallow her up forever.

The door of the nurse's office opened and Sister Mary, the hospital head-nurse, came out. Sister Mary was an experienced nurse, who worked for ten years with patients both inside Namibia and Angola. She stood in the doorway, looking at the faces of waiting patients without saying a word and went back into her office.

Blood drained out of Shekupe's nerves at the sight of the white clothes that Sister Mary wore. 'Shekupe girl, am I dead? Is this worse than the death of my mother and father? No! ... Yes! I am confused. Help! ... Help! Let me die now ... Death, come! Take me away. I ... I am already dead,' Shekupe prayed.

The door of Sister Mary's office opened again. Shekupe jumped. No one came out. There was thunder in Shekupe's heart. But to her relief, the door was closed again. When the door opened the third time, she was called in at once and there was no chance left for her to think otherwise.

'Sit down, my girl,' Sister Mary said, showing her the chair in front of her table. 'What is wrong with you, child?' she asked with a smile. Shekupe could not answer because she wasn't sick at that moment. 'Do you have headaches or body pains, for instance?' Sister Mary asked, following the information she had received from Principal Neumbo and Commander Kalubena.

'I always have headaches and slight abdominal pains. I also vomit every morning and I have lost my appetite,' she said freely. Shekupe did not know anything about pregnancy symptoms and she just thought that there was nothing wrong about her. She was reminded of her painful story when Sister Mary asked her whether she had a boyfriend.

'No! I don't,' she denied with a shiver.

'Relax, my dear. These are normal questions that are meant for every patient who has the same symptoms as you,' Sister Mary explained with care in her voice. She knew that the slightest mistake would put Shekupe into a bad state since she was very young.

'Do you have your periods regularly?' she asked.

'I had them two times but they stopped since three months ago,' Shekupe said.

'Yes ... good,' the nurse said. 'Did any man try to do anything to you?' Sister Mary asked without looking at Shekupe.

Shekupe kept quiet. Her eyes were filled with tears. The tears streamed down Shekupe's face. Sister Mary realised she was touching on a sensitive topic. She then tried to comfort her with sweet motherly words and more simple questions.

'I will not tell anybody about it. Just tell me, okay! I love you. My name is Mary. I think you know me.'

'Yes, I know you,' Shekupe replied.

'Where are you staying now?'

'At the Pioneer dormitories.'

'Where are your parents?'

'They are both dead. Killed!'

Sister Mary was moved. 'Would you like to stay with me and my children?' Sister Mary asked.

'Yes,' Shekupe answered with a hidden excitement.

'Now, go to your dormitory and pack your things. Come and stay with me. Okay?'

'Yes, Sister,' Shekupe said enthusiastically.

On her way to the dormitories, she tried to avoid meeting people because she wanted to have enough time to thank the Lord and the ancestors. 'Shekupe girl, I have passed the test. It is nothing, after all. Sister Mary loves me. I love her too. I will tell my friends, Edith and Erica. They will be jealous of me. Oh, God! I now have a mother. Thank you, God ... thank you so much.'

When she entered in the dormitory, her two friends weren't in. She ran out and saw them coming from the kitchen carrying their *oshifima neeshi* – mealie-pap and fish.

'I have good news for you,' Shekupe shouted to Erica and Edith.

'Why are you so happy?' Edith asked.

'I am going to stay with Sister Mary, the nurse. I love her. She is kind, you know.'

'Farewell!' Erica snapped. She felt bad. But she did not want to believe that it was jealousy.

'Both of you, come and help me pack my things,' Shekupe suggested to her friends.

When Shekupe arrived at Sister Mary's house, the children ran to meet her. They helped her to carry her bundle of things. Sister Mary's first daughter was twelve years and the second one was ten years old. They were almost her age. This was why Sister Mary felt sorry for Shekupe. She knew the pregnancy wasn't her fault since she was still a kid with no adult to take care of her.

The next day, Sister Mary called Shekupe into her room. 'Remove your dress and try on those two dresses on the bed,' she said.

Shekupe was very excited. She did what she was told. Carefully, Sister Mary watched her from her breasts to the navel. There was no doubt that Shekupe was pregnant.

'All right, my child, those dresses fit you very well. You are so beautiful in them. Come and sit by me. Now, tell me about yourself, your schoolwork and what you girls do at your dormitory area. You do sports, I suppose?' Sister Mary asked.

'Yes, we play,' Shekupe replied. She narrated her story from Kassinga and when she received the letter from the front, informing her of the death of her father. She told of the 'moonlight play'. She talked about the boys standing behind the ring, watching the girls singing and dancing.

, 'Those guys just come to call girls,' Shekupe said.

'To where?'

'I don't know.'

'Do you know the girls?' Sister Mary asked.

'I know some,' Shekupe said confidently.

'Has anybody called you too?' Sister Mary went on.

Silence.

'Tell me the truth, I am now your mother.'

Silence.

'Promise you love me and that you want me to be your mother.'

'I promise, I love you and you are my mother.'

'Now, promise that you will always tell me the truth.'

'I promise, I shall always tell you the truth,' at last Shekupe said.

'Good girl. You are lovely,' Sister Mary said, with relief that her message was getting across. 'Do you want to go and show your sisters outside how you look in your new dresses?'

'Yes!' Shekupe replied happily.

'Before you go, tell me whether any man told you that he loves you before.'

Silence.

'I mean, did anyone propose love to you before?' Sister Mary insisted on asking.

Silence.

'My dear Shekupe, you know you have just promised to tell me the truth. Tell the truth then,' Sister Mary reminded Shekupe.

'Only the soldier who came in the convoy the other day.'

'Good girl! What did he do?'

'He sent Deppy, my friend, to call me when we were dancing the traditional dance under the moonlight. Deppy told me that I should accompany her to the soldier's tent. At first I refused, but she told me that soldiers used to bring her sweets, biscuits and sardines because they came from the city,' Shekupe explained.

'Is that all?' Sister Mary asked as she expected Shekupe to tell her more about the story leading to her pregnancy.

'Yes!' Shekupe said.

'What was the soldier's name?'

'Katusha,' Shekupe recalled.

'What was the other name?' Sister Mary continued asking for more information.

'I don't know any other name of his,' Shekupe said.

'Can you describe him?' Sister Mary insisted.

'He was wearing his uniform. He is tall and huge,' Shekupe explained what she could remember about the man she had slept with once. 'That is all I know. I forgot, he was wearing red underwear.'

Sister Mary realised that this was all that Shekupe could tell her. She decided rather to wait for the baby to be born.

'Thank you, my girl. Go and play with your sisters outside,' she told Shekupe with a sigh. Shekupe was an orphan, a victim of love and a victim of war. When she delivered her baby, what would the name of her baby be? A fatherless baby, though the father lived.

A baby's baby.

Elleke Boehmer

They were all at the airport to welcome her. They were the friends who had stayed. They still lived in their old haunts, brick buildings in green streets where night-long parties were once held. At some stage years ago, they'd thought about leaving, about Perth, Brisbane, Auckland, but something had held them, inertia maybe. They stayed on.

She spied Liz first, Liz craning her body over the chrome barrier, the big nest of her hair. And there was Ingrid, waving, and behind Ingrid the dark purple patch of Clare. Alison pushed her luggage trolley more slowly, lifting the handlebar slightly so that the brake was half on. She didn't want to burst in on them. They all needed a bit of time.

But now Ingrid was coming round the barrier, her arms open. Her scarlet shirt was voluminous. The trolley veered off to one side.

'Welcome to the sun, Ali.'

'Man, do you need it.'

'An English woman, that's what you look like.'

Those were Clare and Liz's voices beyond Ingrid's soft shoulder. The men stood further off, Jannie of course in a leather jacket, Chris looking more like a GP than ever. Chris had brought his Indian wife. He introduced her as Susie, which didn't sound like her real name. She was thinner even than Clare. She looked shy, he looked proud, proud maybe of his advanced brand of marriage.

'We're into this new nation thing, Ali,' said Ingrid. 'It's like it's the fashion. I have white friends looking for houses in Coloured neighbourhoods. A girl at work, a white girl, has called her baby Sizwe. We're trying loving and living together these days. In spite of the politicians. It's great.'

Ingrid was talking fast, especially at the traffic lights. She was driving. She cursed the slowness of the lights, calling them robots. Alison had forgotten they were called robots. She had forgotten other things too. Like the smell of bare skin her friends had, also the intense sweetness the women carried on them, the smell of a spray-on deodorant. It was taking time to come back to her, the bright light, the light tar, her friends' sunglasses, greasy frames.

Liz looked for new things to point out, new developments, improvements. There was the extension to the mall, a new flower and crafts market, those townhouse clusters, and white men in their usual short haircuts strolling and shopping with black girlfriends. Further away on the horizon, Alison saw, the big Anglo-American buildings in the middle of town still shone blindingly, like a supernova, like glory.

Jannie was leaning his head against the window as though sleepy. His hair left a fuzzy sweat patch on the glass. After a while Liz gave up talking. Maybe they didn't have much to say to each other, Alison thought, they were pulled back together only by this visit. She looked round to where Chris and the woman he called Susie were following them in a shiny white Honda.

'They're doing okay, those two,' Liz said.

Lunch was at Jannie's house because he was the one who had the space. Look at the tiled patio and walk-through fitted kitchen, Ingrid said, pointing with a raised arm. Jannie's band, still called the Namib Diviners, were doing well. She guided Alison to a frail-looking plastic chair beside the laden table.

The food was mainly mayonnaise salads in Tupperware tureens, side-dishes for a braai. Clare was spooning cream on to a large pink and white fruit pudding in a pottery bowl. Alison recognised the bowl from the time, nearly seven years ago now, when they shared a house.

'That must be Palmerosa pudding,' Liz said. 'I read about it in an American cookbook the other day.'

'Once I thought I would bath my baby in that bowl,' said Clare, pouring herself white wine from a box.

Liz raised her eyebrows at Alison.

In their final year at university Clare tried to have a child. She told everyone she wanted to be a single mother. Every four months or so, regular as a menstrual cycle, she informed them she'd miscarried again. Sometimes she shouted the news from the toilet. Then she spent days locked in her bedroom. Ingrid would leave cups of black tea mixed with Johnny Walker outside her door.

'I wanted us to have the party round the pool,' Liz said. 'But James didn't go golfing today. So he would've been in the way. And the kids too. We wanted to have you to ourselves, Ali.'

'All's not well with the marriage,' whispered Ingrid, giving Alison white wine in a beer glass. She was reciting from one of her most recent letters.

'It must be so strange for you not to have family in this country any more,' Liz was saying. 'Your dad's still in Canada?'

'Yes,' said Alison. Her father was married to a hand and foot model in Toronto. He lectured at the university there about soil erosion. He still used the slides he'd taken years ago in the Transkei. Pictures of red dongas.

'Not so strange as for us to have friends in just about every Western capital of the world,' said Jannie.

The remark was abrupt, it sounded out of place. Liz brought Alison more wine in a plastic party cup decorated with yellow and sky-blue squares. She sat on the carpet beside her chair. She was pretending it was comfortable to sit cross-legged in high sandals.

'I usually don't smoke,' said Liz, waving her cigarette in the air. 'Only on special occasions.'

'We still smoke far too much in this country,' said Clare. 'It's killing the nation.'

She spoke from the kitchen door. Behind her the chicken pieces and chops were blackening on the oven grill. Jannie had forgotten to buy charcoal for the braai.

Chris came in carrying bottles of wine, Susie behind him, also carrying bottles.

'We took a detour to the off-licence,' said Chris.

'They don't drink box stuff,' said Clare.

'We're allowed to smoke and drink without guilt,' said Jannie. 'We're a Third World country after all.'

Liz poked his calf with her sandal heel.

'What is it you do in London, Alison?' said Susie.

She handed Alison a glass of wine, a proper glass this time. Alison now had three helpings of wine on the table beside her, two portions of box wine and the glass.

'Believe it or not, I still do temping,' she said. 'I've been doing it nearly four years.'

'But you earn well on it, Ali,' said Liz, as if she wanted the reassurance.

'This place must look a bit different after all these years,' Chris said.

He didn't look straight at Alison even though he faced her. Chris, Susie, Liz, Clare at the kitchen door were silent now, glasses' rims at lips, lips pressed flat and pink against the glass, looking at her. It was time to declare herself, she saw, tell a story, reward them for the occasion.

Chris arranged mouthfuls of different kinds of salad on a plate. He passed the plate to Susie.

Alison wanted to say, it's not that different, none of you are very different. She wanted to lighten the situation. It was an ordinary thing this coming back, just for a holiday, to see friends. I haven't changed, she could say. When you temp, you don't change, there's no time.

But because she paused Chris must have thought she needed to be filled in. He spoke from where he stood at the table, he had helped himself to three pieces of meat. There was a time when they used to tease him about being serious. Now they listened, no one teased.

'Things are definitely on the mend,' Chris said. 'We can shake the mothball dust off our old green-back passports. Even India will let us in.'

Alison wondered if he said that for Susie's benefit. His eyes were fixed on his plate.

Liz peeled a drumstick like a banana and held it so that the loose bits of skin flopped over her fingers. She tugged them off with her teeth one by one.

'If we try we could all be one happy family,' she said.

'The country needs psychoanalysis,' said Clare.

Clare was on her second bowl of Palmerosa dessert. She had eaten none of the main course. Alison remembered Clare's food fads at university. One week she was a fruitarian, the next week she lived on powdered protein drinks. The protein powder smelt of lavender and soap.

'We desperately need the confidence of the international community,' said Chris slowly, as though making a delicate point. 'We need cash, aid. We don't want to become another poverty-stricken African nation.'

'I don't see the problem,' said Jannie. 'We are an African nation. Let's have black-outs every night. I mean, what will we lose? What has all that wealth done for America?'

'We all need psychoanalysis,' said Clare.

'Anyway, Alison, what do you think?' asked Susie. 'From your outside perspective?'

Alison didn't know what to think. She smiled, she glanced around. Everyone was looking at her again. Plates were empty. They wanted to be put in the picture. There was her life in London, in the ground floor flat off the Holloway Road.

'I've saved a pile of *Weekly Mails*, Alison,' said Chris. 'The most interesting ones from the past few years. If you like you can catch up on our news.'

'I've been following the news,' said Alison.

'But there's nothing like the *Mail* for hands-on opinion,' said Chris. 'I mean, to know about South Africa you really have to be here, you have to see it from inside.'

Clare winked at Liz to fill her glass. She didn't want to interrupt Chris by speaking.

'Anyway, you're looking okay even though you haven't seen much sun,' Ingrid said suddenly.

'I like your top,' said Susie.

She bent over her tightly-folded arms as though over a ledge to look more closely at the appliqué design on Alison's white sweatshirt. The picture was an African mask done in bronze and silver sequins. She had bought the sweatshirt on holiday in Greece.

Everyone bent forward to look at the mask.

'Yes, even I think it's okay,' said Clare. 'And my taste is usually horrible.'

'We have things like that here too,' said Liz. 'Remember the malls? I can take you along whenever you want. I know some of the stores where Winnie Mandela used to buy clothes for her overseas trips. Where Joan Collins shopped when she was here.'

'Thanks,' said Alison.

Jannie's eyes were closed. Clare took the cigarette that was burning between his fingers and stubbed it out in her dessert bowl.

'Your pudding was lovely, Clare,' said Ingrid.

'Yes, you must give me the recipe,' said Liz. 'I want to discover more about foreign cuisine.'

'What shall we do now?' said Chris. 'Remember what we planned? Shall we take Alison on a tour?' His chops were chewed down to the raw bits congealed in the crevasses of bone. 'She can see how town has changed,' he added, responding to the silence.

They had spent time planning this reunion, Alison saw. They didn't want to run the risk of getting bored during the first meeting. Clare now said let's see Soweto, Liz said the Zoo.

'Personally, I'd like to see around Jannie's house,' Ingrid said crisply. 'The times I was here before, I've only been shown the front rooms.'

Jannie stirred at the mention of his name. 'The rooms are really untidy,' he murmured. 'They haven't been done in days.'

'Maybe Alison just wants to come to my house to unpack and settle in,' said Liz.

She was trying to speak cosily but her heart wasn't in it. She sprayed more box wine into her glass.

'Liz said you had some nice garden paving round the back, Jannie,' Ingrid said. 'I'd like to see that.'

Alison decided to help with the planning. 'I'm happy just to sit around,' she said. 'We've hardly even seen each other.'

'That's right,' said Jannie.

Ingrid pulled him out of his chair.

'At least show us your yard,' she said.

They crowded at the kitchen door. To see, Alison had to look to the side of Clare's head. The paving in the yard outside was of silky dark slate. Along the house wall were flowering azaleas in wooden vats. Under Alison's nose was Clare's shirt label. It was sticking out. It said, Cool Wash, Remove Promptly, Made in USA.

'Yes, attractively arranged,' said someone, words from a magazine. Jannie said it must be a professional job. He bought the house this way, with everything that was in it, the furniture, azaleas, the lot.

'Even the dog house came with it,' he said. 'Any of you can take that thing if you want. I don't like dogs.'

To the left of the kitchen steps stood the blue dog house. It had Swiss chalet-style windows painted on either side. The painted curtains were red and white polka-dot. Over the entrance was written, Dom se plek. A heavy chain trailed out of it, as if looking for an anchor.

'The words mean Dom's place,' said Chris.

'Or Dom's spot,' said Liz.

'I'm sure Alison remembers how to translate,' said Clare.

'But if she didn't, she might feel left out if we didn't say,' said Liz.

'No, I remember,' said Alison.

She looked around the yard for something else to say. There were the vats, a hosepipe, a white fence that looked as if made of polystyrene slabs, the outhouse to the garage, painted blue. On the top step of the door to the outhouse a woman was sitting, her legs were stretched out. She wore high gold sandals, stilettos, and an American baseball cap the wrong way round. She was drinking out of a paper cup patterned with yellow and sky-blue squares. On the step beside her was a half-loaf of bread. Chris looked at Alison watching her. He turned away from the door.

'You haven't introduced us to your maid, Jannie,' he said.

'That's Ginger,' said Jannie. 'She's not my maid. She works at a place down the road, a dentist's or something. She must be an assistant. She sleeps here. It's better for her than going all the way home to Soweto.'

'That could be a good idea,' said Chris, 'to turn maids' *kayas* into boarding rooms.'

He stepped back into the kitchen, bumping against Alison. He was somehow uncomfortable, not as confident as when eating. He began to glance over in Susie's direction. She was leaning against the doorframe, her back to him.

Alison wanted to move. Chris had forced her up against the side of the rubbish bucket. A smell rose up out of the bucket of half-digested food, Palmerosa and vinegar, a smell of young babies.

The other women were still collected in the doorway, talking. Something out in the yard continued to attract their interest. It seemed to be the curtain of plastic-coloured strips that hung in the doorframes of Ginger's room. Individual strips blew out, dirty pink and dirty yellow, occasionally flicking Ginger's shoulders. Ingrid remembered they had curtains like that in the sixties in places like butchers and hairdressers. Susie said they had one hanging up in her old home, at the entrance of her parents' bedroom. When she said this Chris breathed loudly.

There was also Ginger's little starched half-moon apron. Ingrid pointed to it. I wonder why the dentist makes her wear that, said Clare. Ginger was using the apron to collect the soft pieces of bread she was plucking from the inside of her loaf. She was eating out of her apron. She was not looking at them. Then the person furthest out, it was Liz, mentioned the garden hose coiled among the azaleas. Everyone liked it, it was transparent, very slender, it looked state-of-the-art. Like transparent straws, said someone. Transparent Coke cans next, said someone else.

Chris nudged Susie by prodding the arm leaning up against the doorframe. He startled her. Her eyes looked back large and confused. Alison dropped her gaze, pretending not to have seen.

Then everyone began to stroll back in the direction of the living room, gathering pieces of food as they went, nibbling. Alison was the last to move. They all filed past her. The rubbish bin edge was wet against her knee. She picked a lettuce leaf off a plate and it doused her hand in dressing. She saw that the woman out in the yard, Ginger, had gone in too. She left her paper cup on the top step.

Liz and Jannie were in conversation at the entrance to the living room. The conversation looked private, Liz's voice was low. 'It's the kids. I could do with a nanny a few days a week. She looks very clean and neat,' Alison heard Liz say as she walked by.

'I've told you what her work is,' said Jannie. Then he dropped his voice.

Ingrid handed Alison another glass. It was box wine again, 'Even Ginger was drinking this stuff,' said Ingrid.

'What I want to know is where she got a name like Ginger,' said Clare. 'What do you think, Alison? Ginger? It's not right somehow. The name's from American movies. It's not African. It doesn't really belong in South Africa.'

Uerieta

Jane Katjavivi

Sarah and Elisabeth sat on the small *stoep* trying to catch the non-existent breeze. Old cans overflowing with plants created a border round the concrete and lined the outside wall of the house. The tin roof creaked. A dog panted beside them, exhausted by heat, not exercise. It was a heavy January day, waiting for rain. Sarah had brought some cooldrink, now tepid after her journey, which they shared in tin cups. In the yard was a child, playing in the dust. Her round face with cheeks only just past the sucking stage. Hair braided in tiny rows. A greyish T-shirt worn as a dress. About thirteen months old.

Sarah wasn't normally interested in children. Too much noise and mess, and if you don't have children of your own you become preoccupied by other things. And after that one time there seemed no chance of her having any of her own. She didn't like the idea of adoption.

But Elisabeth's house was always full of different children, passing through her hands on their way to school, to work, to adult life. It always amazed her how easily Elisabeth would open her home to other people's children.

Other people's property. Yours or not yours. No mixing. No blurring of boundaries. That was what she had always believed. That was one thing she could not get used to in Africa – this constant reshuffling of children. She could understand the economic reasons behind it, but not the human side. How do you really accept a child not of your own blood, and not knowing for how long it might be with you? And how could a mother hand over her child to someone else?

Sarah could remember when she had first heard of someone giving up her child to the extended family. It was a Zimbabwean friend in London who went home with her husband and two-year-old daughter for a visit. When they came back, the little girl wasn't with them. Sarah interrogated her friend about the trip.

'Wonderful. We went through the traditional ceremonies of return. The whole family came from around the country to see John and myself and the little one. There were long celebrations. We found it very hard to leave again to come back here.'

'What about Faith? How did she like meeting her family? How did she cope with the heat, with Africa?'

'Oh well, you know, she may have been born in London but she's an African all right. She acted as if she had known them since she was born. And she was happy to stay.'

Sarah's mind reeled. 'What do you mean? You didn't leave her?'

Leone laughed. 'Yes,' she said, 'we did. Don't look so horrified. It was expected. My mother-in-law is lonely now. Her children are all grown up and working away from home. She wanted our first-born, so we had to agree. Anyway, Faith is with family. We know she is as well loved there as with us. It's a better life for a child, too, in the village, better than in this big city. And we'll be back there again as soon as John has finished his studies.'

Now Sarah was curious to see the latest child at Elisabeth's house. She had come to see Elisabeth in response to her phone call. It entailed a two-hour drive from Windhoek, and Sarah had to get back again that night because of her work in the morning. Normally she would not have gone, pleading her work as an excuse. But something in Elisabeth's voice made her make the effort. And besides, she reasoned, she couldn't get hold of anyone else in the family who might help. Most of them were in Aminuis at a funeral. Obed was in Zimbabwe at a conference for health-care workers.

'You are here,' stated Elisabeth when Sarah had arrived. 'Long time. *Hoe gaan dit?*' They went through the usual greetings. Family. Home. Cattle. Sarah practised her new words – stilted sentences, but an alternative to the English Elisabeth found hard to understand. Sarah knew they must mention many things before they could come to the question of the phone call.

'*Mo ihamua tjinene?*' Sarah eventually asked, unsure how much further she could go with her Herero – Are you in much pain?

Elisabeth nodded. '*Ii,*' she sighed. '*Mba vere* – I am sick.'

Elisabeth never spoke much. Apart from the language problem that always hung between her and Sarah, she was another generation and another kind of woman. Strong and silent, now forced to admit her own weakness. But she was the sister closest to Obed and Sarah longed to get to know her better. Elisabeth was in her late fifties, and by all accounts had helped to bring up Obed after their mother died. She had been suffering from high blood pressure for a long time. Namibia's disease. Now her condition together with the medication she was taking was having a bad effect on her kidneys. The doctors had just told her she must rest more. She had called to speak to Obed about it and to ask his advice on what to do with the child.

'Who is this one?' Sarah asked. '*Mama we uripi?* – where is her mother?'

'*Okanatje ka Frieda,*' Elisabeth replied – She is Frieda's child.

Frieda was a niece of fifteen who had fallen pregnant after her first sexual experimenting. Her mother insisted that after the birth she should go back to school, and Elisabeth offered to look after the baby. Sarah had forgotten all about it. It showed how long it was since she had seen Elisabeth.

Sarah turned to look more closely at the child. Now she could see the resemblance. Frieda's nose and eyes. The family forehead. The child walked over to Elisabeth and climbed onto her lap. Elisabeth shifted her into a comfortable position.

'My little one,' she said. '*Opuwo* – enough – for old lady.'

Sarah wanted to exclaim, to tell Elisabeth she wasn't old yet, but she couldn't find the words. Instead she smiled. The little girl looked at her.

'*Ena rokanatje otjikwaye* – What's her name?'

'Uerieta,' said Elisabeth, 'after our mother.'

Uerieta. The name resonated deep inside Sarah. Her mind went back to her own Uerieta. She could remember the original moment of conception – that particular lovemaking. The next day she had been sure she felt the tiny being attach itself to her womb. She had felt it grow. She had never felt it die. Now the child had returned. Uerieta, her baby's namesake. Obed's mother. Their child.

Living in London at the time, the world had seemed wet and grey for months afterwards. She tried hard to comprehend. She was to have brought forth life but instead she carried death within her – the baby's and her own, for she had nearly died too. It took a long time for her to recover physically, then everyone urged her to get on with life. They tell you it's for the best. They tell you there must have been something wrong with the baby. They tell you to try again. They had done, but after Uerii no one else came.

The worst thing about it all had been the void into which the baby was swept. That, and Obed's emotional closing in. 'We cannot mourn,' he had said. 'This child was not long in our lives. In our culture we cannot mourn a baby we do not yet know.'

Sarah had named the child after Obed's mother. Perhaps foolishly, but she had been sure it was a girl. She had chosen the name because she had never met Obed's mother. Because Obed could not go home to her funeral due to the political situation. Then Sarah wondered if she had actually caused the baby's death by naming it after someone who had died.

'*Suster*, what is it?' Elisabeth asked as she saw the tears in Sarah's eyes.

For some time Sarah could not answer. Then she became practical, telling Elisabeth that Obed would be back soon. She would tell him all about the situation and he would get the family moving on it. She thought about what they would have to do. They must get hold of Frieda and see what she wanted for the little one. They must see who might have space and time to look after her. They must think about schools in the future. Somehow they must sort this all out in between the demands of both their jobs. Yet even as she busied herself with these thoughts, the desire to take the child herself grew inside her. They could not recreate life. But they could carry Uerieta with them into the future. Now they had a second chance.

After promising Elisabeth that she would phone her during the week, Sarah prepared to leave. She picked up the child and held her, breathing in her sweet smell. Then she got into the car and started back down the gravel road.

The light was changing as the sun sank lower, washing the grass yellow, and casting shadows on the hills. It was one of the best times of day – that and early morning. The only times it wasn't hot, so hot Sarah wondered how people managed to live in this dry desert land.

Friends from England asked her how she coped with the heat. At first her feet swelled, she sweated madly and got terrible headaches. Now after three years she had found her own way of coping with it. Instead of the black she had been so fond of in England, she now wore cotton dresses in pale colours that would not absorb the heat. Total sun-block. And she cut her hair and kept it short for ease. Obed had objected, sentimental about her long red locks.

Obed. Never there when she most needed to talk to him. Always heading off to a meeting. Always preoccupied with work, with the intensity of Windhoek, the efforts of transformation.

It was easy to say it would take a long time to build up the country and undo the injustices of the past. But everyone involved in trying to do that was working as if there were no tomorrow. Three years after independence, and still no time for family or friends. Sarah often wondered how long they could keep it up. Obed seemed tireless. She found it harder. Her own escape was through her letters to her sister in England.

'And we thought the struggle was hard!' she wrote. 'We had no idea how hard it would be afterwards. It seemed like there was no time then, because of the political pressure. Now there is no time because of the needs of the nation.'

She wondered whether her own headlong rush into work had merely matched Obed's own, so that she would not be lonely. Yet it was the most exciting and most difficult job she had ever undertaken. There was so much to do in the training project to which she was attached. Trying to overcome the many years of unequal education. Trying to upgrade scientific and technical skills. She joked sometimes with Obed that it was just as well they had no children, since they had no time for them.

Back in Windhoek Sarah collected the mail. A postcard from Obed from Canada – his last trip. Some bills. A letter from her sister. She read it in the car before going home. It had news of mutual friends, an English Christmas, the latest political developments, scandals in the royal family, and offered her the comfort of old familiar ways, a known environment.

She didn't really miss England, but the longer she was in Namibia the more English Sarah seemed to herself. She had never felt particularly English before, never been a patriot. Yet here her Englishness sometimes stood out so much she was forced to question her own sense of self. Here for the first time she felt patriotic, proud of the new Namibia in which she was involved. But it was still a slow process settling in.

Sarah had met Obed in London when they were studying. They were both politically active, and through him she had come to identify with the liberation movement in Southern Africa. When independence finally came to Namibia she had been glad to come, full of the spirit of the revolution. But she had had to face the much harder realities of reconciliation. Not only adjusting to another continent but to those she had easily classified as enemies before. And such a mixture of cultures. For a long time she found it hard to express an opinion in case she offended people.

Now her nearest family was his family, warm and accepting of her, but separated by language and experience.

Obed surprised her two days later by returning earlier than expected. He had managed to slip out of some of the post-conference meetings and leave them to his colleagues.

'I tell you, Sarah,' he said, 'if we think we have a problem with AIDS here in Namibia, you should see the problem elsewhere in Africa. In other countries there are millions of people already infected. That's our future too unless we can get people to change their ways. Now what we have is young schoolgirls getting AIDS from their sugar daddies, and passing it on to their babies. We will have a continent full of AIDS orphans cared for by non-family members or institutions.'

The mention of babies brought Sarah's mind back to Elisabeth and Uerieta. She told him about her visit.

'So,' he said smiling, 'Uerieta has returned. You know that's what the name means, don't you – the one who has brought herself back.'

'Back for whom?' Sarah asked. 'Back to us?'

'Us?' he responded. 'What about your work? It's hardly a time to take on children. You complain already that you're rushed off your feet. A child now will only add pressure.'

'I know,' she said, 'but I can't get the idea out of my mind.'

Obed reached over to take her hand and drew her to him.

'I missed you,' he said. 'I never seem to see you these days, what with your work and my own. So you want a baby to come between us too?' He started to caress her.

She resisted, cross that he didn't take the suggestion seriously. Awkward about switching back to wife and lover the moment he returned from one of his trips.

'I brought you something from Zimbabwe,' he said. It was a bright green and gold African cloth. 'It will go with your hair, and it's just the thing for this heat. Let me wrap it round you.'

This time she did not resist. Caught in the soft cotton, she then undressed him and wrapped them both together. It felt good to hold him again, and their lovemaking was heightened by their enforced abstinence.

'This is the good part of separation,' Obed murmured.

One morning later that week Sarah got another call from Elisabeth. She had decided to move back to where she grew up, deep in Hereroland, and wanted someone to look after Uerieta in town, nearer a school. Sarah's mind raced. She arranged to call back.

'*Okanatje mo kevanga?*' Elisabeth had asked Sarah – 'Do you want the child?'

'*Ii, me kevanga,*' Sarah replied – I want her. Very much. How had Elisabeth known?

She went to work in a daze and couldn't concentrate at all. She checked with Obed. He had been in touch with Uerieta's mother, Frieda. She was still only in Grade 9 and was hoping to train to be a nurse. She had no means of supporting the child herself for many years.

That night she phoned her sister in London.

'What would you think,' she asked, 'if I told you I wanted to take in a child?'

'It's all a question of space,' was the answer. Space in the home or space in the heart? Sarah wondered. She did not have the problem of cramped London terrace houses.

'Help me,' she said to Obed. 'I need Uerii. I feel she's part of us.'

'What about your work?' Obed asked again.

'I don't know,' Sarah answered. 'Maybe I can get someone to job share. We'd have to get some help at home.'

'You, the one who refuses domestic help because you don't want to be labelled a Madam?' Obed responded.

'Yes, me. Yes, us,' was her reply.

'What about the language?' others asked. 'What about her culture?'

'She'll become a black Englishwoman, not an African.' Sarah echoed her friend's words from long ago.

'She's with family. You know she'll be as well loved here as with Elisabeth.'

Sarah went to collect the child, leaving in the early morning to avoid the heat. As it got lighter she became less nervous about the possibility of kudus leaping across the road. She took coffee and brötchen to share with Elisabeth.

As she gathered up the small bundle of clothes, taking Uerieta in her arms, breathing her in, Sarah thought of the English home she had long left behind and the future she was embracing. She sang in the car in spite of the heat, and the journey home seemed to take no time at all.

When she got back to the house, Obed was waiting for her, a meal ready on the table.

'Welcome home,' he said, taking Uerii from her and giving them both a hug. 'Welcome to Africa.'

Crossmatch

Farida Karodia

Sushila Makanji sat on the step of the veranda at her parents'
home in Lenasia, an Indian township just outside
Johannesburg. On her lap, face down, lay the script for a stage
play, *Love under the Banyan Tree*. It was a fascinating story, a
tour de force of emotional torment. From the moment she
saw the script she had felt a strange connection with the main
character. It was as if the role of the young wife, trapped in a
loveless marriage, was created specifically for her. She could
hardly wait to get back of London to audition for the lead.

Reflecting on the character, she leaned back against the
veranda wall, tilting her face to the sun. She could just imagine
what it would be like to be forced into marrying someone
she despised.

Through the window, Sushi caught a glimpse of her mother
and her sister Indira, six months pregnant with her second
child. Although Indira was making a valiant effort to disguise
it, Sushi had sensed a sadness about her that she had not
detected on her previous visit. She had sensed this change in
her sister almost immediately, but her mother, around her all
the time, seemed to suspect nothing. Indira had always been
good at hiding her emotions. They were so different, the two
girls, both in looks and in temperament: Indira the pretty
child with the endearing shyness; Sushi the wilful one,
disconcertingly frank. Her large intelligent eyes fixed one with
their bold gaze, with intensity, always challenging.

Paradoxically some of these traits, unsettling as they might
be, were what made her such a sought-after actress. In the
five years that she had been working in the theatre, she'd
never been without work. Her success had not changed her
in the least, however; she was still as arrogant, intractable

and tactless as ever. She was a born cynic and her earlier rebelliousness had merely intensified with age.

When her mother asked her why she always went out of her way to be rude to family and friends, Sushi said, 'I have no time for all this crap. I know what they think and say about me behind my back.'

'They all like you, darling. They think you're fabulous,' her mother had said. 'You mustn't be rude.'

'Bullshit!' said Sushi.

Her mother had gazed at her in astonishment, the language totally unexpected, even from Sushi.

'Those are the people who chased me home. They thought I was a bad influence on their daughters because I smoked and swore.'

'You smoked?' her mother had asked, aghast.

'We all smoked, but I was the one who took the rap.'

Sushi had an uncanny knack for attracting trouble. It was impossible for her to keep a secret. Somehow or other, her secrets were always discovered. This was not for lack of wanting to be secretive, but it all just seemed to spill out. She had tried to hide the photograph of her and Kevin in an embrace, but Indira had found it, had ferreted it out. Indira studied the photograph and had made some choice comments about the way Kevin had his bare chest crushed against the spandex of Sushi's gym suit. The two of them were pressed so close they might easily have been joined at the hips, Indira remarked. 'Look at it,' she remarked. 'You guys are practically doing it for the camera.'

'Oh, come off it. We're just kissing. Some idiot took the picture.'

'Some kiss. There'll be hell to pay if Ma or Papa sees this.'

Sushi could well imagine the furore. The mere thought of her living with a man, let alone an Englishman, would drive her parents crazy. She snatched the picture out of Indira's hands and tucked it away under the newspaper lining in the bottom drawer of her bureau. She was confident it was safely hidden.

'Don't even mention Kevin or this photograph again. Walls have ears and if Ma ever gets wind of this picture and has the slightest suspicion that something is going on, she won't let go until she drags the truth out of us.'

'God, Sushi ... If they ever find out ...'

But Sushi cut her short. 'Find out what?' she demanded. 'The only way they'll find out anything is if you tell them.'

Sushi thought about that conversation as she sat outside sunning herself. Deep down, she knew her sister was right. It wasn't so much the fear of discovery which constrained her, but the energy required to deal with the commotion which would result from such discovery. Not only was she exhausted, but also emotionally burnt out from her last role. It was with great reluctance that she had finally agreed to visit. She hoped that the time away from her work would restore the passion drained on all those nightly performances. The mere possibility of a confrontation with her mother was too exhausting even to contemplate.

She closed her eyes and turned her face to the sun, drinking in the warming rays. She missed London. She missed Kevin and the comfort of his arms. For a while she basked in the ripple of anticipation that accompanied the thought of seeing him soon. She opened her eyes, leaned forwards and gathered her damp hair, tying it in a knot on the top of her head.

Her mother watched as she tied her hair back. She feared that Sushi had grown apart from them and that it was too late to bridge the gap. Sushi knew that her mother worried about her. Her mother had this idea that everyone living abroad, and particularly in London, lived a debauched lifestyle.

It was true that thoughts of Sushi in London preoccupied Mrs Makanji. Although she tried not to dwell on them, they crept into her every waking thought. Sometimes, at night, the anxiety awakened her and she would lie in the darkness thinking about Sushi. It was difficult for her to watch her youngest daughter drifting beyond her sphere of influence. Even more difficult was the possibility that Sushi might have abandoned her Hindu traditions. What to do? she wondered. The question repeated itself, like a mantra echoing through her thoughts. What to do? What to do?

She turned to Indira. 'We should never have let her stay in London. Just look at her. Who dresses like that, eh?' Mrs Makanji inclined her head to where Sushi was sitting on the veranda.

Sushi, dressed in black leggings and a brief top, sat absorbed in thought.

'Slacks are okay. I wear slacks too,' Mrs Makanji said. 'But what is that she's wearing? Those tight, tight pants? You can see the shape of everything. Has she no shame to go around in public like that?'

'It's the fashion in London, Ma,' Indira said.

'Those people in London are all *Mangparas*! It would be much better for her to be wearing decent clothes, good dresses, so she can look decent like a nice Hindu girl should. Why don't you and she go to the Sandton Shopping Centre, eh? The driver can take you.'

'Me and my big stomach. Who wants to go shopping with me?' Indira said.

'She'll go. She'll go. Just talk to her. If she doesn't want to buy dresses, let her get a couple of Salwar Kameez or Sari, or dress slacks even from the Plaza in Fordsburg. It's okay. Anything but what she is wearing now,' Mrs Makanji said, her lips curling contemptuously. 'I'll phone my friend Shantiben. She'll pick out some good stuff for her.'

'Forget it, Ma. You're dreaming. Sushi will never do it. Why don't you take her?'

Mrs Makanji shook her head. 'You know how stubborn she can be with me. Whatever I say, it's the opposite of what she will do.'

The expense of a shopping trip was of little concern to Mrs Makanji, who spent quite lavishly. The old argument of Sushi's that she was saving them thousands of rands in wedding costs just didn't wash with her parents any more. By local standards she should have been married already. Mrs Makanji had never scrimped on her children. There was never any need to do so. In the days of rampant apartheid, when there had been no choice about where they could live, she and her husband had built their dream home here in Lenasia. It was at a time when Lenasia was designated a residential area for Indians.

'What do they care?' Mr Makanji had asked when he spoke about the Group Areas Board. 'They are going to implement their policies of Separate Development, whether we like it or not. So why fight it?'

Mr Makanji had grown tired of the uncertainty. He had wanted to provide a decent home for his wife and his family, and so had moved before the evictions began.

'I had to give up,' he explained with a wan smile, when asked why he had been among the first to move.

Sushi and her father often discussed the changed face of the country. It was still unbelievable that all of this had happened within the space of a few years. Her last visit had been about a year ago and now elections were over and there was a new government. Things had already started changing some time before the election, Mr Makanji had told her. As things had begun to change, people who had made their money in the new liberal atmosphere had moved out of the townships into affluent white areas. Places like Sandton, Houghton and Rivonia had become neighbourhoods of choice for those non-whites who could afford to live there. Never having had the opportunity to own land, they set their sights on the biggest properties they could find. At first, many had moved to so-called grey areas, others bought in white areas, using a white person to front for them. In exchange for this kind of service, many had to give the persons they used as fronts an interest in the property.

Now, of course, fronts were no longer needed. People were moving around and buying wherever they chose to live. Admitted to these once-hallowed neighbourhoods, the new rich sported all the trappings of their wealth. Electronic gates swung open to admit their brand new Mercedes-Benzes and BMWs.

For the Makanjis, Lenasia was home. Although the crime rate had increased after the elections, Mr Makanji was quite content to stay where he was. There had been some incidents. Some break-ins. Sometimes these incidents were nerve-racking, especially when violent crimes happened so close to home. And once a woman had been murdered only a few blocks from where they lived.

Mr Makanji was protective of his wife and daughters. He worried about them when he wasn't home. Mrs Makanji was a very youthful-looking woman. She was tall with a good figure and a certain elegance which one noticed immediately. Her husband felt flattered by the attention his wife received. He was always thoughtful of her. Whenever he went on his business trips to India and Taiwan, he brought back exquisite gifts for her, seeking out the finest silk saris money could buy.

In all honesty, Mr Makanji considered himself fortunate to have found a woman like his wife. He had often expressed the hope that Sushi would turn out to be more like her mother. Sushi was his favourite, even though she was stubborn and wilful, not at all like Indira, who had never given them a day's trouble. Sushi, it seemed, was always stirring the trouble-pot.

Now that Sushi was home for a visit, her mother eagerly sought a good match for her. Mr Makanji had reminded his wife that they had not been successful before, and that there was no reason why they should be now. Mrs Makanji was adamant that this time would be different. He was not so sure. They had already arranged three meetings, none of which had turned out well. Sushila had been rude and indifferent towards the boys and their families. It was embarrassing for Mr Makanji, who had known the families of two of the three boys for a long time.

'What kind of parents do you think we'd be, if we didn't try to find someone for her?' Mrs Makanji demanded, when her husband remarked that Sushi would only frustrate all their attempts. In the next breath she shifted responsibility to her husband. 'You have to put your foot down, Arun. You're her father. She has to obey you.'

'When has that ever happened?' Mr Makanji asked lamely.

'We have lost her, Arun,' Mrs Makanji despaired. 'We have lost her. I can't bear the thought of her going back to London, to work on that stage.' She spat out the word 'stage' as though it were an obscenity. 'What kind of life is that for an Indian girl from a good home?' she demanded.

At a loss, Mr Makanji shook his head. It was obviously too late to forbid her from continuing her acting work. The mistake had happened right at the beginning, just after she graduated from college, and they had given in to her pleas to stay in London. Then she was only supposed to stay for a few months, but the few months dragged into years. He was sorry now that they hadn't insisted she come home at once after getting her BA degree.

When she didn't come home right away, and they had heard she was working as an actress, Mr Makanji had gone to London immediately to see what was happening. 'A BA degree to do this?' he demanded, horrified.

'Papa, please, just for a little while longer?' she pleaded. She had put up such a tearful scene that he didn't have the heart to deny her request. He returned home without her. He and his wife worried themselves sick about their youngest daughter.

One day she sent them a copy of a review in the *Guardian*. Although Mrs Makanji hid it in a drawer, she couldn't help thinking about the good things the article had said about her daughter. Eventually, after showing it to a few friends and receiving a favourable reaction, she left the review lying around where everyone could see it.

All her grey hair, she often complained, was due to Sushi. She was as convinced as ever that the only solution to all their problems was to get her married.

Mrs Makanji had heard that Dilip Vasant was in town visiting his family. He was a Chemical Engineer, teaching at Stanford. The boy sounded like an answer to their prayers.

Mr Makanji did not know the Vasants very well. He had only met them at one or two social gatherings. Now, pressed by his wife, Mr Makanji was making enquiries.

Sushi entered the front room, wearing her tights and the scandalous little top, even shorter than the *choli* blouse worn under a sari. She became aware of her mother's disapproving gaze.

'Are you talking about me again, Ma?' she asked, winking at her sister.

Mrs Makanji threw up her hands and rolled her eyes.

Indira grinned. 'Think we have nothing better to do than to sit around gossiping about you?'

'Come sit here,' Mrs Makanji said, patting the seat next to her, but Sushi ignored her mother's invitation.

'I see you've hired two more security guards,' she said.

'You know your Papa,' Mrs Makanji replied.

This was so typical of her father, Sushi thought. Her mother didn't have to do a thing. He took care of everything. Others envied her mother, but it was not a life that Sushi would have wanted for herself. Her mother only had to speak once, to voice a thought, or a desire, and her father would respond. Her mother had a safe-deposit box full of jewellery, diamond rings and gold necklaces to attest to his generosity. She had all that jewellery and couldn't show it off. Even the ring with the enormous diamond had to be locked away. Instead, she wore a piece of coloured glass on her finger – a trinket made in Taiwan. Mrs Makanji complained constantly about the exploding crime rate. Nothing was sacred any more, not even the gold chains around your neck. 'Thugs just walk by and yank them right off. If they come off easily, you are lucky, otherwise they drag you by the chain until they break either the chain or your neck,' she said.

Costume jewellery was preferred. Big pieces, so gaudy that it was obvious to any fool that they were worthless. Women flaunted them, wore them brazenly. No one was interested in stealing the junk. Sushi's father had cashed in on this trend; he'd seen it coming. Now his company sold tons of the junk jewellery, imported from India and Taiwan.

Mrs Makanji sat on the sofa in the living room, which had all the trappings of wealth. Behind a secret panel that opened with a flick of a switch were the TV and stereo. It was one added feature of security. Just in case ... one could never be too careful.

Since she could not display her wealth on her person, she had lavished it on her home. The furniture was leather, the carpets from Afghanistan and Iran. The pictures on the wall were of Hindu deities: prints of Krishna playing the flute with the *gopies* dancing around in their colourful skirts, pictures of Lakshmi and Ganesh – all in the best-quality crystal frames which her husband had bought on one of his trips.

Sushi sat on the floor with her legs crossed, still wearing the clothes her mother found so offensive. She was applying the final coat of scarlet passion to her toenails, with as much care as an artist finishing a canvas.

Mrs Makanji sat with her legs crossed on the sofa, her gold bracelets jangling as she gestured with her hands. Sushi surreptitiously watched as her mother's long, elegant fingers fluttered and curled, jabbed and sparred in the air as she spoke. Her mother had been a dancer. One could see it in the graceful way she walked and moved.

In the background the sound of music seemed to rise into the dead spaces of the room. *The Ghazals,* by a popular Indian singer, was a tape she had brought from London. She was familiar with the words and sang along under her breath. Mrs Makanji, drawn by the plaintive wail of the singer, stopped talking to listen. Better this, she had said to Indira, than the other unbearable loud pop music which was Sushi's other passion.

'Sushi, I think on Sunday you ought to wear a pale-blue sari. What do you think, eh, Indira?'

'I told you, Ma, I'm not going to dress up for anyone. I'm not interested in this idiot from Blythe or wherever it is he comes from,' Sushi said, without taking her attention from her toenails.

'He's from California,' her mother added.

'Just so you get your story straight, Ma ... his brother is from Blythe, he's from Stanford,' Indira said. 'Both places are in California.'

'Well, same thing. No difference,' Mrs Makanji said, tossing her head.

'Who cares if he's from the bloody moon!' Sushi cried, her gaze shifting from her mother to her sister. 'And how come you suddenly know so much about him, Indira? Have you been in on this, too?' she asked suspiciously.

Indira did not respond. There was a time when Indira would have risen to the bait; lately, though, Sushi noticed that her sister was more subdued than usual. She had complained about the baby being too active and that she was constantly tired. Sushi had noticed, too, how edgy she was and had assumed that it was because Ravi was away. Sushi finished painting her nails. She screwed the bottle shut, carefully got up and padded into the next room.

Indira exchanged glances with her mother.

'She has turned down every eligible young man. What is wrong with her? One of these days she'll be too old. Then what?' Mrs Makanji asked. 'You speak to her, Indira. She'll listen to you. This is a nice boy. He's an engineer, teaching at Stanford. Good-looking too, or so I've heard. He's just visiting with his parents. He's not going to be around forever. We have to get the two of them together for an introduction.'

'You know you're just wasting your time,' Indira said.

Mrs Makanji called out to Sushi in the next room, 'He's a nice fellow. You're making a mistake not wanting to meet him. He can have any girl he wants.'

Sushi returned. 'If he's such hot stuff, why isn't he married yet?'

'Perhaps he's fussy,' Indira said.

Sushi went over to the stereo to change the tape. 'Or perhaps there's something wrong with him. Have any of you considered that possibility?'

Mrs Makanji threw up her hands in frustration. 'Better that I would have had a dozen sons. Boys are much less trouble!'

Sushi laughed. 'Ma, you're so quaint!'

'What does that mean?'

Sushi continued to laugh. Indira joined in, despite her attempts at self-control.

'What does it mean, this being quaint?' Mrs Makanji's glance moved from Sushi to Indira.

'It means sweet, Ma. Sweet,' Indira said.

'A little old-fashioned, too,' Sushi added.

Mrs Makanji thought about what her daughters had said. Old-fashioned wasn't exactly the way she perceived herself.

'You should've asked for a snapshot, Ma,' Indira said.

'I did. Mrs Lalji, who is his mother's cousin, said she'd send me one. But I never got it.'

'Likely story. He probably thought we'd figure out he looks like the rear-end of a jackass.'

Indira laughed so hard she almost lost control of her bladder. She struggled out of the chair and waddled over to the window, still laughing. She gazed out into the yard as she pressed her hands into her back.

She was six months into her second pregnancy and enormous. Most of their friends took one look at her shape and promptly declared, 'Another girl!' Ravi, however, had set his heart on a boy. One girl was enough. Now he wanted a son to carry on the family business.

When Sushi left the room, Mrs Makanji turned to Indira, patting the seat beside her on the chesterfield. 'Sit, Indira. Are you all right?' she asked, leaning forward and gently lifting a strand of hair out of her daughter's face. 'You don't look well.'

'I'm fine, Ma.'

'Listen, my darling, talk to your sister. One of these days she'll be too old and then no man will want her.'

'She doesn't have to worry, Ma. She has a career ...'

'What career?' Mrs Makanji snorted. 'What is acting? That is not a career!' She paused, her glance softening as she gazed at her daughter. 'Why can she not be more like you? Look how happy you and Ravi are. We knew the instant we saw Ravi that he was the one for you.'

Indira's glance flickered away. She just couldn't bring herself to tell her parents about the problems she and Ravi were having. Her mother gazed at her affectionately.

'And now the baby is coming too,' Mrs Makanji added. 'Maybe this time it'll be a boy, eh? Not that we're unhappy with having a girl for our first grandchild,' she added quickly. 'We love Nita so much. She's a darling child, but it would be nice to have a boy, eh?'

Indira seemed to brace herself against her mother's words, and then slowly raised her head. 'Boy or girl, it doesn't matter,' she said.

'Of course not. We're so happy for you, Indira. We know how long you've waited for this second pregnancy.

Indira nodded and smiled wistfully. 'I know you are,' she said, patting her mother's hand.

'I just wish you would speak to your sister. She has great affection for you and Ravi.' Mrs Makanji's hands fluttered to her lap as gracefully as a butterfly settling on a delicate flower. 'Better we talk to her now than have trouble when Dilip Vasant comes with his family on Sunday. Go, please, Indira, my dear. See what you can do, eh?'

With a boost from her mother, Indira got up off the chesterfield, but did not go after her sister.

'I don't know what to do with her any more. Stubborn! You will not believe how stubborn that girl is. I don't know where she gets such stubbornness,' Mrs Makanji said. 'Your Papa is not like that.'

Sushi heard this comment as she went upstairs to her room. She needed some quiet space to concentrate on the script. There was obviously not going to be any peace and quiet until this whole issue of meeting this boy was over.

'God,' Sushi muttered as she flung the script onto the bed. 'I should've stayed in London.'

At breakfast the next morning Sushi listened indifferently to the conversation at the table. Her father had left for his office already and her mother was making plans for Sunday. It was hard to believe that her parents had gone to so much trouble, even consulting with an astrologer to fix an auspicious date and time for the meeting. Though Sushi might have found the situation amusing, her parents were proceeding in all earnestness.

'I know this time will be different, Sushi,' her mother said. 'I have a feeling about it.'

Sushi exchanged glances with her sister, who smiled encouragingly. She wondered for a brief instant about the boy, imagining that he was probably being subjected to the same pressures as she.

While Sushi reflected on her fate, across town the Vasants had just finished their breakfast. Dilip, sitting in an easy chair, enjoyed his second cup of tea while listening to a CD on the brand-new stereo system. He seemed distracted and drew a hand through his hair in a characteristic gesture of frustration.

Mrs Vasant watched her son. A robust, traditional Indian woman who always wore·a sari, she sat cross-legged on the sofa. On her lap was a *thali* tray, holding an assortment of relishes, chutneys and pickles. Mrs Vasant seemed quite unperturbed by the loudness of the modern Indian music as she nimbly picked at the food on the tray.

Her son was thirty-six years old and still unmarried. A fact, she feared, that might raise questions in the minds of others. She had prayed that he would return to stay, but he was home only for a short visit. Her sari slipped off her shoulder. As she raised an arm to carry the food to her mouth, she revealed a too-tight bodice that exposed the upper rise of her breasts. Around her midriff, pinched pale folds of skin were visible. Her hair hung loose to her waist.

Dilip got up and walked over to the stereo. He had the easy, fluid grace of a dancer. Although his face was pocked with acne scars, there was still something very attractive about him, something in the expressiveness of his eyes. He was thirty-six and unmarried. Try as she might, his mother could not get beyond that fact. She studied him as he leaned over the stereo and for the first time noticed that his hair had receded.

Mr Vasant, seated in an easy chair, seemed preoccupied.

Mrs Vasant paused in her eating to gaze fondly at Dilip. 'I have told everyone about our son who is an engineer at Stanford, in California, USA. I wish you could stay here with us and not go back there,' she said.

Dilip raised his head and smiled distractedly at his mother. Mr Vasant seemed to rouse himself from his thoughts. 'Arunbhai Makanji has invited us on Sunday. It seems he has expressed great interest in meeting you. He's heard about you.'

Dilip glanced up from where he was sorting through the CDs and shook his head. 'There's a cricket game on Sunday. I promised some friends I'd go with them.' He selected a CD and slid it into the player.

'Your father and I are very proud of you, son. You cannot refuse such an invitation,' Mrs Vasant said to Dilip. She turned her eyes on her husband in a mute appeal for help.

Mr Vasant frowned disapprovingly. 'Forget cricket. On Sunday you will come with us.'

Dilip felt his throat tighten. His parents tended to have this effect on him. Sometimes he felt as though he was going to choke, but he suppressed his feelings and turned his head to hide his expression. He hated it when they made decisions without consulting him. Above all, he hated the way they still treated him like a child. His visit had been nothing but an aggravation. First they criticised his taste in music, then it was the earring. To keep the peace he had removed the stud from his ear. Now they were putting pressure on him to meet this girl. He opened his mouth to protest, but saw the look of eager anticipation on his mother's face and his anger dissipated. He wished that they didn't have so many unreasonable expectations about him, and that his mother didn't always give him this guilt trip. She had cried when she discovered he was eating meat. The underlying issue, he realised, was not only marriage, but also their desire to keep him at home.

'I wish you'd drop this idea. I've told you: I'm not interested in finding a bride,' Dilip said, returning to his chair.

'What makes you think we're finding a girl for you?' Mrs Vasant asked coyly.

'Because I know you. I'm not stupid, Ma. Don't you think I've noticed what's been going on around here lately?'

His mother smiled. 'I hear this girl, Sushila, is very educated and very beautiful. You'll see. You'll change your mind once you meet her,' she said.

'I'm not going to change my mind.'

'Don't worry about liking her or not liking her, just come along so we can meet the family. If you don't like her, it's okay,' his mother said.

'Ma, please ...'

'We will not utter one more word about it, *dikra*. See, I've sealed my lips.' Mrs Vasant put up her hand to silence any further discussion. Then she laughed and gave her son an affectionate glance. Dilip shook his head in resignation and smiled, tightly.

'Your brother phoned from Blythe this morning. He says you don't visit much any more,' Mr Vasant said.

'I told you that I've been busy. I've had my hands full with my new job,' Dilip replied.

'That's why you need a wife ... to help you,' said his mother.

'I don't need a wife. Now will you please drop the subject,' Dilip snapped.

Mrs Vasant's startled gaze sought her husband's. She sensed a new element. Something was wrong. 'There is someone in your life already?' she said, turning the statement into a question.

Dilip got up abruptly, almost upsetting his cup of tea. He walked to the window and gazed out. He wondered how he could tell them. They would never understand. Never. He had to lie again. His whole life had become a lie. His parents waited. 'There is someone at Stanford ...' he said.

Mr and Mrs Vasant exchanged troubled glances.

'I was going to tell you about it,' he muttered.

'Who is she?' Mrs Vasant asked.

'Why have you not mentioned this before?' Mr Vasant demanded, leaving his chair with startling agility.

'Who is she, my darling? What is her name?' his mother asked, her shrewd gaze studying her son's face.

Dilip tried to remain calm. He had opened the sluice gates; now he had to control the flow.

'Well,' his father said, 'why don't you answer your mother?'

Dilip regretted that he had given them an opening. They were obviously not going to let go of it. His mother was like a dog with a bone.

'Who is she, Dilip?' she asked.

'Where is she from?' his father asked.

Dilip felt the room closing in on him. 'It's someone from California,' he said, affecting nonchalance. The music ended and he went over to the audio system to change the compact disk, turning up the music a little more, to make conversation awkward.

'What is her family name?' His mother had to shout above the music. Dilip mumbled something.

'Turn the volume down!' his father cried.

Dilip hesitated. He needed time to get his thoughts together. His father glared at him. His mother put her hand to her head.

Dilip turned down the volume. 'Sorry,' he said, smiling sheepishly. He glanced at his mother. Her arm was poised above the *thali* tray. He could feel the noose tightening. 'Ma, I was going to tell you all about it, but not right now. Why don't we meet this lady on Sunday and we'll see ...?'

'We'll see what?' his father asked, still perturbed by the way Dilip was avoiding their questions.

For the moment, however, Mrs Vasant was satisfied. 'Okay,' she said. 'It's a deal. No problem now, eh? We go to the Makanjis on Sunday.'

Mr Vasant watched his wife eating.

'I wish you would stay here instead of going back to the USA. There are good prospects here for engineers. It's not like it used to be before. Now we need South Africans to come back. We need our own people at the universities. Our young people need role models. We all have a responsibility to this country. We can't just run away. We have to give something back to make this country work now.'

'It's ironical, isn't it, Pop, that there was a time when blacks couldn't even enrol in engineering. It was a faculty closed to them because the government figured they could never work as engineers in this country. Now here we are ...' Dilip said with an ironic shrug.

'So, what do you say? You don't need to rush back to California,' Mr Vasant persisted.

'My life is in California, Pop. Not here.'

'I was hoping that some day the business would pass on to my sons,' Mr Vasant said. 'But now you have your engineering job and your brother has his motel in Blythe ...' He paused, his expression pained. 'Work, work, work, all my life and for what? Who will be there to take over the family business? I fought to stay here; I went to jail even,' he said, shaking his head at the recollection. 'I spent my life building this business, expanding it ... and for what?' Mr Vasant shook his head. His heart ached with disappointment and a tear gathered in the corner of his eye as he gazed at the food tray on Mrs Vasant's lap. 'We'd better get to the shop,' he said.

Dilip said he'd join them later. He didn't feel like going with them. He'd never imagined his visit home would be so stressful. It was as though he were in a fishbowl, everything he said or did was subject to scrutiny by his parents. In a matter of three weeks, his mother had somehow managed to reduce him to a twelve-year-old boy again. Although he hated it, resisted it, he was no match for his mother, who was an expert at manipulation. She'd had years of practice on his father. He was anxious to get back to Stanford and his life there. He had only been home for three weeks, but it already felt like months.

At home in Lenasia, Sushi shared these sentiments. She glanced into the mirror and with a start saw her sister. 'I didn't hear you come in,' she said. She examined her image in the bedroom mirror, turning her head this way and that way, holding her hair up in a knot at the top of her head. 'What do you think?' she asked. 'You think I should cut it? I've been thinking of cutting it and maybe getting a perm. I'm so tired of the way I look.'

'Don't be silly ... You look wonderful. I like your hair the way it is,' Indira said,

'You're so old-fashioned,' Sushi snorted. 'You're just like Ma.'

Indira groaned. 'I don't think so. But never mind me,' she said. 'What are you going to do when they find out that you're shacked-up with an Englishman?'

Sushi shrugged. She gazed into the mirror and caught her sister's eye. 'I don't know,' she said to her sister's reflection.

'He's cute. I suppose you're being careful?' Indira said, with the same habit as her mother had, of turning a statement into a question or vice versa.

'Oh, come on, Indira! What do you think? I'm not that stupid!'

Indira grimaced and leaned back against the pillows. 'This is the fourth boy they've invited,' she said.

'I don't care. It's their problem. Anyway, I'm only humouring them. In another ten days I'll be out of here and all of this will just be a bad memory.' Sushi glanced at her sister who looked so forlorn. 'You okay?' she asked, sitting beside her on the bed.

Indira nodded and was silent for a moment. She scowled at Sushi, her expression darkening with pent-up frustration. 'Oh damn ... No! I'm not all right! My back hurts. I'm exhausted. I don't sleep well. I eat like a pig and I throw-up like a fucking sick-dog!'

Startled, Sushi glanced at her sister – Indira's strongest expletive was usually 'Shoot!', which under extreme conditions translated to 'Shit'. But this! Sushi fell back on the bed, howling with laughter. 'If Ma could hear you she'd have a fit!' Sushi said, amid peals of laughter.

Indira started to laugh, holding onto her belly, tears of mirth and pain leaking from her eyes. Finally she caught her breath. 'God, I hate being like this. I forgot what it was like with Nita,' she said, dabbing at the tears with a crumpled tissue. 'Look at me, only six months and I can't even get my shoes on by myself. I have to ask Ma or Anna. What am I going to be like when I'm eight or nine months?'

Sushi saw the sad look returning to her sister's eyes. 'I think Ravi is a jerk,' she said. 'He doesn't know what a wonderful wife he has. I sure as hell would never put up with his crap. Where is he? ... He's jetting around while you're struggling to function with this ... this enormous belly.' She put her hand on her sister's stomach and felt the baby move. 'Why do you put up with it, Indira?'

Indira's glance slid away. She took a shuddering breath. 'Ravi is away on business. It's not like he's deliberately staying away ...'

'Bullshit! When are you going to stop covering for him? He took off the moment you started your morning sickness! It's easier to send you gifts and make long-distance phone calls than to be here supporting you through this time. And what about those tests he wanted you to take?'

'How ...?'

'You wrote to me, remember? I inferred from your letter. I know you too well, sister.'

Indira picked at the edge of the bedspread, twisting and untwisting the corner around her finger. 'I don't care about the sex of the child ... but Ravi wants a son. When I refused to take the tests, he went on a business trip to the UK and India.' She paused, glancing away. 'Sometimes Nita and I used to go with him, but now it's like he's punishing me because I didn't want to take the tests.'

'The bastard ...' Sushi muttered.

Indira glanced up with a disconsolate expression.

Sushi's glance softened. 'Never mind, it'll all be over soon and, whatever it is, it'll be adored by all. I'm glad you refused to have the tests,' she said.

'I almost agreed,' Indira confessed. 'I heard him telling his mother, if it was another girl he'd persuade me to have an abortion in the States.'

'Crafty bastard, he knew that if you came to London, he'd have to deal with me. Do Ma and Papa know about this?'

Indira shook her head and shut her eyes, too ashamed to look at her sister, who was sitting cross-legged, looking for all the world like a vengeful Buddha.

'You're too soft. Too easy to manipulate, that's why everyone thinks you're such a good daughter.'

Indira was silent, uncomfortable both physically and emotionally. She swung her legs off the bed, looking so miserable, so unhappy, that Sushi could only feel sorry for her. Indira had leaped directly into marriage. She had never had the opportunity to explore her potential, to see what she was capable of, or to determine her own worth.

Sushi got up and returned to the dresser. She caught her sister's eye in the mirror and quickly glanced away.

'Ma and Papa,' Indira said, 'are wondering why you've been turning all these men away. You should tell them something ...' She knew her parents would persist. Things might have been different for her if she'd had the strength to stand up to them.

'You're right,' Sushi said. 'I'll talk to them. Isn't it incredible? I'm twenty-eight years old. I've walked in off the street and auditioned stone-cold for major roles. I've played to tough audiences, and yet here I am worrying about telling Ma and Papa that I'm living with a man.'

'Yes, but this isn't just any man. It's an Englishman...'

Sushi grimaced wryly, picked up the brush and started to brush her hair again.

On Sunday Mr and Mrs Vasant and Dilip arrived at the Makanji house in Lenasia. Mrs Vasant gazed around curiously. It was obvious the Makanjis were rich, though this, of course, was no surprise – she and her husband had made discreet enquiries about their hosts. She maintained that it was always good to be prepared, so no time was wasted fumbling around. This definitely had the possibilities of a good match.

Mr Makanji and his wife welcomed them. The men shook hands. Mrs Vasant put her hands together. '*Namaste,*' she said. Her glance travelled around surreptitiously before she raised her head. In that brief instant she had made a mental note of the entire entrance hall and the living room.

Nita, dressed prettily in a dress of flounces and bows, shyly joined her grandmother in the entrance hall. Mrs Makanji gently urged her forward to greet the visitors.

'Come inside, please,' Mrs Makanji said, taking Mrs Vasant's arm and escorting her to the smaller entertainment room. The men remained in the care of Mr Makanji, who led them into the living room.

'You have a lovely home,' Mrs Vasant said.

Mrs Makanji beamed. 'Thank you,' she said. 'We'll sit over here and I'll bring my daughters to meet you. Go call your mother and Sushila,' she said to Nita.

Nita hesitated, her grandmother waved her on and she hurried away to call her mother and her aunt.

Mrs Vasant sat down. 'She is a darling,' she said.

'My daughter Indira's little girl,' Mrs Makanji replied proudly.

Mrs Vasant smiled, glancing around the room at the pictures on the wall while she and Mrs Makanji made polite conversation. Mrs Vasant sat back in the sofa, but her legs were too short and dangled uncomfortably. She tried sliding forward, perching on the edge of her seat so that her feet touched the floor, but she was still uncomfortable. She would have loved to draw her legs up on the sofa, but she couldn't; it wouldn't be polite. She shimmied back in her seat, and, reaching for a pillow, placed it behind her back.

Indira waddled in, looking pained and uncomfortable. She greeted Mrs Vasant and sat down. Sushi sauntered in a few moments later, looking unconcerned. She had resisted the pressure from her mother to wear a sari. 'Not on your life, Ma,' she had said. 'I'm not wearing a sari just to impress anyone. I'll wear one because I want to, and I don't want to wear a sari today.'

Mrs Makanji had wrung her hands, had put on a tearful performance, but Sushi was adamant.

'You're not going to wear any of the stuff you brought along with you, are you?' Mrs Makanji had asked, in a small pained voice.

'I'll wear slacks,' Sushi tossed back casually.

Having feared something even more outrageous, Mrs Makanji refrained from critical comment when she saw Sushi's white tight pants and long Nehru-style blouse.

Sushi greeted Mrs Vasant, noting the woman had none of her mother's elegance. Mrs Vasant was fat and squat. From her sister's expression, Indira knew that there was no hope for Dilip Vasant.

The wives took Indira and Sushi into the living room to introduce them to Mr Vasant and Dilip. Sushi was extremely polite and Mrs Makanji could find no fault with her behaviour, except that she was so cold and aloof. It was as though she were deliberately putting the boy off.

What is wrong with this girl? Mrs Makanji asked herself as they sat with the men. 'Anna will bring some refreshments in a moment,' she said. The words were hardly out of her mouth when Anna came in with a tray laden with cold drinks and snacks.

'How's business, Chimanbhai?' Mr Makanji asked Mr Vasant.

'Not bad for me, but many shopkeepers in town are complaining. They say that the African vendors are ruining their business. They are opening stands everywhere. If there is a fruit shop, right in front of the fruit shop they will open a fruit stand. If there is a dress shop, right in front of that dress shop they will have a rack of dresses on the pavement, selling it much cheaper than the shop because they don't have to pay any rent.'

'Some people would admire such entrepreneurial spirit,' Dilip said.

Mr Vasant shrugged. 'It depends on how you look at it. If you were a shopkeeper, you wouldn't be saying that.'

'I wouldn't be downtown if you paid me to go there. Too many robberies lately,' Mr Makanji said.

Dilip laughed and shook his head. 'It's a sign of the economic crisis here and elsewhere. People have to survive somehow. It's the same problem in the States.'

'I hear you're an engineer there,' Mr Makanji said.

Dilip nodded, his gaze straying to Sushi, who had not as much as given him a second glance. Mr Makanji noticed the glance and was hopeful.

'So you're a university teacher?' Mrs Makanji said.

'Yes. I'm teaching at Stanford.'

'Are you thinking of coming back to South Africa?' Mr Makanji asked.

Dilip glanced at his parents and shook his head.

'It was my question to him as well,' Mr Vasant said. 'Just the other day I was saying, now that things had changed, it might be a good idea to come back home.'

Sushi glanced over at Dilip. She couldn't help feeling sorry for him as both sets of parents put him through the third degree. She and Indira excused themselves and went to the kitchen. Neither of them was there when Nita sidled over to her grandmother holding the picture she had found in Sushi's drawer. Nita, fascinated with everything about her aunt, enjoyed rummaging through her possessions and playing with her make-up. She had been going through Sushi's bureau drawers as usual when she found the photograph of Sushi and Kevin.

Nita quietly waited in adult company for the opportunity to show off the picture. She leaned up against her grandmother's lap, the photo in her hand, waiting for a break in the conversation, knowing her grandmother would be annoyed at her for interrupting.

'Nani, see this picture of Aunty Sushi,' she said, the moment her grandmother paused to take a breath.

Distracted, her grandmother took the photograph from her, smiled indulgently and glanced at it. The picture was a blur without her glasses. She still held the picture in her hand as she gestured, her gold bracelets clinking with every movement. Dolefully, Nita gazed at the two women, disappointed about being ignored by her grandmother who was merrily laughing at something Mrs Vasant had said. Mrs Vasant paused as she noticed the expression on Nita's face. Mrs Makanji became aware of Nita still waiting beside her chair.

She glanced at the photograph again. 'Later, darling. I'll look at the picture later. I don't have my glasses,' she said, handing the photograph back to Nita. Sushi entered the room as Nita slipped away, feeling slighted. She didn't notice the photograph in Nita's hand, or notice Nita pausing at the sideboard to put it in the top drawer.

Meanwhile, Mrs Vasant observed the glance Sushi had given Dilip as she entered the room and was relieved. The match would be an excellent one. The girl had a good face and was respectful. She seemed like an obedient daughter, just the kind of girl Mrs Vasant was hoping Dilip would meet. It would have been better, though, if she had worn a sari instead of those pants. She would have preferred a more traditional girl for Dilip, but at this stage she wasn't going to let minor details distract her.

Mrs Makanji thought that everyone was getting along splendidly. Still, she held her breath. Although Sushi was on her best behaviour, Mrs Makanji wasn't prepared to trust her luck. Any moment now she expected her happiness-bubble to burst.

After dinner they sat talking again. Sushi had managed throughout dinner to avoid glancing at Mrs Vasant, who was eating with such uninhibited relish. Once or twice she had caught her mother's eye and her mother had shaken her head unobtrusively to discourage any comment from Sushi. Dilip had intercepted the exchange. Embarrassed, he had glanced away.

Later Indira, Sushi and Dilip went out onto the veranda. Dilip and Sushi were a bit awkward with each other at first.

'When is your husband coming back?' Dilip asked Indira.

'In about two weeks,' Indira said,

Sushi studied Dilip. He wasn't too bad, she reflected. Of the four men, or 'boys', her parents had introduced her to, Dilip was the least offensive, but ... his mother was definitely a different story.

They spoke for a while. Dilip asked her about her work in London. She asked him about his work at Stanford. He was easy to talk to. She was genuinely beginning to like him and felt relaxed and comfortable in his company. There was something non-threatening about him and she listened with great interest as he described his life in California. Indira, feeling left out of their common experiences and anecdotes, went inside.

'It's crazy, isn't it?' Dilip said to Sushi. 'I'm glad you're not taking any of this seriously.'

Sushi grinned. 'They're just buzzing with excitement now,' she said.

'Each time I come for a visit, we go through the same routine. That's why I don't get back too often,' he said.

'I know what you mean,' Sushi chuckled, imagining how their parents would probably be interpreting the exchange she was having with Dilip out on the veranda.

They sat outside, perched on the wall, talking as though they had been friends for years. Mrs Makanji smiled, the brilliance of her smile spreading around the room until Mrs Vasant felt it too, and smiled in return. Things were going much better than either of them had hoped for.

Eventually Dilip and his parents left. There was no firm commitment from either family to meet again; there was hope, however. It was there in the smiles as the two families said goodbye to each other; it was in the sparkling air and in Mrs Makanji's laughter, so rich in undertones. Mrs Makanji was anxious to find out what Sushi thought about Dilip. She thought he was perfect, but, knowing her daughter, she didn't dare ask in case Sushi turned him down out of contrariness. So Mrs Makanji went to bed that night, bristling with questions and anxiety. She was so highly strung that Mr Makanji had to sit up half the night, reassuring her.

'They were talking so much. Didn't you see?' Mr Makanji said.

'Darling, you don't know her as I do,' Mrs Makanji said, 'Don't worry. She'll decide.'

'When, Arun? When she's an old woman and no one will want to marry her?'

Mr Makanji laughed.

'If only she would be as easy to please as Indira,' Mrs Makanji muttered.

'We have given her an education. We have taught her to think independently. Now we have to trust that she will make a good decision.'

'If we had boys we might have had less problems,' Mrs Makanji grumbled.

Mr Makanji smiled. He knew not to take her seriously.

'Look at Indira. I can see that something is wrong, but she is not telling me,' Mrs Makanji continued.

'She will tell us when she is ready. Only then can we help her,' Mr Makanji reassured her. 'For now, I am satisfied and thankful that we all have our good health.'

Meanwhile Indira and Sushi were awake as well, talking. Indira, unable to sleep, had sneaked into Sushi's room.

'He's not too bad, but I don't think I could take his mother!' Sushi said, laughing. 'My God!' she cried, giving a mock shudder.

'She wasn't that bad ...' Indira said.

'What!' Sushi cried. 'I'd rather be dead ...' She threw her hands up into the air with all the drama she could muster. Then she leaped onto the bed and bounced up and down with child-like exuberance.

'How come you're taking the meeting with Dilip so lightly?' Indira asked, puzzled by her sister's lack of concern. She had expected her to be angry.

Sushi laughed. 'He's very sweet and... he's also very gay.'

'You're joking. Right?' Indira said.

Sushi shook her head. 'I'm not.'

'How do you know?'

'I have lots of gay friends in London.'

'I can't believe it. Are you sure?'

'Of course I'm sure. Why?'

'Well ... Hindu boys ... I mean ...'

'Come off it, Indira. Why do you find it so hard to believe that a Hindu boy can be gay?'

'I don't know. I've just never known any.'

Sushi smiled and shook her head in gentle reproach. 'You're still very naïve, you know.'

Indira smiled. 'I suppose so.' She paused and met her sister's glance. 'I'm going to miss you,' she said, suddenly serious again.

'If things here get really rough for you, come and spend some time with me,' Sushi said. 'And bring Nita. You'll like Kevin. He's a lot of fun. Don't worry. We do have a spare bedroom.' She paused for a moment. 'I'm going to miss you and Nita. I'll probably miss Ma and Papa, too, but it's better to keep my distance from them. We get along much better that way.'

Indira sighed and leaned back against the cushions. 'God, I can't get him out of my mind,' she said. She just couldn't get over the idea that Dilip was gay.

'Who?'

'Dilip.'

'Why?' Sushi asked.

'I can imagine what it's going to be like when his parents find out.'

Sushi was silent. She, too, had been thinking about it.

'I'd better get back to my room. If Nita wakes up she'll feel insecure if I'm not there. She's been difficult lately,' she said, getting up and waddling to the door in her bare feet.

Mrs Makanji sat up and turned on her light. 'I can't sleep, Arun. I think I'll go make myself some warm milk.' She got up and went to the kitchen to warm some milk in the microwave. She usually kept a small box of sleeping powder in the sideboard drawer. It was an ayurvedic remedy for insomnia and the only thing that helped her through those awful nights when she couldn't get to sleep.

Mrs Makanji opened the drawer. Lying right on top was the picture of Sushi and Kevin in their passionate embrace. She found her spare glasses in the other sideboard drawer and took the picture into the light. Stunned, she felt her knees weaken. Her hand flailed behind her for the chair and she sat down heavily. She studied the picture and then turned it over.

On the back of the picture was the corny message – *To Sushi. My lips, my heart and all those important parts, love you forever! Kevin.* Mrs Makanji's face was ashen.

'Sushi. Oh Sushi,' she moaned, clasping her chest, writhing. 'Such a curse! ... Oh, my God ... Oh, my God,' she cried softly.

Sushi lay awake in the darkness, thinking about Dilip. It was going to be a shock to her parents when she told them the truth about him. She knew that somehow she was going to have to tell her parents about Kevin, too. She wanted to ease into it, slowly, though. She wasn't quite sure how, yet. Sushi sighed wearily. She was too tired to deal with it now. There would be time enough the next day.

I'd sell my horses

Sheila Roberts

In June 1977, when Kirstin and her daughter Robyne went to Jan Smuts Airport to board a flight for the USA, all the family were there to see them off – Kirstin's parents, her ex-husband Matthew, her cousin and closest friend Sue with her first husband Kosie and their daughter Marissa. Marissa, Kirstin's godchild, was then fifteen and as delicately pretty as a Royal Doulton figurine, if not as fragile. And milling about were various other cousins and friends, and even the couple who were to rent Kirstin's house while she was away.

All Kirstin knew at that stage was that she had a one-year's appointment at an American university, a small college in the mid-west. Everyone believed that Kirstin and Robyne would be back within the year, replete with tales of the nonsensical decadence of American life. They would probably be aping for a time that laughable Yankee way of talking, tossing out zany street-slang. There would be names-dropping, the pretended familiarity with soap-opera stars, and breathless narrations of those TV programmes still banned by the South African Broadcasting Corporation. They would tell grandiose yarns of immense snowfalls, of Arctic storms that killed people even as they valiantly pressed ahead in their pick-up trucks, wanting to get home to their hotdogs and beer. But the family knew that they could soon good-naturedly mock Kirstin and Robyne out of any assumption of travellers' superiority, that within a matter of months it would seem as if they'd never been away at all. Thus they could all afford to be generously celebratory as they waved at the travellers through the glass-barrier as they boarded the escalator to go down to Passport Control and Customs.

Kirstin and Robyne looked back, waving too, Kirstin kissing her hand to Sue and then to Marissa, her favourite.

Kirstin and Robyne did not return, though Kirstin did visit regularly, up until her parents died. The terrible 1980s came, and still Kirstin remained away, immune from the violence, the states-of-emergency, and, in her family's opinion, untouched by their problems. Kirstin, perhaps naïve, couldn't understand why as time passed the members of her family distanced themselves from her. They barely replied to her letters and, when they did, they implied curtly that she no long understood them or the condition of the country and, therefore, it wasn't much point their going into details. Eventually Kirstin got the message: she had, with so many others in the wake of the Soweto Revolution of 1976, ostensibly taken the 'chicken run'. She'd deserted her country, deserved to be considered some kind of traitor, and could no longer presume to any real familiarity with those who'd stayed behind. By the early 1990s, the only person writing fairly regularly to Kirstin and occasionally phoning her was Sue, for even Marissa had got tired of exchanging cards and thank-you notes. From Sue's letters Kirstin could follow to some extent the course of Sue's life: her divorce from Kosie and remarriage to Joe; Marissa's marriage to Dannie and the birth of her twins; the worsening economic situation of the 1990s going hand-in-hand with a new political optimism. Not that Sue's letters were always satisfactory. They were brief and barely factual and never fully explained the ramifying causes of events.

One such letter arrived in early December 1993:

Dearest Kirst,

It's as if I don't have enough problems already, but Marissa's landed on Joe and me with the two kids. Don't get me wrong, I fancy my grandkids, I think they're cute, but I don't want them here day in day out. And Joe's not impressed.

It's not as if they're *his* grandkids, you know? But Marissa and Dannie have broken up and Marissa needed to find a job and get some money together before she could go on her own. So I've put them in the cottage, you know the one you've stayed in when you've visited, so don't expect to stay here if you visit any time soon. But that's not the whole of it. Mar's been having period problems and she went to the gynaecologist and was told she had cancer of the womb. She needs to have a hysterectomy pretty-damn-quick. But listen to this – she's found a job selling photocopy equipment and she's on the firm's medical aid but the medical aid won't pay for any operations until she's been on their books for six months. So what with the drought and the water restrictions and the fact that Joe's not getting much work in, the building-trade's in the doldrums New South Africa and all, I'm up to my eyes in worries. Now in addition I've got Marissa not looking too good and the two kids who run around making a row every afternoon after kindergarten. Oh well, there's no use complaining. I just wish I had more money coming in. My horses' bedding is worn and I've got humungous vet bills from when Calypso had colic. But this must all sound like French to you. How's the snow?

Kirstin was shocked as well as dissatisfied by the letter. She read it through several times, then sat staring through the lace curtains at the thick fuzzy white outlines of snow on the branches outside. Why was Joe's business not doing well? What caused Marissa and Dannie to break up? *Wasn't* Dannie paying Marissa support for the children, for God's sake? Had the doctor not given any explanation as to why Marissa, so young, should have contracted uterine cancer? Then, it seemed inconceivable to her that anyone needing a hysterectomy because of uterine cancer had to mark time untreated until medical insurance became available. She thought of Marissa, her dear godchild, and was soon haunted by a vision of the cancer ranging around, malignly exploring other parts of Marissa's tissue. She could see it leaving spots like the yellow mould in summer that ate into things, softening Marissa's chances of recovery. She recalled Marissa, how she'd looked the last time Kirstin had seen her some years before; a small-framed young woman with frail slender bones and still the same soft blonde hair she'd had as a child, quite unlike her strong athletic horse-loving mother. Marissa wore only size 3 shoes, for God's sake! remembered Kirstin, and her thin hands with their bitten-down fingernails hardly looked womanish. *Oh God, Marissa,* thought Kirstin; oh God, so young and to have cancer.

Kirstin decided to telephone Sue.

'Sue,' she said urgently, 'Marissa needs that hysterectomy right now. There must be no delay ...'

'Kirst, didn't you read my letter?' demanded Sue; 'or are you losing your mind? I told you, didn't I, that there's no money for the operation? Mar hasn't got any money and Joe and me can't afford to pay for it. End of story!'

Kirstin had lived long enough in the States to have imbibed ideas of *Yankee ingenuity*, of belief, whether mistaken or not, that anything can be taught, anything can be learned, and, especially, anything can be fixed. But then this was not so very different from the South African idea of *'n Boer maak 'n plan*, except that she'd forgotten that old adage. So she felt called upon to find a way to fix Marissa's problem. Not sure where to start, she pondered whether there mightn't be someone able to advise her. Then of a sudden she recalled Anne Davies, an old university chum; yes, Anne Davies, now a psychotherapist working with children at Baragwanath Hospital, someone she hadn't had much contact with over the years but who mightn't mind a telephone call. She remembered Anne as a highly sympathetic woman, bright and enthusiastic in her work, and with a good knowledge of the South African medical system. Kirstin found Anne's telephone number and dialled.

'Anne,' she said, after the surprised preliminaries had been got through; 'Anne, my godchild Marissa has cancer of the uterus and nothing can be done about it because the medical insurance she has now applied for will not kick in to pay for major surgery for another six months ... What? Oh, yes, she's thirty-one, I think. But I wanted to ask you whether you knew of anything that could be done. I thought you might be able to suggest something, working at Baragwanath and all. You know, Anne, I remember in the old days if one hadn't any money one could go to the Johannesburg General. That time in second-year when I had my appendicitis attack ...'

But Anne had interrupted her, not brusquely but tiredly, her voice strangely low and chilling. Anne said:

'Kirstin, do you know that there are millions of people in South Africa these days, as in all of Africa, who have terrible diseases, new diseases and old ones, and no means of getting medical treatment? And the numbers are growing every day. I'm sorry, Kirstin, but I have to ask you *this*: why should your godchild, white and once very privileged and who, I'm assuming, never saved a brass bean in her life, why should she be offered any special treatment as an indigent?'

'Anne, Anne, please, wait up!' gasped Kirstin. 'I just thought there might be ... that you might know of ... of some medical scheme for folks without money. I'm not asking for ... for charity.' Kirstin's voice had risen high and dry with immediate hurt and shame. It sounded to her ears like a boy's at adolescence, and she was beginning to wish she hadn't phoned, wished she'd phrased the question differently, wished Anne Davies didn't have to sound so accusing.

'Kirstin, what *are* you asking for?' Then Anne's low taut voice returned to normal. 'Listen, I'm sorry, I've got a lot on my mind. Of course, there are no distinctions made here now between black and white indigents. It's just that, well *surely* your godchild's family among themselves can come up with the money?'

'Anne, I don't really know. I know very little about all this, really. I only know that Marissa has cancer and can't pay for surgery. The whole thing seems like an unnecessary mess to me ...'

'Kirstin, you don't know what the word *mess* means. Isn't it time you paid us another visit?' said Anne, her tone dropping again. 'I'd like to take you around some of the wards here. It'd be an eye opener for you.'

'Anne, give me a break,' breathed Kirstin.

There was a momentary pause, then Anne said in a smooth but dull voice, 'I'm sorry for your godchild, don't think I'm not. Let her try the Johannesburg General. But also let me warn you, the service isn't what it was thirty years ago when you had an appendectomy. I really don't have any other suggestions to offer, I don't have much to do with medical cases *per se*. I only see people once their bodies've been patched up. Kirstin, please understand, I've several patients to see, I've had no time for lunch and although it's only three o'clock I'm already dead tired. To tell the truth, I haven't the energy to think about any adult white person at the moment. I've just examined a four-year-old Xhosa boy who, as an infant, suffered horrible ritual mutilation. I think you probably remember the sort of thing, it's been going on in the rural areas here since God-knows-when. Anyway, during the ritual, they cut off his thumbs and penis and ...'

Kirstin could only groan, 'Oh Lord ...' and then listen quietly as Anne told her the full story about the boy. Then she went on to describe the conditions in her clinic and her far too many traumatised patients needing therapy. She had little funding and fewer resources. She was worn-out, discouraged.

When the one-sided conversation had ended, Kirstin went and again sat at the window and just stared out at the snow-swathed lawn and the white-decked shrubs. It was as if something of Anne's own exhaustion had slipped into her mind and she too could barely think.

As the dusk deepened beyond the windowpane, she could see the outline of her head with its grey-blonde hair bristling upwards in the dry blow-heat of the room. Her face was not clearly reflected in the glass but she could see it as she knew it to be, the pale soft skin, the mottled cheeks and the gently falling folds. She knew it was no longer the face of someone who'd grown up under the Highveld sun. It was as if her face declared that the years of her childhood and life in South Africa were receding deep into the past; as if soon those years would no longer exist; as if with age she was metamorphosing into one of her own remote Scottish ancestors. Kirstin hugged her arms to herself as she faced a question she usually evaded: had she made a mistake leaving South Africa in 1977? Wouldn't she and Robyne have had happier, more useful lives had they remained?

But how can one ask oneself such questions? There are no answers to them. Only if she were capable of living a parallel, simultaneous life, one in the American mid-west and another in the Transvaal, could she make a judgement as to which was better. She could only conjecture that if she were there now, in a South Africa newly made free and democratic, she might find ways in addition to her teaching-job of contributing to the common good, and thus earn the approval of people like Anne Davies. And, of course, she'd not be considered 'chicken' by most of her family; would still be accepted by them and have her opinions listened to. Yet, when she thought back to 1977, she had no recollection of being chicken at all. She'd been fearful for the country at large but not about her personal safety. She'd simply jumped at the chance of gaining a year's experience teaching in America, and when the job was converted to a permanent one, being then integrated into the life of her department and her village, she'd gladly kept it. By such chance events can a life be altered, she told herself, rising from her seat by the window. So why did she feel so agitated and guilty? Because, let's face it, she *had* accepted the permanent job, *had* chosen to stay away from home.

One evening over dinner, Kirstin said to Robyne, 'You know, Robyne, what I ask myself is, where is Dannie, Marissa's ex-husband? Why couldn't he contribute toward the cost of the surgery? After all, if she should die, he'd have to take the kids, wouldn't he? But I don't think that's something he'd want to do. Aunty Sue's complained about how he reneges on his commitment to take the children every second weekend. And where is Uncle Kosie, Marissa's own dad? Can't he help his daughter with some money?'

'Don't ask *me*, Mom. Ask Aunty Sue when next you write or speak to her on the phone?' said Robyne, no longer interested in a subject her mother had been wearing thin over the past couple of weeks.

'Well, I would but ... I'm kind of nervous. I'm afraid that Aunty Sue'll dismiss my question by saying something like, *Oh Dannie can never be relied on to do anything.* But then her voice'll take on a challenge and she'll say, *You never did meet Dannie, did you, Kirst? You couldn't manage to get out here for the wedding in '85, could you? You were poep-scared of the ANC violence, weren't you?*'

'Well, were you?'

'No, I wasn't! It really was a question of money, Robyne. It seems to me that the family sometimes thinks that because we live in the States, we've an endless supply of ready-cash. But as you know yourself, that's absolutely not the case. I badly wanted to attend Marissa's wedding, but I ask you, how could I just drop my work, take you out of school, and fly us to Jo'burg for it, especially when it was so sudden? I would've spent about four grand on airfare and who knows how much on other expenses, for God's sake!'

'You know, Mom,' said Robyne, 'you're lettering this matter of the hysterectomy really bug you. Can't you forget about it, put it out of your mind? Let it go. After all, it's their business, not yours.'

'I can't let it go,' said Kirstin. 'Marissa's my *godchild* and I'm worried about her.'

'Mom, she's a grown woman in her thirties, and you hardly have any contact with her anymore. Let her worry about herself!'

Kirstin had been about to raise another matter that'd been nagging at her, but hearing the impatience in Robyne's voice, she remained silent. The question on her mind was how Sue could possibly live with the daily awareness of Marissa's cancer and not make efforts herself to raise money for the surgery. Sue kept horses; three horses, as Kirstin recalled, one an expensive and well-trained dressage horse. Why not sell the dressage horse, or all three for that matter, and solve the problem? She'd wanted to suggest this solution to see how Robyne would react to it; had wanted to point out that if Robyne, God forbid, had been in Marissa's situation and she Kirstin had horses, she would immediately sell her horses. But how could she make such an assertion without seeming to contrive a moment of self-praise and, at the same time, force Robyne into thanking her for something she hadn't had to do?

But the question why Sue didn't sell her horses was, the more Kirstin thought about it, certainly not a frivolous one. Why hadn't Sue, even before hearing about Marissa's cancer, sold the horses to relieve the bad financial situation she and Joe were in? Dwelling on this enigma, Kirstin reflected on the huge property Sue and Joe owned in Kyalami. She recalled how from the house, built on a rise, one could see the spacious sweep of a valley where other homes and grounds and paddocks nestled, and above that the immense blue of a sky more often than not banked by dramatically high cumulus clouds. She recalled the silence and the beauty. Sue employed servants and grooms and, apart from the horses, kept several dogs. It was all very expensive, so Kirstin imagined. In recent months Sue'd been forced to take an office-job, the worst kind of job for an outdoorsy woman like Sue, having to sit at a computer in a travel agent's and planning for *other* people to go to gorgeous places, scuba-diving in the Red Sea or off Phuket, or relaxing on the beaches of Bali. Such a job couldn't bring in much money, could it? But then, maybe the bond on the Kyalami property had long been paid off. Had it?

'Don't get up, Mom,' said Robyne kindly, breaking into Kristin's musings, 'I'll do the dishes ...'

The next morning Kirstin telephoned Sue.

'Sue,' she said, 'I'm just asking ... as a matter of interest. This is not an implied criticism, you understand, just a *question*. I just want to ask you ... I thought ... wouldn't it make sense to sell one of your horses to pay for Marissa's hysterectomy? I mean, have you thought of that? I was just wondering ...'

There was a brief pause during which the vague electronic hum along the line began filling Kirstin's ear with foreboding. Then Sue spoke, her voice thin:

'You know, Kirst, the longer you stay away from South Africa, the more stupid your remarks and suggestions get. You don't understand nothing! Let me tell you, the only thing that keeps me going, keeps me sane in this *New* South Africa, is my horses. If I sell my horses, then I may as well go lay down and die. You don't know what things are like here anymore. You haven't any idea what it's like to worry all the time about bank-overdrafts and humungous car-insurance because of all the hijacking, not to mention the huge food bills and water bills and the fines we've had to pay for using more water than we should've. And then there's the vet bills for Saskia and Ben and Mimi. Now don't tell me to get rid of the dogs as well. We have to have dogs here for protection in this place. This is not small-town America, you know? We have *crime* here, in case you've forgotten ...'

'Sue, Sue ...' begged Kirstin.

'Exactly what kind of life do you expect me to lead? To go to work in that boring office Monday to Saturday and then get home to *nothing*? To sit on my backside of an evening and do nothing but worry, worry, worry? Is that the life you want me to lead? Jesus Christ, I would've thought by now that you understood that I love my horses, I *need* my horses.'

'Sue, Sue, yes, I do understand ...' Mortification had thickened Kirstin's tongue but she managed to apologise, insisting that she'd merely been *asking*, was just *wondering*. Everything was okay, okay, she *did* understand. Then she managed to switch the talk to Christmas looming and the pity that they all couldn't get together, and then to her snow and Sue's drought and the exciting cricket South Africa was playing. A worm of humiliation still churning in her guts, Kirstin kept her voice light until they rang off.

Letter from Kirstin to Sue dated 13th December 1993:

Dearest Sue,

Again I apologise for my phone-call yesterday and my stupid questions about your horses. I wish I did understand all the ins and outs of your life, honestly I do. Being so far away, I can't possibly know all you have to cope with, all the daily irritations. Things at Joe's firm sound awful, and it seems as though you're holding up the whole Kyalami edifice with your own two hands. And I worry that something, one final thing, might break you Sue, some terrible worry or something [Kirstin had wanted to mention the danger to Marissa's life but, not finding a way to express this, her sentence limped on], and I do wish I could be of some help. As you know from way back when, I've never understood the appeal horses have for some people, but I respect your love of them. God, we all need things, sometimes unnecessary things, as I well know. Even King Lear said to his daughters, *Count not the need*. So I would never try to count your need, Sue, believe me.

Talking about need, you know I have a friend here in Michigan who says she *needs* to live in a place that gets sub-zero weather and heavy snowfalls in the winter! That I really

don't understand. I also have a colleague who needs to smoke
a small black ball of rolled Indian hashish before classes,
otherwise he's incapable of teaching. Crazy, hey? But that's
need for you!

Anyway, I don't need these terrible winters, but I do need
to know you're fine and that you're not angry with me. Do
write soon.

Letter from Sue to Kirstin dated January 4, 1994:

Dear Kirst,

Don't worry, I'm not still cross with you. *Ag* Kirst, I'm
used to you. I've told you before, even as a girl you were
always a bit of a know-all, always bossy. But that's all right.

You know what happened the other night? Joe and me'd
been out to supper with the Deventers and we'd just let
ourselves in through the electronic gates and were
disentangling ourselves from the dogs, they're always so jolly
glad to see us, and there was Mar looking rather like a dog
herself all crouched over on the grass at the fishpond. Her
face was all wet and dirty and her hair looked terrible. It was
late, hey, but there were the two kids in their pyjamas standing
nearby. Mar, what's going on? I said, and then Lucy piped
up something about mommy's been crying and flinging her
hair up and down. Then Dirkie has to have his say and says
mommy's been drinking and now she's pissed. That was his
very word, pissed. Kids these days. So what does Mar do?
She leaps up and smacks the kid through the face saying he
must never speak about his mother like that.

Man, I was sorry for the kid. But really they're both a
handful. They're supposed to stay with Sanna at their cottage
when they get home from kindergarten and not get under
my feet. But they won't listen, or rather they try to but they
can't. I get home from work earlier than Mar does and then
the kids follow me about, but at a distance, they're guilty
you see, but they watch every damn thing I do. They follow
me to the stables and try to stand on tiptoe to see me and

Stephen brush the horses down. I know they like the smell of the stables, you know that sweet musty smell and the hides of the horses. I like it myself, but I can't let them in to get in the way. They also stand at the fence of the paddock when I give the horses their exercise. I know the little buggers want to climb up but if they do, I bring the animal around and head towards them and then they jump back down.

It's like being tailed by the police, man. They watch me do what I'm not supposed to. I turn on the spigot so more water from the well (which we sank illegally two years ago) can flow into the fishpond. I don't want my fish to die. And then I carry out the morning's bathwater in buckets to water my plants on the patio. Sometimes if I'm not feeling too *bedonderd* I call the kids and let them come and chat to me. But that's hardly a relaxation. They jabber away and they fight to get closer to me and then it's sticky hands touching me and wet kisses and I was never one for that. But I did hear something the other day that aggravated me. Lucy said that Mar will not hug or kiss them anymore. *Mommy says she does not want to give us a bazeeze,* she said. She meant of course *a disease* and though I laughed I felt flat-eyed with Marissa. Doesn't she know at her age that cancer is not contagious?

Well, Kirst, my hand's getting tired so I'm going to close. But you can't say that I never tell you anything.

Kirstin sat holding the appalling letter. Oh, poor Marissa, poor, poor woman! Didn't Sue realise that she wasn't worried about contagion, she couldn't be. It was something else that caused her to push away her own children. Maybe, aware minute by minute of the crawling menace, the churning danger in her body, she couldn't bear to have hands touching her, not even the hands of her own children; couldn't bear to be reminded of the *fleshness* of her flesh. Oh, good God! And to think of Marissa, crouched like a dog and weeping, flinging her head up and down, howling while her children watched. Kirstin's heart went dark and her eyes burned.

When she could think clearly again, she went yet once again to the telephone and dialled, longing to hear Marissa's voice. She started off brightly, warmly, asking Marissa how she was doing, and how the twins were, but soon realised that she'd made another tactical mistake. What she got was Marissa's putting on the typically cute female South African voice, a voice women assume when they want to appear brave or upbeat or just plain young. Or when they want to tell someone to get lost. It was a bright clipped voice, studiedly girlish. *No, Aunty Kirstin,* Marissa said, *everything's fine. No really, I'm fine and no, no, the kids are fine. It's so nice of you to ask. But Mommy's been writing to you, hasn't she, so I won't repeat what she's told you about my problems. Everything's going to be all right, Aunty Kirstin. This call must be costing you a fortune ...*

Whenever members of Kirstin's family warned her that her calls from the States were costing her a fortune, she knew that they wanted to bring the conversation to a speedy end. They couldn't care less about her fortune, she knew that; they just didn't feel like talking to her on the phone, that was all. So Kirstin put the receiver down. She was breathlessly annoyed at Marissa's sweet but brief and high-voiced rebuff, but also in a squirm of helplessness that added to the sick feeling in her stomach.

Why the rebuff? she asked herself. Why does Marissa want me to back off? Is she motivated by pride? But then where was the pride coming from? Was Marissa afraid that Kirstin would offer to pay for the surgery and she would be tempted to accept, whereas she didn't want to accept? Was it a matter of not taking money from an aunt she hadn't seen in some years, one who, as far as the family was concerned, had run off like a traitor? Did Marissa see Kirstin's money as tainted? None of this made much sense to Kirstin, which didn't mean that it couldn't make a kind of sense to Marissa.

Kirstin, however, was not ready to back off, not yet anyhow. All the phone-call with Marissa had done was cause her to think about money, about her own finances. She sat down with a recent bank statement and her savings-book and did some calculations, taking into account the coming year's property taxes and the fact that the furnace in her basement might not hold out if the winter continued as severe as it was through February and March. She came to the conclusion that she could probably pay for Marissa's hysterectomy immediately and not wait until that benighted medical insurance gave their say-so for the operation. Not wanting to risk Marissa's pretend-Barbie-doll voice on the phone again, she went to telephone Sue, brushing away the thought that this month's telephone bill was going to be, what was Sue's word, *humungous*.

'Sue,' she said, 'you know Marissa is my godchild ...'

'Kirst, did you phone me all the way from America to tell me that?' laughed Sue.

'No, I just want to emphasise that Marissa is dear to me.'

'Kirstin,' said Sue heavily, 'out with it. Why *are* you phoning?'

'Listen, I've worked it out that I can afford to pay for Marissa's hysterectomy. Sue, I have the money and I want to pay for it *now*.'

Sue inhaled and then exhaled audibly, as if her lungs had taken in too much disappointing air. She said slowly, 'You know, Kirstin, Mar is somebody who has to help herself.'

'What d'you mean?'

'Well, the doctor told her that while she's waiting for the medical aid to make her eligible for the operation, she should build up her strength. She's supposed to give up smoking and drinking and to be eating a healthy diet...'

'But she's not doing that,' interrupted Kirstin, 'is that what you're telling me?'

'Yes, that's what I'm telling you. When she does eat, she eats nothing but pizzas and hamburgers and doughnuts. She says she can't give up her ciggies, which means not ten a day but sometimes thirty. And, I can tell you, three nights out of four she gets so drunk she can't see to walk straight. I hear her celebrations, man, all the damn noise coming from the cottage. Sometimes I hear her singing like a duck with a sore throat, and I'm sure she dances round the place.'

'Sue, have you spoken to her; seriously, I mean?'

'What must I say? She's heard what the doctor said. She must now co-operate.'

'But is there any reason why she can't have the operation now, even though she's not built up her strength? I mean, Sue, if she's not co-operating now, she'll not have co-operated by the time the medical insurance okays the surgery. But she'll *have* the surgery then, won't she, cigarettes, booze, and all?'

'Yes, but by then the medical aid will pay for it. I don't see why anybody else should give money for her when she won't do her part.'

Kirstin couldn't believe what she was hearing. Sue's callousness was like something revolting served up to her on a plate. Indignation rushed up her gullet and she blurted out, 'Sue, what you mean is, you don't want to sell a horse and you don't want me to pay for Marissa's surgery!'

'Look, Kirstin,' yelled Sue, 'lay off my horses and lay off my daughter. We don't need your interference here.'

'Look, Susan,' Kirstin shot back, 'Marissa is my goddaughter. And why must you be so goddamned rude to me when I'm only trying to help?'

The minutes and the money ticked away as both silently fought to find the right words. Kirstin could hear Sue breathing audibly and suspected that she was trying to find a way to say something that she didn't want to end up being ashamed of or something that was meant to be insulting but which she wanted to sound like words of wisdom. Tired of waiting, Kirstin said, 'Sue?'

'Do you remember, Kirst,' said Sue in a suddenly placating voice; 'do you remember mentioning a couple of years ago that you might one day send me airfare to visit you … if ever you had the spare cash?'

'Why, yes …' murmured Kirstin.

'I've always wanted to visit you in the States, you know that, don't you?'

'Well, I've not been sure. You never have anything good to say about the place, Sue.'

'That's because I think you racist Americans have been great hypocrites towards us white South Africans. But I'd still like to see where you live. And, you know, Kirst, I really need a holiday away from my depressing life here. I need to take a break and soon. There's just too much on my shoulders. Kirstin, I *need* a break!'

Kirstin was nonplussed. The concern she'd been nurturing for Marissa she had to allow to submerge as she tried bringing to consciousness the sudden implication that Sue was calling on her for rescue. But the turn-around was hard to bring off.

'Are you suggesting, Sue,' she asked in a hard voice, 'that I send you the money I have so that you can visit me, and that I do not send it to Marissa for her surgery?'

'All I'm saying, Kirst,' said Sue, 'is that sometime I'd like to visit you. I'd like to see you again. Have some heart-to-heart talks. That's all I'm saying.'

'Well, I'd also like that a lot, Sue. But you've caught me off-guard. I can't talk about this now. Let me give it some thought and get back to you, okay?'

After the two women had rung off, Kirstin found herself pacing the living-room with short staccato steps, trying to jog her body into helping her mind to discover the sub-text of the conversation that had just taken place. She thought of Sue, her hard dry humour, her grit. She was, like Marissa, also a neatly-built woman, though taller, and she'd developed very strong arms and rippling back muscles from all the horse-riding. Her legs were hard and her hands, large for a woman of her size, were big-knuckled, lined, and capable. When she was young, her skin used to be, again like Marissa's, delicately beautiful. But she was different now, beautiful in a different way, deeply suntanned and rugged, her intense blue eyes compelling, and her straight greying hair cut like a schoolboy's. Oh, how regal she could look, remembered Kirstin, when she was dressed in her jodhpurs, pink coat, white ruffled shirt, and black hunting hat; sitting, riding-crop in hand, high up on the back of a golden-brown horse all shimmers and shivers and nervously ballet-footed. How many falls from horses hadn't she taken, how many broken bones hadn't she suffered? But, undaunted, she'd always climb back up on those horses.

Yes, Sue was tough and fearless. If she was not always exactly kindly, she was loyal to her family and friends, and it was impossible to believe she was not beside herself with anxiety over Marissa. Was that it? Was the nature of the anxiety so intense that it was debilitating her, causing her to want to run away, go someplace else, take a vacation? Did the problem of raising money for Marissa's surgery seem insoluble, at least temporarily so? But *why*?

Having no answers, eventually Kirstin stopped pacing, went back to her desk, and did more calculations. It was possible, by not replacing the furnace, that she'd be able to pay for Marissa's surgery right then and for Sue's visit to America in six months' time. But what would she *do* with Sue in Marshall, her village? It was one of those small towns which one drove through without realising that it was a place where people actually lived and worked, and that some miles out of the town there was a good Lutheran college and a world-class golf-course. In August, Marshall baked and soaked under a steamy sun. After dark, aimless kids in pick-up vans, radios blaring, cruised the main drag, then ended up in the McDonalds' parking lot. Nobody Kirstin knew kept horses.

Then, suddenly, Marissa took matters into her own small inept hands. Two days later Kirstin got a phone-call from Sue to tell her that Marissa had taken an overdose of sleeping-tablets.

'Oh God, Sue, is she all right?' gasped Kirstin.

'Yes, she's alive, but feeling very sorry for herself. It's no picnic having your stomach pumped, you know.'

'What *happened*?'

'Kirst, it's a long story but I'll try cutting it short. Mar put the kids to bed and then started drinking. When she saw that Joe and me were in bed and the lights were off, she carried the rest of her wine to her favourite spot which don't ask me why is the grass near the fishpond. Then, it seems, she drank a whole bottle of sleeping-tablets and went wading in my fishpond. She must have been in a strange state, sort of dazed with joy or something, because she danced over my pots of water-plants, kicking some over. I'm not happy about that, I can tell you. And she jumped up and down and splashed the water, churning up a hell of a lot of mud and killing some of my fish. It seems she was chanting or singing something, because that's when Sanna woke up in her room.'

'Didn't you or Joe hear her, Sue?'

'No, man, our bedroom is at the other end of the house. But Sanna's a light sleeper. She told me at first she thought it was drunken burglars and wondered where the dogs were. But then she recognised the Young Madam's voice and tried to go back to sleep again. But she couldn't. Then she got up to go and tell Mar to go to bed but was just in time to see Mar collapse back onto the grass. Meanwhile, the dogs in the house were becoming restless and whining deep in their throats, you know the way dogs do, and Joe got up to investigate. Immediately me and Joe threw Mar into the back of the van and drove her to the emergency room.'

'Thank God you got to her in time ...'

'*Ja*, but you should have seen her, hey. She had on some tiny shorts but with no panties underneath and the shorts were riding up her backside. And her boobs were falling out of her halterneck, and her bare feet and legs were just one smear of mud and slush and dead grass. I can tell you, Kist, I was not proud of her!'

'Sue,' yelled Kirstin, pushed to her limits by the calm tones of her cousin, 'Sue, she's desperate! Can't you see that? She's desperate! It's goddamned time somebody ...'

'Don't shout at me, Kirstin!' Sue yelled back at her.

'Are you blind, Sue?' asked Kirstin, lowering her voice.

'No, I'm not blind. And yes, I do see that she's desperate. *You* don't have to tell me that.'

There was another of those living silences along the line but when Sue spoke again her voice was back to normal. She said, 'Listen, Kirst, I'm not selling Calypso my dressage horse, but I've decided to sell the other two. I've spoken to the doctor and he'll schedule the operation as soon as I have the cash in hand.'

Kirstin felt a rush of words beginning to agitate her tongue, but controlled herself, sensing that at that moment any exuberance on her part would merely serve to irritate her cousin. When she could speak steadily, she said, 'I'm so glad to hear that, Sue, really glad. I think you're making the right decision and ... and I know you won't be sorry. Sue ... Sue ... you'll let me know immediately, won't you, the date of Marissa's surgery?'

'Kirst, don't hold yourself stupid,' Sue said. 'How can I not let you know when it'll be and how things go? Christ, if I don't call you, you'll keep calling me until you drive me nuts.' Then Sue laughed, a sort of grunt in her nose, and added, 'And how do you know, Kirst, that I won't be sorry to sell my horses?'

'Oh Sue,' said Kirstin weakly, 'Sue ... In the meantime, please give Marissa my love and tell her ...'

'Yes, yes, yes, I know what to tell Marissa from you.'

Kirstin, confused, hesitated, trying to guess the source of Sue's mocking impatience with her but sensed that Sue was waiting for her guess. At last she thought she understood. 'Sue,' she said carefully, 'I know this is not the time to be planning a holiday, but you know I've been thinking … I get about a week off over Easter. That might be a good time for you to visit. It'll be spring here, cold still but spring, and we could spend a few days in Chicago or someplace …'

'Why isn't this a good time to plan a holiday?' interrupted Sue.

'Well, what with our concern over Marissa and all …'

'All the more reason why it's a good time, I should think.'

'There's lots of time. We can talk about it later,' said Kirstin.

'Let's talk about it now,' said Sue. 'When I have to sell horses, I need something nice to think about to take my mind off seeing their rumps as they're led into the horsebox and driven away. Do you have your schedule handy? Look at it and tell me when in April you get your break.'

Kirstin reached over and pulled the calendar towards her. Thoughtfully, not quite comfortable with being hurried along by Sue, she took her time to page. As she did so, she questioned Sue, to mark time, asked her about the drought. Sue actually seemed grateful to talk about it, about how hard the veld was on the horses' hooves, how, in the unusually intense heat, dormant animal sicknesses were cropping up again. She spoke about her dying plants, giving them their botanical names, spoke as if Kirstin remembered the plants individually; spoke about the poor maize crop in the Free State, about veld fires.

But Kirstin wasn't herself comforted to hear Sue chatting away in her everyday voice, for she couldn't dispel a vision of Marissa lying in front of a large window, unconscious on a hospital stretcher. She was waiting to be wheeled into the theatre for surgery. From the window behind her Kirstin could see only greyish-black burnt veld, the dead pink of grassless sand, and the whiteness of an empty sky. Why was Marissa just lying there? But Sue was continuing to speak and Kirstin had to concentrate on the holiday plans. She blinked her eyes hard. Sue needed to plan and maybe Sue understood something profound about human survival that she might have understood once.

Ethel, the sensible

Gcinaphi Dlamini

You know her when you see her. She who is skilled in the art of the hunt. You may or may not be like her, but Ethel knows she is not. Like Ethel, perhaps you have done your homework, primed your mind and shown the warmth of your heart but you are still too ... too anxious, too deep, too ... just too ...

Marginalised, mumbling to yourself, fumbling through life, trampling toes, nibbling on nerves, blowing to make it better. Apologetic for your existence. It is not often you open up your heart but when you love, it is always ... too ...

Ethel muses, she must be one of those women who love too much. In her honour and yours, if you know what I mean, you have a book dedicated to you and the men that hate you. You are the ones who have forgotten the art of the hunt. A wounded fighter, Ethel has returned to her lair to lick her wounds, nurse her pathetic longing.

Political correctness has let her down once more. She refuses to admit she is gutted, walking away with her bleeding heart clutched in her hand. Heart, she will not let you break, even as you strain at the seams leaking bitter tears. She will not fight.

Ethel is in a state of shock and bewilderment, watching the one that got away, as she fumbled, intellectualising, while another, strong and sure, sleek and supple, moved in for the kill.

How can she explain to the happy captive that she knew him before she saw him? When she saw the light in his eyes, and marvelled at the soft smile, does he imagine how her heart soared? And how she caught her breath in mid-sentence, as she embraced the changing seasons in the world of his face?

Her sorrow is a punctured lung.

Ethel wants to wail like a banshee, streak naked through the streets of her small hometown and tear her hair out, knowing that that man is lost forever.

Her mother never told her that women are hunters. Ethel had no sense of it, having spent many years of her life in captivity as a circus performer – standing on her head, jumping through hoops, in an effort to please, smiling and waiting for the applause that never came. But every show had to end. The audience had to leave before the lights went out and the smiling clown faces turned to ones of surly depression. They had to go. He had to go. But who would have thought she would lose him to a woman like that?

She, who has laid her trap carefully, skilfully concealed poison, bone-breaking snares, soul-destroying venom, in the mists of beauty and grace and patience. There is only one outcome – she captures, scores, reels in the big fish. If she can do it, why not Ethel?

Ethel is crippled by the stifling convention of political correctness and gender sensitivity! Hey! Ethel comes from the school of thought which holds that men and women are equal, different but all the same really but lately, she's been thinking, a hundred years of a feminist revolution later, many battles fought on her behalf, that she's more than likely to throw in the towel, give up the fight and succumb to convention and stop being ... too ...

It was just a few weeks ago that she realised with blinding clarity that all she wants is to be wanted. Up against the kitchen sink, bent over a hot engine, in bed, in the shower – any which way. Desired. Not for her so-called intellect. She's pretty tired of being told about this intangible intellect and feeling like she has to perform like a circus attraction to hold a man's attention. She wants somebody to look into her slightly bored, vacuous eyes with deep desire. She wants someone who will perform circus tricks to amuse her, desperate to keep her interested. She wants to be somewhat cool but smouldering, the innocent bitch, the one who needs to be protected.

Is it too late, she wonders, to learn to play the game so well men will die defending her honour and sincerity? That they will cast away lifelong friends who dare to see through the veneer? Is it too late to learn to lie with such skill about the number and timing of other lovers? Is it too late to learn the sultry, smoky look practised in front of the mirror? Is it okay to laugh at herself alone in front of that mirror, smiling coyly, pouting profusely, licking her chops seductively ... No! No! No!

Ethel wants to apologise to Barbie and friends – for casting them to one side, with a dismissive nod of her intellectual head. Now that head must hang itself in shame and admit to not even being that smart after all. Barbie has got it all, and she can't even string an intelligible sentence together, has never had one original thought but the thing is: who the fuck cares?

Ethel also wants to apologise for her passion for the politically correct. For telling women really stupid things like it's not what you look like that matters, it's who you are inside.

Ethel will emerge after many months of incubation. She will move to a place where nobody will know her as that smart and sensible girl. Pared down in body and mind, schooled in the ways of the hunt, she will swan in and introduce herself as something light and lovely – very carefree yet deeply new age spiritual, that is how Ethel is going to be.

Soft and gentle, she will laugh at stupid jokes and not think too hard. She will muster grace and charm. She will be attentive and understanding but not original – anything but original! She will let someone else do the running for a change. She will be unavailable but loving. Mysterious but uncomplicated. She will pretend to have a busy, busy life. She will not speak out of turn, she will laugh at the right time, but she will not be so easily taken. For even as women are the hunters who lure their prey, a great hunter will never give the game away before she is well prepared for the kill.

We are many millions of years into evolution, and Ethel, young (and smart) and beautiful, is only just about to learn to play the survival game.

ETHEL! What are you thinking? Do you vaguely remember a word 'feminist'? In the seventies and eighties, your mothers fought hard to maintain the image of Superwoman. Having it all was the buzzword. They fought for you, so that you would never have to choose this way, compromise yourself like this.

All Ethel knows is that in the end, her only desire is to love and to be loved back. Are you going to tell Ethel that there is something wrong with her? That she lacks self-love and confidence? You are going to tell her to be herself and love will find her. Ethel maintains she has seen the light. Fuck political correctness and gender sensitivity. New age man is also an animal. This is what you forget. Ethel doesn't want her brain fucked any more. She wants to be adored, worshipped and cherished for just Being a woman.

In truth, Ethel lives a rich and rewarding life, like many of you. She is a warm and wonderful human being but she has unlearned what you all instinctively know. That she is a woman and wants to be wanted. She doesn't want to live her life alone, filling her house with some or other form of animal to fill the spaces. She doesn't want neat bookshelves lined with clean, well-dusted books because there are no children to flip through them, or glass ornaments filling the rooms as if to attest to some kind of hollow victory that she has no children, therefore she can fill her house with crystal vases and white couches.

Has Ethel tried therapy? Especially for women who love too much? How is this possible? asks Ethel, How do you love too much?

There are many ways to love too much, Ethel. Bending over backwards, until your back breaks. Kissing the feet of your loved one so that he can kick you in the teeth, loving someone who thinks you are too ... or not enough, like Goldilocks trying out Bear things, looking for Just Right.

This is no fairy tale.

Ethel is limping away from a war she never wanted. In her lair, dark and warm, she readies herself for self-imposed exile. The victor takes all. There can be no political correctness here of being friends. How can she be friends with the one who has ripped out her loving heart and thrown it in her face? Can you? It would be like living her life out as a slave captured in battle. She will sling her breaking heart, her perforated lung, over her shoulder and venture out into the world.

One day, she will open the sack and examine the discarded contents, with a detachment and a peace she never thought possible. She will laugh that she ever wanted to change, to shrink and disguise the light of her soul and the shadows in between.

Maybe one day, she will find the one who will love her odd beauty. The one who will not fear the depth and breadth of her love, who will run towards this open book, eager to learn. Someone who will reach out to her happy but grappling soul that we know little of because we have only seen her at this low point, when her pain is too real. Someone who will cheer the sincerity and courage, and revel in the passionate and sensual woman who is Ethel. Maybe.

For now, she will be alone. She will breathe, she will keep her eyes focused, her ears sharp. She will put one foot in front of the other and she will go on.

Supermarket soliloquy

Moira Crosbie Lovell

There's a queue of empty trolleys lined up outside. Like wire prams. The one you choose has a gammy wheel, which seriously affects your gait and reminds you that you are not a spry young mother with a comatose cutie out for a walk, but a middle-aged woman with a bare cupboard and intimations of mortality.

Entrance is free. 'Welcome to a walk in the supermarket park. Where the sun never sets (fluorescent lighting); the air's fresh and bracing (air-conditioned); and the band's always playing (on tape). No dogs allowed.'

But there is a catch. It's just like life. Entrance is free. But you accumulate debts on the way. And you have to pay before you exit.

Just like life.

On the right, as you enter, eggs, bulging in their trays, lie like wards of pregnant women waiting to deliver the contents of their stomachs. You take down a tray. One egg's already broken in its bed. Stickily. Prematurely. And the porcelain womb, cracked, can't be repaired with glue. It's finished. Like yours.

A little further on there's a refrigerator shelf stacked with great plastic breasts of milk. You hold one in each hand, feeling the weight, pressing them gently. They are as full as yours used to be. A brimming cup of C. And nippleless. As yours are now, awaiting reconstruction. For a moment, weighing the smooth packets in the scale of your palms, you think you won't bother, after all, with that final artifice. You have no need now of nipples. Either for feeding or for flirting.

You drop the two bags into the trolley. They sag against the wire. As you move towards the cheese trough, you catch a glimpse of yourself in an unexpected mirror. You have an urge to charge it with gross misrepresentation. A distortion of yourself leers up at you as you lean over. Your face is a creased feta cheese white.

Other cheeses present a range of past complexions; chubby, baby-smooth Mozzarella; freckle-faced Pepato; bride-white Camembert; tanned Red Cheshire; jaundiced Cheddar. You cast a furtive eye on the blue-veined Gorgonzola up ahead and settle, after all, for the feta.

There's a trolley obstructing your way. A child sits in it, sucking at the wire. Spittle slides down the bars. You imagine her gnawing a hole big enough to escape through. For a moment you remember a broken cage. It's in the back garden of your childhood home. Your pet rabbit has gone. 'Mummy! Mummy!'

'Mum-mee!' the child is wailing, suddenly. You try to manoeuvre past the cage with your club-footed trolley. You find yourself pinned against the meat container. Rows of maroon fillets, shrouded in transparent clingwrap, lie like skinned rabbits. 'Mummy! My rabbit's gone! Matilda's gone ...!' And you see, as you are running wildly to the kitchen door, the gardener patting the ground under the mango tree with the shovel.

'It's all right, darling.'

'Matilda's gone!'

The dog slinks into the kitchen with red teeth.

You avert your eyes. But they are professionals and have already photographed the meat container. As you move away, about as fast as a geriatric with a walker, slides flash on the screen of your mind. Limbs and flesh.

There is a landmine. Buried in the bush. A relic of the guerrilla war. Your father is out walking with some of his labourers. *Blwadoom!* That piece over there. That's a bit of him.

Limbs and flesh.

You don't eat meat.

Someone in a wheelchair whizzes past.

You manage to twist the trolley into an aisle. For some reason, as you straighten it out, it takes to a brief stretch of gliding. And you think, 'Here comes the bride!' In the pews on either side, cans rise in their designer wrappers like a congregation of wedding guests. Some are, inevitably, over the top. There's a bunch of maiden aunts with pot-scourer perms on the right. Old Uncle James is a leonine mop. Aunt Martha is as plumed as a feather duster.

In the distance, where the bread has been put out, is the altar. You can see the priest there, in his white surplice. And your young husband waiting, tall and slim as a broom. Bridegroom groomed, smiling like peppermints.

At the top, you stretch for two loaves of wholewheat. 'This is my body which is broken for you.'

You turn around. Aislewards. Rows of bottles catch the light like stained glass windows. Oils glow rich in gold and ochre and green. Vinegars are deep burgundy and brawn. Or transparent, like a sudden pane of clear glass. Tomato relish is a saucy red.

The chutneys are bronze brocade.

Suddenly your trolley wheels lock. A bag of rice has burst across the floor. You remember your bronze brocaded bridesmaids throwing handfuls of rice as you reached the church door. Man and wife. And rice falling out of the sky like light pellets of rain.

A shop attendant has already arrived to sweep up the rain. 'Excuse me, Madam,' he says, because you are standing in it. He tries to push your trolley. Of course it won't push. He tries a bronco-busting tactic. It bucks away round the corner.

And you are in collision with ranks of dishwashing liquid. Green for go. And stretching to infinity. Boxes of washing powder across the aisle rise foaming into a massive cloud filthy with the threat of floods. Ahead, there's a gauntlet of polishes to slip you up.

As you make it to the far end, you catch sight of boxes of tea, serene as books on their shelves. You run your fingers along the familiar titles and take a favourite volume down.

Quite suddenly you are back in the university library, reading. The young lecturer, who's mildly in love with you, takes the chair next to yours.

'What are you imbibing?' he asks, pressing his spectacles at the bridge of his nose.

'*A Cup of Tea*, by ...'

'Ah, yes,' he interrupts. 'Very stimulating.'

He wants to tell you he thinks you're beautiful, but he has neither the valour nor the vocabulary. He mooches off, mute as a cabbage, folding knowledge page by page into his head. You marry someone else. So does he.

Funny to think about the ones you might have married. There was the youth your father called Kreepy-Krawly. He crept round your folk and crawled over you, giving you those long slow love-bites that a dysfunctional kreepy-krawly doles out to the walls of a swimming pool. *Sch-loop; sch-loop.*

You mustn't forget the swimming pool chemical. It's about all that goes into the pool these days. Besides hadedas, which leave downy underneath feathers like dirty-grey underwear in the water. Your husband's a hydrophobe and you don't swim much anymore. Probably because the world's grown colder.

You think of Superglue. The fellow who made you feel like a Siamese twin. Everyone knows the type. It's all right initially, but in time you start getting desperate for separation surgery. The best technique is probably a spongeful of turpentine words. You have a memory of him trailing tissues as he departed for a distant continent to convalesce.

Suddenly you discover your trolley has sidled up to a demo table. You're stuck. Forehead to forehead with a woman promoting a new brand of canned mushrooms. She has a tray of them – like little bronze medals. She plunges a cocktail stick into one and pins it to your lips. You can hardly refuse it. It's salty and you want more. A whole shelf of them shines strategically from behind her left shoulder. You reach for a can. The woman's dentures momentarily blind you. Like the flashlight of a photographer. Like love.

Talking of love, there was the other boy. Schwarzenegger. Who ate mushrooms to make his muscles like mountains.

'They're called the Schwarzenegger of vegetables,' he said. Which was how he got his name. Later, he slipped over a rock ledge and fell to his death when he couldn't hold on long enough for his friend to heave him up.

A sign is swinging above you. 'Fruit and veg.' Presumably the signwriter can't spell 'vegetables'. Or the board's too small. The potatoes look like a gang of garden service employees. Their brown faces dotted with moles of earth.

'Okay, dahl …' says a man into his cellphone. He's almost kissing it with his lips. You catch the carrots stalking by on long man-hunting legs.

'Y'okay, dahl …?'

It's you he's talking to.

No wonder. Your trolley, turned Pamplona bull, is butting him in the back.

'Sorry.'

'No problem.' He sounds the 'p' as a 'b'. Turning on the beast, he swings it through the air. A gold chain flies round his throat. You have the idea he might be a ballroom dancer. The trolley glistens in her silver net and sequins. Or a discus thrower. The trolley turns disc and spins off.

'Thank you!' you yell, scurrying after it.

'No broblem!' He turns, 'Hey, dahl …' into the machine.

The trolley is nuzzling the breadspreads. Beef extract has taken over. Masses of jars, like tight little black buttocks, toyi-toyi across the shelf, holding colourful banners.

You think of the garbage workers' strike, just last week. How suburban avenues were littered for days with bulbous black dustbin bags lying like giant turds at the tops of driveways. The crap of fat-cat consumerism.

The bags made you feel branded. Someone with enough to throw away. Someone with too much. Someone...

Someone with neon lipstick greets you. 'Hi!'

'Hello.'

'You always look miles away. So distracted. Busy writing something, I suppose. Mind elsewhere.'

'Um. Yes, I suppose that's it.'

'What is it?'

'What?'

'That you're writing.'

'Oh. It's a ... a short story.'

'I see.'

'And you? What are you doing?'

'We're off to Australia ...'

You're standing next to a fridge of frozen fish. The ice thaws into a sea. Over a wave comes an army of prawns. Medieval knights in tarnished armour waving their lances like antennae. A giant crab has pincers of frozen crab-stick wrapped in cellophane bandages ...

'Excuse me.' It's another demo woman. She has a full plastic apron that makes her look like a crustacean. Her fingers are crab-sticks. She chops them into bite-sized pieces. 'Would you like to try some?' she asks. 'Dip it in the mayonnaise.'

It tastes like a piece of finger. You feel like a cannibal. 'I don't eat meat,' you say.

'It's seafood,' she says. As if you're a half-wit.

You swim off, the trolley with a bad screwkick.

Soap. Shampoo. Toothpaste. The expense of keeping clean. A rope of dental floss, coiled, is your grandmother's white curl in the heirloom locket that a burglar trophied off through the bedroom window a little time ago. Along with other antique irreplaceables. Classy thief. He broke the window with a stake that was supporting the standard iceberg rose outside the bedroom. When you came home, the rose was bending over, touching its toes. Balletic. Anna Pavlova with her back broken. The shattered window was lying in glinting jewels on the bedroom carpet; and the jewels were gone.

The house has had a lot of orthodontistry since then. All the mouths wired up. And razor-gut spiralled across the garden wall. It looks as if a giant spider from an extra-terrestrial locality has spun its metallic web across the wall. 'Come into my parlour,' says the spider to the fly. You picture black-balaclava-ed burglars buzzing their last on the barbs.

Don't forget the fly-spray.

You ought to make lists.

Most of the loo rolls are stacked in packs of a dozen. They look like mattress springs. But a solitary one, quite impulsively it seems, falls from the shelf. *Phlock!* You pick it up. You imagine it unravelling itself. Like a Christmas streamer. You see the whole place festooned with loo paper decorations. And smile. You are Father Christmas in a lopsided sleigh carrying sackloads of surprises home to your husband. 'Ho, ho, ho.' Another flimsy supermarket packet bursts on the kitchen floor.

A solitary roll of loo paper falls to the floor. *Phlock!* You pick it up. It unravels itself and winds around you. Like bandages. Like a shroud.

Intimations of mortality.

'Just a moment,' you think. 'I'm not quite finished. I haven't done everything I was intending to do.'

I have the bread. 'This is my body.' But not the wine.

The wine cellar runs blood. You limp in, anaemic, hoping for a transfusion. Someone says, 'Cheers.' You turn around. It's not a toast. It's a farewell.

You take some wine by the throat. 'This is my blood.'

You look at your watch. Time is at a premium. There are deadlines to be met. Post offices. Publishers.

A priest overtakes you. His robe is licking up a wind.

You think fast. The last items. 'Cleaning agents. Stain removers. Scourers.'

Absolution. Last rites.

Miraculously, there isn't a queue. The trolley, apoplectic, collapses at the till. You pay the bill. And waft out. Trolleyless. Trailing loo paper like Lazarus.

Biographical notes on contributors

Elleke Boehmer (South Africa) She was born in 1961 in Durban, and studied at Rhodes University. In 1985 she went to the United Kingdom to study at Oxford. She now teaches at the University of Leeds. Among her novels are *Screens against the Sky* and *An Immaculate Figure*.

Gcinaphi Dlamini (Swaziland) She was born in 1968 in Mbabane, and went to school in Swaziland and Wales. She has a BA degree in Psychology and French from the University of South Africa. Currently, she works as a trainee director and producer for a video production company in Swaziland. She is currently working on two scripts, and editing a completed manuscript.

Nadine Gordimer (South Africa) She was born in 1923 in what was then the small mining town Springs, where she attended a convent school. She studied at the University of the Witwatersrand. She is South Africa's most distinguished and honoured novelist and short story writer. In 1991 her writing career was crowned by the award of the Nobel Prize for Literature. She has published more than ten novels, including *A Guest of Honour, Burger's Daughter* and *The House Gun*, and many collections of short stories.

Bessie Head (South Africa-Botswana) (1937-1986) She was born in the Pietermaritzburg mental hospital, as a result of a liaison between her white mother and an unknown black man. Her difficult childhood was spent moving from a white foster-family, to a Coloured foster-mother, to a mission-orphanage. She trained as a teacher, and worked as a journalist. After a failed marriage in Cape Town, she left South Africa on a one-way exit permit, and she and her son settled in Botswana. She was twice refused Botswanan citizenship and lived for some time as a refugee in Francistown. Eventually granted citizenship, she remained in exile in Serowe village until her death from hepatitis. Her novels are *The Cardinals, When Rain Clouds Gather, Maru* and *A Question of Power*; and her short pieces are collected in *The Collector of Treasures and Other Botswana Village Tales, Tales of Tenderness and Power*, and *A Woman Alone*.

Kaleni Hiyalwa (Namibia). She was born in the 1960s in Ohangwena region of northern Namibia. She completed her school education in Zambia and Cameroon, after going into exile. She taught Namibian refugees under SWAPO's care in Angola. Having completed a diploma in journalism in Ghana, she has worked professionally in the fields of journalism and gender, and currently works in the Department of Women's Affairs in the Office of the President. Forthcoming is the publication of her first novel.

Farida Karodia (South Africa) She was born in 1942 and grew up in the small town of Aliwal North. Having taught in Johannesburg and in Zambia, in 1969 she emigrated to Canada, where she worked as a teacher and as a radio writer. Later, after 1990, she returned to South Africa. Her novels are *Daughters of the Twilight* and *A Shattering of Silence*; her short stories are collected in *Coming Home* and *Against an African Sky*.

Jane Katjavivi (UK-Namibia) She was born in 1952 in Leeds in northern England. She did African Studies at Sussex and Birmingham universities and then worked for organisations supporting the southern African liberation movements, and in journalism and publishing. She married a leading SWAPO activist and, after independence in 1990, they resettled in Namibia. She founded and runs the publishing company and bookshop New Namibia Books. She has two children.

Doris Lessing (Zimbabwe-UK) She was born in 1919 in Iran (then Persia) and grew up in Zimbabwe (then Rhodesia) from 1924. Twice married and divorced, she and her son left Rhodesia for the United Kingdom in 1949; her first novel *The Grass is Singing* was a considerable critical and sales success. In the 1950s she was declared a prohibited immigrant in both Rhodesia and South Africa. She has had a most distinguished career as a novelist and short story writer. Her African novels are the Martha Quest 'Children of Violence' sequence, and her African stories are collected in *This Was the Old Chief's Country* and *The Sun between Their Feet*.

Moira Crosbie Lovell (Zimbabwe-South Africa) She was born in 1951 in Zimbabwe (then Rhodesia), and moved to South Africa in 1976. She now lives and teaches in KwaZulu-Natal. She has had two collections of poems published, *Out of the Mist* and *Departures*, and has written a number of stage and radio plays.

Sindiwe Magona (South Africa) She was born in 1945 in Gungululu, a village 18 km from Umtata in what is now the Eastern Cape province. As a small child, she moved to Blaauvlei, near Retreat in Cape Town, and later to Guguletu. She worked as a domestic worker, studied to be a teacher, and was granted a bursary to study at Columbia University in the United States. She has degrees from the University of South Africa and Columbia University, and has been awarded an Honorary Doctorate from Hartwick College, New York. She works at the United Nations. Her published works include *To My Children's Children, Forced to Grow, Push-Push!, Mother to Mother*, and the collection of short pieces *Living, Loving and Lying Awake at Night*.

Gcina Mhlophe (South Africa) She was born in 1958 in Hammarsdale near Durban. She attended high school in the Transkei in the present Eastern Cape province, and began writing poems and stories in Xhosa. She has achieved international success as an actor, theatre director, playwright (*Have You Seen Zandile?*), and, above all, as South Africa's finest storyteller. She has also published a number of books of stories for children, including *Hi, Zoleka!*, *The Snake with Seven Heads* and *Queen of the Tortoises*. Forthcoming is a CD called *African Lullabies for Khwezi*.

Sheila Roberts (South Africa-US) She was born in 1951 in Johannesburg, and was brought up in the small town of Potchefstroom. She studied at the Universities of South Africa and Pretoria, and emigrated to the United States in 1977, to teach creative writing at the University of Wisconsin. Her works include *He's My Brother* and *Outside Life's Feast*

Agnes Sam (South Africa) She was born in 1942, and was brought up in Port Elizabeth, where she had a Catholic Christian education. She attended university in Lesotho and Zimbabwe, and then taught in Zambia. In 1973 she went to the United Kingdom, and studied English Literature at the University of York. In the 1990s she made a number of return visits to South Africa. Her short stories were collected under the title *Jesus Is Indian*.

Yvonne Vera (Zimbabwe) She was born in Bulawayo. She studied at York University in Toronto. She is now the Director of the National Gallery of Zimbabwe in Bulawayo. She has published a number of novels, including *Nehanda*, *Without a Name*, *Under the Tongue* (winner of the 1997 Commonwealth Writers' Prize, African region), and a collection of short stories *Why Don't You Carve Other Animals*.

Zoë Wicomb   (South Africa)   She was born in 1948 in the Cape. She completed an Arts degree at the University of the Western Cape and then studied English Literature at Reading University. She lectured in English at Nottingham, and was writer in residence at Glasgow and Strathclyde, where she now lectures, specialising in feminist and cultural theory. She spent some time lecturing at the University of the Western Cape in the early 1990s. Her inter-related stories form a novel, under the title *You Can't Get Lost in Cape Town*.

Glossary

ag	expression of irritation
aia	old Coloured woman
Boers	Afrikaner whites
bedonderd	bad-tempered
braai	barbecue
bredie	stew of meat and vegetables
choli	bodice worn under sari
dagga pils	marijuana cigarettes
dikra	term of endearment
doekie	headscarf
dominee	church minister
dongas	washed out gullies, ravines
Gogo	grandmother
gopies	maidens
Hama	mother
Hayi!	No!
Hoe gaan dit?	How are you?
imbongi	a praise poet
ja	yes
kayas	slang for servants' quarters
Khawulele! Wenk'umntu!	Stop her! Everyone!
klawerjas	fourhanded card game
knobkerrie	a knob stick
kopjes (koppies)	small hills
lobola	bride price
makoti	new bride
mangparas (mamparas)	incompetent greenhorns
mealies	maize
melktert	custard tart
Miesies	Madam

Mholo	Xhosa greeting
moffies	effeminates, here referring to theology students
mos	actually, indeed (redundant)
'n Boer maak 'n plan	a farmer devises a solution
namaste	a formal greeting
ou	fellow, chap
Ounooi	elderly female employer
Ousie	family term, lit. elder sister
platteland	rural countryside
plaasjapie	farm yokel
poep-scared	lit. fart scared
pondokkies/pondoks	huts, shacks
saamberani	incense burnt during prayers
sies	expression of disgust or contempt
skollie-boys	unemployed street youths
Slams (pl. *Slamse*)	Muslim Coloured of Malay extraction
sousboontjies	haricot beans in sweet-sour sauce
spek en boontjies	to no effect; here, child for whom rules of game are bent
stoep	veranda
suster	sister
Tali	gold bridal pendant
thali	food platter
Tata	father, here used for grandfather
veld	open countryside, landscape, grazing land

Acknowledgements

The compiler and the publishers are grateful for permission for non-exclusive use of copyright material in this book as follows:

Elleke Boehmer: 'Ginger', first published in *The Penguin Book of Contemporary South African Stories* (ed. Stephen Gray), 1993; Gcinaphi Dlamini: 'Ethel, the sensible', unpublished, included by permission of the author; Nadine Gordimer: 'No place like', from *Livingstone's Companions*, Viking Press, New York, 1971 and Jonathan Cape, London, 1972, and 'The ultimate safari' from *Jump and other stories*, David Philip, Cape Town; Bloomsbury Publishing plc, London; and Farrar, Straus & Giroux, New York, 1991, both reprinted by permission of the author; Bessie Head: 'The collector of treasures' from *The Collector of Treasures and other Botswana Village Tales*, David Philip, Cape Town, and Heinemann Educational Books, London, 1977; Kaleni Hiyalwa: 'The baby's baby' from *Coming on Strong* (ed. Margie Orford & Nepeti Nicanor), New Namibia Books, Windhoek, 1996; Farida Karodia: 'Crossmatch' from *Against an African Sky*, David Philip, Cape Town, 1995; Jane Katjavivi: 'Uerieta' from *Coming on Strong* (ed. Margie Orford & Nepeti Nicanor), New Namibia Books, Windhoek, 1996; Doris Lessing: 'The De Wets come to Kloof Grange' from *This Was the Old Chief's Country, Collected African Stories, Vol 1*, Michael Joseph, London, 1951, and Simon & Schuster, New York, copyright 1951 Doris Lessing, reprinted by kind permission of Jonathan Clowes Ltd, London, on behalf of Doris Lessing; Moira Crosbie Lovell: 'Supermarket soliloquy' from *New Contrast 100*, included by permission of the author; Sindiwe Magona: 'Flight' from *Living, Loving and Lying Awake at Night,* David Philip, Cape Town, 1991; Gcina Mhlophe: 'Transforming Moments' from *Love Child,* published only in German by Peter Hammer Verlag, included by permission of the author; Sheila Roberts: 'I'd sell my horses' from *New Contrast 94,* included by permission of the author; Agnes Sam: 'High heels' from *Jesus is Indian and other stories,* Heinemann Educational Publishers, a division of Reed Educational and Professional Publishing Ltd, Oxford, 1989; Yvonne Vera: 'Independence Day' and 'Shelling peanuts' from *Why Don't You Carve Other Animals,* Tsar Publications, Toronto and Baobab Books, Harare; Zoe Wicomb: 'A clearing in the bush' from *You Can't Get Lost in Cape Town,* Virago Press, London, 1987.

Every effort has been made to trace and acknowledge copyright holders. Should any mistake have been made, the publishers and the compiler apologise and undertake to correct the mistake in any future impression.